THIEVES' WORLD™

is a unique experience: an outlaw world of the imagination, where mayhem and skulduggery rule and magic is still potent; brought to life by today's top fantasy writers, who are free to use one another's characters (but not to kill them off . . . or at least not too freely!).

The idea for Thieves' World and the colorful city called Sanctuary™ came to Robert Lynn Asprin in 1978. After many twists and turns (documented in the volumes), the idea took off—and took on its own reality, as the best fantasy worlds have a way of doing. The result is one of F&SF's most unique success stories: a bestseller from the beginning, a series that is a challenge to writers, a delight to readers, and a favorite of fans.

Don't miss these other exciting tales of Sanctuary: the meanest, seediest, most dangerous town in all the worlds of fantasy. . . .

THIEVES' WORLD
(Stories by Asprin, Abbey, Anderson, Bradley, Brunner, DeWees, Haldeman, and Offutt)

TALES FROM THE VULGAR UNICORN
(Stories by Asprin, Abbey, Drake, Farmer, Morris, Offutt, and van Vogt)

SHADOWS OF SANCTUARY
(Stories by Asprin, Abbey, Cherryh, McIntyre, Morris, Offutt, and Paxson)

STORM SEASON
(Stories by Asprin, Abbey, Cherryh, Morris, Offutt, and Paxson)

THE FACE OF CHAOS
(Stories by Asprin, Abbey, Cherryh, Drake, Morris, and Paxson)

WINGS OF OMEN
(Stories by Asprin, Abbey, Bailey, Cherryh, Duane, Morris and Morris, Offutt, and Paxson)

THE DEAD OF WINTER
(Stories by Asprin, Abbey, Bailey, Cherryh, Duane, Morris, Offutt, and Paxson)

SOUL OF THE CITY
(Stories by Abbey, Cherryh, and Morris)

BLOOD TIES
(Stories by Asprin, Abbey, Bailey, Cherryh, Duane, Morris and Morris, Offutt and Offutt, and Paxson)

AFTERMATH
(Stories by Abbey, Brunner, Drake, Morris, Offutt, and Perry)

UNEASY ALLIANCES

Edited by
ROBERT LYNN ASPRIN & LYNN ABBEY

ACE BOOKS, NEW YORK

This book is an Ace
original edition.

UNEASY ALLIANCES

An Ace Book/published by arrangement with
the editors

PRINTING HISTORY
Ace edition/August 1988

ISBN: 0-441-80610-4

10 · 9 · 8 · 7 · 6 · 5 · 4 · 3 · 2 · 1

CONTENTS

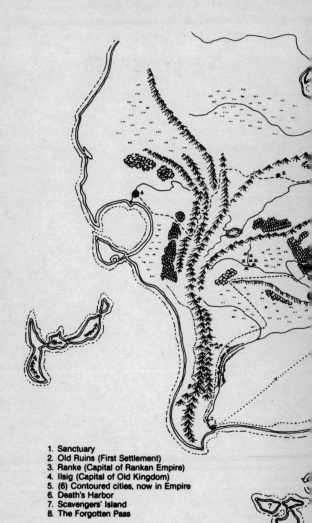

1. Sanctuary
2. Old Ruins (First Settlement)
3. Ranke (Capital of Rankan Empire)
4. Ilsig (Capital of Old Kingdom)
5. (6) Contoured cities, now in Empire
6. Death's Harbor
7. Scavengers' Island
8. The Forgotten Pass

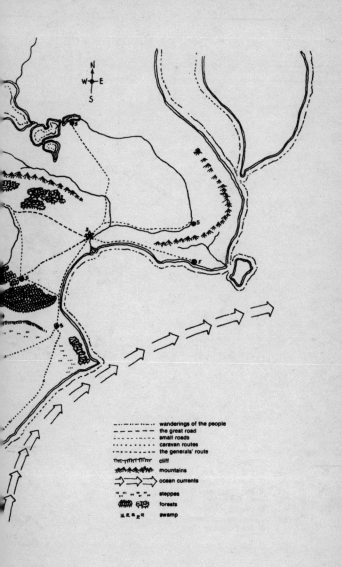

wanderings of the people
the great road
small roads
caravan routes
the generals' route
cliff
mountains
ocean currents
steppes
forests
swamp

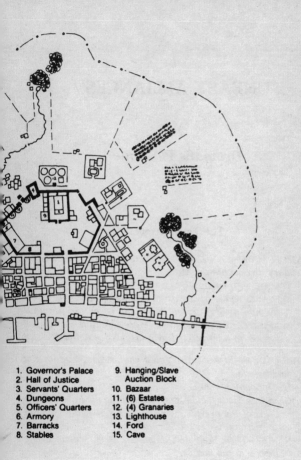

1. Governor's Palace
2. Hall of Justice
3. Servants' Quarters
4. Dungeons
5. Officers' Quarters
6. Armory
7. Barracks
8. Stables

9. Hanging/Slave
   Auction Block
10. Bazaar
11. (6) Estates
12. (4) Granaries
13. Lighthouse
14. Ford
15. Cave

~1 mile

UNEASY ALLIANCES

Dramatis Personae

The Townspeople:

AHDIOVIZUN; AHDIOMER VIZ; AHDIO—*Proprietor of Sly's Place, a legendary dive within the Maze.*

    THRODE—*An employee at Sly's Place.*

    CLEYA; JODEERA—*The woman Ahdio loves, and who works for him at Sly's Place. Since she is far too beautiful to travel safely through the Maze, Ahdio has arranged for her to be protected by a disguise of ugliness.*

LALO THE LIMNER—*Street artist gifted with magic he does not fully understand.*

GILLA—*His indomitable wife.*

    GANNER—*Their middle son, slain during the False Plague Riots of the previous winter which signaled the end of severe civil unrest in Sanctuary.*

    VANDA—*Their daughter, employed as nursemaid to the Beysib at the palace.*

    WEDEMIR—*Their eldest child and son. A member of Walegrin's guard patrol.*

    LATILLA—*Their youngest daughter.*

    ALFI—*Their infant son.*

HAKIEM—*Storyteller and confidant extraordinaire.*

    HORT—*Son of a fisherman and Hakiem's apprentice.*

JUBAL—*Prematurely aged former gladiator. Once he openly ran Sanctuary's most visible criminal organization, the Hawkmasks, now he works behind the scenes.*

  SALIMAN—*His aide and only friend.*

MORIA—*Once one of Jubal's Hawkmasks, then a servant of Ischade. She was physically transformed into a Rankan noblewoman before the magic died, and the transformation endures. She is in hiding with Stilcho.*

MYRTIS—*Madam of the Aphrodisia House.*

SNAPPER JO—*A fiend who survived the destruction of magic in Sanctuary. Once employed as a bartender in the Vulgar Unicorn.*

STILCHO—*Once one of Ischade's resurrected minions. He was "cured" of death when magic was purged from Sanctuary.*

ZIP—*Bitter young terrorist. Leader of the Popular Front for the Liberation of Sanctuary (PFLS). Now he and his remaining fighters have been designated as officials responsible for peace in the city.*

The S'danzo:

ILLYRA—*Half-blood S'danzo seeress with True Sight. Wounded by PFLS in the False Plague Riots.*
DUBRO—*Bazaar blacksmith and husband to Illyra.*

THE TERMAGANT—*Oldest of the S'danzo women practicing her craft in Sanctuary.*

The Magicians:

ILSIGI MAGES:
  MARKMOR—A powerful, ambitious, youthful wizard.
  MARYPE—*His arrogant, yet blundering, apprentice.*
  MIZRAITH—*Marype's father, slain by Markmor shortly after the Prince arrived in Sanctuary.*

RANKAN HAZARDS dwelling at the Mageguild:

> RANDAL; WITCHY-EARS—*The only mage ever admitted into the Sacred Band of Stepsons or trusted by them. Now a teacher at the Mageguild.*

Those who adhere to no hierarchy or discipline but their own:

> ENAS YORL—*Quasi-immortal mage cursed with eternal life and a constantly changing physical form.*

> ISCHADE—*Necromancer and thief. Her curse is passed to her lovers who die from it. Since the diminution of magic in Sanctuary, she has been in isolation at her house on the White Foal River.*

> STRICK; TORAZELAN STRICK TIFIRQA—*White Mage who has made Sanctuary his home. He will help anyone who comes to him, but there is always a Price, sometimes trivial and sometimes not, for his aid.*

Visitors in Sanctuary:

THE SHEPHERD—*A figure of considerable mystery. By his panoply he might be an Ilsigi warrior—but all such men have been dead for years.*

The Rankans Living in Sanctuary:

CHENAYA; DAUGHTER OF THE SUN—*A beautiful and powerful young woman, the Prince's cousin, who is fated never to lose a fight. In her arrogance and innocence she made more enemies in Sanctuary than even fate could handle and has left town until her reputation repairs itself.*

> DAYRNE—*Her companion and trainer.*

> LEYN, OUIJEN, DISMAS AND GESTUS—*Her friends and gladiators at her father's school.*

DAPHNE—*Rankan noblewoman and first wife of Prince Kadakithis. Ostensibly sent to safety before the arrival of the Beysib, she was actually kidnapped and sold into slavery on Scavenger's Island where Chenaya rescued her. She is estranged from her husband.*

PRINCE KADAKITHIS—*Charismatic but somewhat naive half-brother of the assassinated Emperor, Abakithis.*

LOWAN VIGELES—*Half-brother of Molin Torchholder, father of Chenaya. A wealthy aristocrat self-exiled to Sanctuary and hoping to return to the Rankan capital in triumph someday. He operates a gladiator school at his Land's End estate and has built a small, temporary arena there.*

MOLIN TORCHHOLDER; TORCH—*Archpriest of Sanctuary's wargod (whichever deity that is at the moment). Architect for the rebuilt walls of Sanctuary. Supreme bureaucratic administrator of the city.*

RASHAN; THE EYE OF SAVANKALA—*Priest and Judge of Savankala. Highest ranking Rankan in Sanctuary prior to the arrival of the Prince, now allied with Chenaya's disaffected Rankans at Land's End.*

STEPSONS; SACRED BANDERS—*Members of a mercenary unit loyal to Tempus. Their years in Sanctuary were among the worst in their history and all but a few of them have gratefully left town.*

    CRITIAS; CRIT—*Longtime mercenary in the company. Tempus left him in charge of peace-keeping in Sanctuary when everyone else left. Also the partner of Straton, though that pairing has been in disarray for some time now.*

    STRATON; STRAT; ACE—*Partner of Critias. Injured by the PFLS at the start of the False Plague Riots. He has been Ischade's lover and though her curse has not killed him, most of his former associates count him among Sanctuary's damned.*

WALEGRIN—*Rankan army officer assigned to the Sanctuary garrison where his father had been slain by the S'danzo many years before. He is now one of three officers responsible for the peace in Sanctuary. He is also Illyra's half-brother.*

The Beysib:

SHUPANSEA; SHU-SEA—*Head of the Beysib exiles in Sanctuary; mortal avatar of the Beysib mother goddess. Lover of Prince Kadakithis whom she wishes to marry.*

INTRODUCTION

Lynn Abbey

"No! No more blood! Make it stop!"

Shupansea awoke at the sound of her own scream. The nightmare had propelled her out of bed and to the window of her bedchamber. With a trembling hand she pulled the casement shut. This wasn't the first time she'd found herself before an open window; wasn't the first time she shed a cold sweat wondering what would happen if some night she did not scream herself awake.

"O Beysa, forgive my intrusion. I—I heard you scream . . ."

Shupansea turned to the lamplight and faced the frightened eyes of Kammesin, the woman who had cared for her since infancy. "It was nothing—a noise in the dark. Nothing at all."

Kammesin did not relax. The old woman's eyes remained wide, round and steadily unblinking. Mother Bey! Had she been exiled so long among the fluttering Rankans that her own people looked strange and unnerving? Was her soul forgetting that the fixed stare was a gesture of honesty and transparency as much as it was a measure of

1

uncontrolled anxiety? And had she, herself, blinked even once since waking from the nightmare?

"Yes, Kam-sin," she admitted, forcing the membrane to withdraw and her eyelids to descend. "It was the nightmare, again. But I'm all right now. Just light my lamp then you go back to sleep."

The woman gave a shrug that every servant knew. It meant the same to both Rankans and Beysibs: disbelief and resignation. "As you wish, O Beysa." She lit the lamp beside the bed as she left.

A flush of shame burned across the Beysa's face as she heard the door close. Those folk who believed aristocrats were unaware of their servants had no understanding of the matter at all. Shupansea felt her old nurse's censure as a sad, painful twinge in her heart. All her life she had confided in Kammesin, but now, when she was overflowing with despair, she could speak to no one.

In point of fact, the Beysa wished to speak to the goddess Bey. She wanted to know why, after all these seasons in Sanctuary, her sleep was haunted by memories of the final, bloody days of her brief, unsanctified reign over the Beysin Empire. But it had been more than a year since the Mother's voice had resounded within her head. Mother Bey, like everything else magical or divine in Sanctuary, had been reduced to shadow strength.

The town which had been god-ridden was now virtually god-less. Mother Bey was the merest whisper of empathy in Her avatar's mind. A calming whisper nonetheless, and it seemed to say that the goddess was content with exile and did not plan to return home soon.

That's not enough, the Beysa thought loudly enough, she hoped, for the goddess to hear. *I can't stay here and remember the past, too.*

The flicker of empathy shifted, resonating love and the smiling face of Prince Kadakithis. Shupansea grit her teeth and shook the feeling away. Mother Bey had strengthened every cynic's hand when She tumbled into a divine infatuation with the wargod, Stormbringer. Half the people in Sanctuary—if not the known world—had shared hot frustration in their dreams as the would-be lovers contended with a mismatch of immortal anatomy.

Such divine emissions had ceased when the magical *nouma* of Sanctuary was burned away, but Shupansea knew the pair chased each other still and she was more than slightly embarrassed by her progenitor's lusty behavior.

Though Shupansea purged the goddess from her thoughts and feeling, the prince was not so easily removed. Surely it was no coincidence that the nightmares had started right after they'd announced their intended, but still unscheduled, marriage. Right after she'd decided to abide by Rankan standards of acceptable behavior and moved her personal entourage out of Kadakithis's suite.

Love had never been part of Shupansea's emotional vocabulary. Indeed, no Beysa had ever dared to love—not when her blood was venom and all her male offspring were condemned to death in her womb. At home they sacrificed the royal consort, and the Beysa insured her line with casual, guilt-free affairs.

Could she doubt for one heartbeat that the nightmares—the cold fear that lived in her belly—were the underside of her love for an unlucky Rankan prince?

Shupansea shivered from the fear, and the everpresent dampness that permeated the palace. She shrugged her gown over her shoulders and looked beside the bed for her slippers. It was no wonder that Rankan women swaddled themselves in layer upon layer of cloth. Sanctuary was always damp; it was hot and damp in the summer, then chilly and damp the rest of the time. Either way you wrapped yourself in soft, absorbent cloth for comfort.

She opened the door quietly, half expecting to find Kammesin crouched beside the latch-hole. The corridor was empty, but her lamplight caught the final sway of a nearby drapery. Despite her age, Kam-sin had retreated to her alcove and, after another moment, began snoring gently.

A faint smile crossed the Beysa's lips as she headed for the sunrise wing. Twice a year everyone who was anyone changed residence from one side of the palace to the other—adjusting the social hierarchy in the process. The best people had sunrise suites in the warmer months and sunset suites in the dreary winter.

At first Shupansea and her comrades-in-exile had taken all the good rooms for themselves—winning themselves no friends among the Rankans. Moving days had been tense, bristly affairs with frequent brawls between the servants and the occasional duel between the incoming and outgoing residents.

The palace, like the city, had mellowed in the last year. Some of the Beysibs had moved to renovated estates beyond the walls; some of the Rankans had as well. Those who remained got along better—as well as any court in either empire—and Beysibs began mixing with Rankans on both sides of fortune's wheel.

The man whom Shupansea sought could have had an apartment on the sunset side, but he chose, for reasons of his own, to live in counterpoint to both the Beysa and his prince.

"Ambitious people have stronger stories," Hakiem always insisted when moving day found him marshalling his possessions against the tide. "And unhappy people have tragic ones."

The Beysa never argued with the storyteller, who was her closest friend among the natives. Privately she thought he was wrong, at least about tragedy. She knew her own story, and that of Prince Kadakithis, and she'd gladly have changed with a sunrise resident whose life was both comfortable and dull.

Trusted servants slept in alcoves and on pallets beside their masters' doors. The more alert and reliable managed to be wide-awake as Shupansea walked by with her lamp. Most of the Beysibs kowtowed to her shadow, some of the Rankans glowered with scant respect—but not as many as once had done. The Beysa ignored them, which was what they all expected anyway.

Hakiem's knotted latchstring was drawn to the inside of his door, and Shupansea was suddenly aware of the late hour. The storyteller said he was always ready to be her ears—any day, any night—but he wasn't a young man. Men and women offered themselves to a Beysa or a Prince in the sublime confidence that their gift would never be called.

Twice Shupansea pulled her knuckles soundlessly back from the door. The third time she touched the wood, but still there was no sound as the door swung open on well-oiled hinges.

"Hakiem? Friend?"

The room was empty; the storyteller's pallet was rolled up into a day-cushion. Shupansea felt awkward and foolish. Hakiem *was* old enough to be her father, but that didn't quite make him *old*. Certainly he was charming, witty, and—now that he was better groomed and bathed regularly—cut a handsome figure among the court ladies who commonly complained that men talked only of war and politics. Surely he had offers—no doubt his assignations were more easily arranged from this side of the palace.

She resolved to make no mention of her untimely visit and was about to leave when the lamplight fell on a pile of drawings. She saw her prince with a bloody sword, and herself with bloody hands—and curiosity got the better of her good sense.

Lighting Hakiem's lamp from her own, Shupansea settled down to examine the colored sketches more closely.

Not all of Sanctuary ran on palace time. The Street of Red Lanterns was ablaze well past midnight. The Maze didn't start to get interesting until respectable people pulled their shutters in. And a dive like the Vulgar Unicorn hit its stride a good deal later than that.

Through all Sanctuary's vicissitudes, the Vulgar Unicorn had been a touchstone of a sort of stability. Its bartenders—human and otherwise—were uniformly ugly; its wenches were invariably on the downside of careers that had never looked promising. Its food was uncompromisingly vile, and the swill they tapped from their kegs . . . The beer at the Vulgar Unicorn was generally regarded to be the worst of mixing sludge from the harbor and goat urine; the wine—well, the beer was better than the wine.

Irony of ironies: Hakiem the Storyteller, who had spent the better part of his adult life in a drunken stupor, begging coppers to squander on the vulgar wine, now had enough money to buy the tavern's entire cellar, and he could no longer drink the bilge. The taste was the same in his mouth, and it brought back bittersweet memories of a vanished Sanctuary, but he dared not swallow. Fortunately no one noticed when he hawked the bloody liquid at the floor.

He was in disguise—that is, he wore the old clothes he'd sworn to incinerate years ago. Most people knew he'd come up in the world; most people didn't recognize him when he looked liked his old self. A few even worried about him and warned him away from the Unicorn now that he had a few coins in his pouch and access to the palace. Those few were probably right, but he could no more live without the Vulgar Unicorn than he could . . . Than he could live in the palace day after day.

Late at night, long after his respectable patrons had shut down their respectable soirees, Hakiem eased back to the Sanctuary they could not imagine and harvested another crop of tales. He had an apprentice of sorts, the fisherman's lad, Hort, who did the first winnowing and pruning, but nothing could replace his own senses. And nothing could replace the parade of life in the Vulgar Unicorn.

He let his eyes go out of focus—an easy task since his hair had begun turning white as well as gray—and was struck by a wild insight that shook him in his shoes: *His beloved Unicorn and the palace weren't so very different after all*. He gulped his mug of wine and blamed his seeping eyes on it.

But, no, the comparison was in his mind and the similarities would not go away. The Vulgar Unicorn and the palace were both places where style was generally more important than substance. They were both places where you belonged, or you didn't belong—and where you had to always prove that you still belonged. Both had reputations which exceeded reality, and—might as well admit it—both were parasites in the city's lifeblood.

Dark Shalpa knew how many honest men it took to support a thief—even one who lied as all thieves lie. Hakiem guessed it took about as many as it took to support an aristocrat.

"You look like you've seen a ghost," Hort said cheerfully as he took the chair opposite his mentor.

Hakiem raised his head to see twins smiling at him. Futtering Nether-gods! What *did* these people put in their wine? Old habits, however, died hard and stood him in good stead as he reestablished conscious control over his body with slow, deliberate gestures. Old habits, and the fact that he had drunk no more than half a mug of sour wine.

"You've forgotten everything I've taught you," he said, using drawling sarcasm to mask the stiffness in his tongue. "What sort of introduction is that? Make a point, Hort. Get your audience's attention. Add color. What manner of ghost; what sort of look—"

They had played this game before. Hort puffed up his chest and spread his arms wide. "Ye gods, old sot, your eyes are as red as the gutters in Shambles Cross; you're as pale as a man who's seen his mother's ghost dancing naked with Vashanka's tent peg!"

Hakiem swallowed hard, and not because of the wine. The boy had talent; had learned everything he'd been taught. He didn't need a mentor any longer.

"Better, lad. Much better. You do yourself, and myself, proud. Now, tell me, what have your pointed little ears heard this week?"

"Tales of vengeance: brothers for brothers, fathers for sons. Ordinary folk are confident that the worst is over and are stepping out to settle their own scores."

Hakiem nodded. He'd sensed as much himself. The

Nisibisi-funded PFLS anarchy was over and there was a sense that the future would not be like the past. But debts had to be evened before the future was embraced.

"What else?"

"A whole new society growing in Shambles where the rousters who moved Torchholder's stones make their homes. They think the streets of Sanctuary are paved with gold—or at least the walls are—and, dammit, if they don't seem to be right. Everybody's swinging a mallet or smoothing mortar, even our Prince and the common folk think the world's getting better each day."

"Are there *any* clouds on our cheerful horizon?"

The young man shed his expansiveness. His eyes grew intense and he leaned across the table. Still good storytelling, but Hakiem sensed there was something more in Hort's eagerness.

"Men are vanishing, maybe five or six a week. And they're not turning up in any of the usual places. Some say it's the Mageguild trying to get power back, but I've found a blind alley there. Best guess points toward the harbor."

"You've checked that out?"

Hort drew back a hand's breadth. He was the son of the best fisherman in town, and, while he had no taste for salt water himself, he had the confidence of those who did.

"We're taking more trade up and down the coast: stone for the walls and pretties for Beysib gold. Most goes where it should, but some sails west and hooks about the Hag Banks—and you know what that means."

It galled a bit, but Hakiem had to shrug and shake his head. He'd heard of the banks, where the Beysib fisherfolk had taught Hort's people to set their nets for deep water fish, but he knew nothing more.

Hort's smile deepened. "Catch the current there," he

whispered, leaning further across the table. "And you bring up in the lee of Scavenger Island with a harbor as deep as ours, twice as wide—and no law at all to interfere with your gold."

The master storyteller twirled a grey tuft of his beard. He knew the history of Sanctuary better than any other man. These days the Rankans were the tyrants and the townsfolk pointed with underdog pride to their Ilsigi ancestry; it hadn't always been that way. Not far beyond the reach of living memory the Ilsig kings had been the enemy, and Scavenger's Island had been the sanctuary toward which the oppressed fled.

Scavenger's Island—pirate haven. A place which made Sanctuary at its worst seem serene and orderly by comparison. Scourge of the seas, Harrier of the coast, and, also, a place which had generally regarded Sanctuary as a poor relation and left it alone. But Sanctuary wasn't poor any longer.

"How does this tie to the missing men?" Hakiem asked, completely sober now.

Hort shrugged. "Some go willingly as recruits, the rest as galley slaves."

"And no one else suspects that we're being harvested by pirates?"

"Did you?"

Again Hakiem had to shake his head. Sanctuary had always been downtrodden—a home to thieves, not the target of pirates. Old habits died hard, indeed.

"The Old Man," Hort continued, speaking of his father, "says you can always trust kings and princes to build their walls in the wrong place."

I suppose you can, Hakiem agreed in silence.

"You'll tell them, won't you?" Hort asked, no longer a

storyteller but simply a young man who was afraid for his home and his life.

Hakiem nodded. He would, of course, nevertheless, a tale like this was wood-ripe for burning and required special care. There were people in Sanctuary who could confirm the substance of Hort's suspicions, and few of them owed an old storyteller a favor. He'd get started tomorrow, but without Hort. There were some tricks to his trade Hakiem hoped the younger man would never need to know.

"Anything else, my boy? Scandals, magic, two-headed calves?"

Hort relaxed and began one of many tales, about a love charm gone remarkably awry.

It was nearly dawn when Hakiem made his way out of the Maze to West Gate Street. He'd stayed out later than planned, drunk more than he should, and could practically feel his plump bed beneath his cheeks. A group of tired guards hailed him as he came through the gate, then looked the other way as he took a candle from the rack and slipped into the backways.

The backways were always the fastest, most discreet ways through the palace. A warren of hidden stairways, corridors and cul-de-sacs had been built in order to be officially forgotten at the end of each burst of palatial expansion. Like the Maze and the sewers, they were rumored to be more mysterious than they actually were. Beneath the Hall of Justice, Hakiem passed not one but three courtiers scurrying back to their proper beds; he didn't even try to count the servants.

There was only one protocol along these backways: silence. One might look, but never see; hear but never speak. Hakiem remembered what he saw, but unless he saw the same event in a public area it stayed locked forever within him.

As the storyteller rounded the dusty corner where the backways merged with the public ways, he was minded again of the similarities between palace life and criminal survival. There were seeds of an epic tale sprouting in his mind and no room for other thoughts.

Later on Hakiem would say of those next few moments that he was neither a kowtowing Beysib nor a stiff-backed Rankan courtier and so he looked the Beysa straight in the eye as a proud Ilsigi. Truth was, though, that the sight of Shupansea—with her dark gold hair night-braided, her soft wool gown and slippers, and her deadly emerald beynit draped across her shoulder—sitting on his cushions completely unnerved him.

"O—O—O Bey—" Words failed him as they had never failed before.

The Beysa reacted with little more aplomb. She tittered like an apprentice handmaid and scattered a pile of drawings clear across the floor. Only the slender serpent retained its dignity; it yawned, showing its ivory fangs and crimson maw, then wove itself deep into her hair.

Shupansea grabbed the nearest of the drawings. She got to her feet and held it out as a peace offering. "I'm sorry, Storyteller . . ." Her lamp was guttering. A swathe of pale light came through the narrow window. She realized she'd spent the night in his room—with him or without him. "Oh, I'm really sorry."

Hakiem bent down to pick up another drawing, and to look at something besides her face. A successful drunk learns that death is not the likely consequence of embarrassment. He had mastered that lesson years ago, but the

Beysa, obviously, had not. She was redder than her serpent's mouth.

"Had I known it was you, O Beysa," he tried to keep the absurd amusement from his voice and reached for another drawing. "Had I but known, I would have come home much sooner."

Time froze for a moment, then thawed as Shupansea exhaled in a long, trembling sigh. "I—I had nightmares. I thought you might be able to help . . . If I could think of an ending for the dreams, perhaps they'd go away. You always seem to know how things should end."

Hakiem shook his head sadly. "That's because stories may end while the hero—or heroine—is still alive. Life is different, O Beysa. But I would be glad to listen."

"No, I guess I understand that they're my dreams, and I must conquer them." She crouched down and gathered more of the colorful parchment scraps. Her fingers paused above a portrait of Prince Kadakithis standing uneasily beside a corpse. "I think maybe I learned something just looking at your pictures. It's strange—I've never thought of Ki-this using his sword. I mean, he's not weak, but I love him because he's gentle. He's strong and gentle—and someday maybe his people will realize that. But looking at this—well, I could *see* it happening. I knew this man was a traitor, and that Ki-this had to kill him. He was proud and disgusted both at the same time—and he grew up that night.

"I'll have to do the same thing—well, maybe not with a sword, but I've got to grow up if I'm to help him turn Sanctuary into one city for everyone. You should draw more pictures and put them where everyone can see them."

Hakiem made a sour grimace and took the scraps from her hand. "That, I fear, is the general idea. I tell stories while an artist sketches, and then the Torch—excuse me, Lord Torchholder—intends to have them painted on his new walls.''

Shupansea straightened as if the priest had entered the room. She had a half-dozen contradictory opinions about the omnipresent bureaucrat. Not that anyone claimed to understand Molin Torchholder. He was a black-haired Rankan, a dedicated priest of a vanquished god and the driving force behind the resurrection of a city he openly loathed.

''It's a good idea. He hasn't mentioned it yet, but he will, and both Ki-this and I will tell him so. He'll grumble something about doing what's necessary and walk away under a dark cloud. It must be hard, I think, to work as hard as Lord Torchholder does, and get so little satisfaction.''

''They say hate is as satisfactory a mistress as love.''

''I prefer love.''

''Lord Torchholder does not.''

The last drawing had slipped beneath the cushions. They both saw it at the same time and Hakiem, who recognized the subject from the visible corner, dove to retrieve it first. He would have had it, but his sudden lunge aroused Shupansea's serpent. Discretion was always the better part of valor, still a lump hardened in his throat as she pulled the sketch out.

Torchholder's orders had been precise: illustrations from Hakiem's stories of the events that had shaped Sanctuary since the Prince had arrived as governor. There had been few occasions more momentous than the afternoon when Kadakithis had handed the Savankh to the Beysa and her court-in-exile for ''safe-keeping.'' Hakiem liked Shupansea now—the Prince wanted to make her his wife—but they'd

hated her that afternoon and it showed clearly in Lalo's
sketch.

Draped in jewels and cloth-of-gold, hard-eyed, her face
and naked breasts painted an iridescent green, Shupansea
had been the archetype of arrogance. The storyteller sel-
dom connected the young woman he'd come to know and
the alien creature he remembered, but he could not deny
that the Beysib, with their abundant gold and equally
abundant contempt for all non-Beysib things, had been the
prime cause of Sanctuary's horrors. The Rankan campaign
against the Nisibisi in the north would scarcely have touched
the city—much less divided it—if the Beysib hadn't riled
it first.

"Does he intend to have them all painted?" Shupansea
asked in carefully measured tones, her gaze never rising
from the picture.

"With the Prince's approval, and yours—of course."

The parchment fluttered in her hand. Her eyes went
wide and glassy, the beynit rose from her hair, and Hakiem
began to doubt that she had, in fact, truly changed during
the years he'd been advising her. She had returned the
Savankh to the prince's keeping, but not the power behind
it.

"We looked like that, didn't we?" Shupansea whispered as she put the parchment on top of the pile. "And
nothing I ever do will erase that picture, will it?"

Hakiem caught her hand and squeezed it gently. "I
don't tell stories about the future, you know, but it's my
guess that Lord Molin means to leave the largest space—
the space above the main gate—for a commemoration of
your wedding with Prince Kadakithis— "

Shupansea sighed and pulled her hand away. "If we
marry. Maybe hate is stronger than love." She stood in the

doorway, looking over her shoulder waiting for Hakiem to deny what she did not believe could be denied.

"Hope is the strongest of all," he assured, and watched her walk slowly down the corridor.

SLAVE TRADE

Robert Lynn Asprin

Saliman did not have to stretch his acting talents to maintain an air of disdain as he carefully picked his way through the rows of chained slaves. He had performed this task hundreds of times before, so though unpleasant, the odor of so many close-packed, unwashed bodies was not new to him. The fact that he was on board a ship only added a new batch of musty smells to the proceedings. Pulling his cloak high to keep it from the filth on the floor would do no good. The air itself would invade the fabric until it would either have to be thoroughly cleaned or discarded altogether. One didn't wear one's best clothes to shop for slaves.

No, it was not the distasteful nature of the job that had Saliman in such a vile mood, but rather the hour. The fact that he had been rousted from a warm bed shared by an even warmer bed partner to carry out this mission in the pre-dawn hours virtually guaranteed that he would be less than generous in his negotiations with the slavers.

"I shouldn't be doing this," the man holding the lantern

grumbled loudly. "I got better things to do, what with the ship to get underway and all."

This was, of course, the reason for this sudden assignment. The ship was due to sail on the morning tide, and it was important to carry out this mission before it left Sanctuary's waters. Still, it gave Saliman a focus for his irritation.

"Do you want me to tell that to Jubal?" he said, his expression bland. "I'm sure if I alert him to your inconvenience, he'll be careful to only bother you with important matters in the future."

The thinly veiled threat was not lost on the slaver.

"No! I . . . that won't be necessary."

The slavers had paid well to be sure that Sanctuary's crime lord did not interfere with their operation, and did not wish to raise that price by denying his request. Particularly not when Jubal's prices were known to occasionally include blood as well as money.

"If you could simply speed your selection?" The man was pleading now. "This is the third time we've been through the rows, and if I don't set sail soon, I'll miss the morning tide and lose a full day's travel."

Saliman ignored him, not deigning to dignify the whine with a response as he peered around the darkness of the ship's hold. Sailing ships were not noted for their punctuality, not when winds and storms could affect their schedules by weeks, not just days.

Still, he was secretly in agreement with the slaver. This was taking much longer than was necessary. Of course, the search was slowed by his reluctance to admit that he was searching for two particular men rather than two slaves in general. If he were to impart that piece of information, the process would be speeded, but the price would doubtless increase with the implied importance of the individuals in question.

Surprisingly enough, it was the man Saliman only had a description of who had been the easiest to find. While his features and hair had been obvious enough, that slave had been rocking back and forth, hugging his knees and moaning his own name as if trying to cling to his pre-slave identity. It was the other man, the one Saliman knew on sight, who had thus far eluded his search.

A movement in the dark caught his eye, and he grasped the slaver's arm, redirecting the light of the hooded lantern.

"What's that?" he demanded, gesturing toward a large sack, its mouth secured by ropes.

"That? Oh, that's a special deal we made. A fellow and a couple of his friends brought that one by . . . said they were getting rid of his wife's lover. They made me promise not to let him out of the bag until we were at sea."

"You bought a slave without even looking at him?"

"They weren't asking much for him." the slaver shrugged. "If he's alive, we'll show a profit, and from the way the bag's been jumpin' around it's pretty safe to say he's alive."

"Well, open the bag and let me see him."

"But I just told you—"

"Yes, yes. You promised. But if you're about to sail, who's to know whether you opened it early or not?"

The slaver drew a breath to argue, then shrugged and gestured to the two burly sailors who had been standing by to insure that none of the slaves attempted either attack or escape while the hold was open. Those stalwarts seized the bag, kicking aside any slave who happened to be in their path, and began fumbling with the ropes that secured its mouth. There were a few underbreath grumbles about

landsmen who didn't know proper knots, then the bag was
opened and its contents jerked upright for display.

The slave was a slim youth, still clothed—which confirmed the slaver's claim that he had been untouched since
being brought aboard. His wrists were bound and his
mouth gagged, and he blinked painfully in the sudden light
of the lantern's glare.

Saliman knew him instantly, though he was careful not
to let any sign of recognition show on his face. Shadowspawn.
One of Sanctuary's homegrown thieves who had stolen
and fought his way to the top of his profession.

The thief gave no sign of recognizing Saliman, though
whether this was from any cunning on his part or from
simple lantern-blindness and drug-confusion, was hard to
tell. Whichever it was, he decided to act before the scene
had a chance to change.

"Well, he's not much . . . but he's the closest I've
seen. I'll take him."

He made a point of turning away before the slaver could
even begin the anticipated protest.

"But . . . I can't do that!" came the expected sputter.
"I told you, we weren't even supposed to open the sack
until we were at sea! If the ones who sold him to us see
him walking around town—"

". . . You won't care one whit because you'll already
be at sea with your profits," Saliman finished loftily.
"Spare me your efforts to wheedle a higher price. Remember, I'm not some landowner who only buys one slave a
year. I'm too familiar with the trade to be convinced of the
worth of a slaver's word."

"But—"

"I'll give you fifty in gold for him. If that isn't sufficient I'll just have to review the rest of your stock again. I

was trying to be considerate of your schedule, but if you prefer to spend time haggling I have nothing else to do before midday.''

Faced with logic, an ebbing tide, and a more than generous offer, the slaver surrendered . . . as Saliman had known he would. Still, by the time the money had changed hands and the slaves hauled out of the hold and offloaded onto the wharf, the sun had already begun its slow climb into the heavens.

A wagon was waiting there, and the slaves were put in the load and covered with a tarp, the thief still secured in his sack. Saliman had a healthy respect for the youth's talents, and did not wish to return to Jubal with one slave and a tale of escape. The one called Shadowspawn would have to wait until they were in more secure quarters before his bonds were loosened . . . quarters safe not only from escape, but from prying eyes as well.

Despite his offhand manner with the slaver, Saliman kept a careful watch until his cargo was covered from sight. The fishermen had already left for their day's task so the wharf was deserted, but that could only serve to focus attention on his own activities. Though he had had no specific instructions for secrecy, he could see no advantage to letting it be known that the two slaves were still in Sanctuary, and countless disadvantages.

The driver clucked to his team and departed without a wave or a backward glance, leaving Saliman to find his way to the rendezvous on his own. Again, this was as planned. While it would have been easier to ride in the wagon, there were too many in town who recognized him on sight and knew him for Jubal's lieutenant. Shopping and hauling were not among his normal duties, and his presence on the wagon would have drawn unwanted attention to the cargo and its destination.

He was not normally awake, much less about at such an early hour, and as he trudged through the streets Saliman peered about him curiously as the shops and stalls of Sanctuary came to life, preparing for the day's business. There seemed to be more people in town now, a lot of strange faces what with the work being done on the walls. Work meant money in the pockets of the laborers, money which was quickly transferred to the coffers of shopkeepers, tavern owners and whores. The old hopelessness of Sanctuary and the more recent fears during the street wars and magic upheavals seemed to have disappeared in the light of the new prosperity. There was even a light, mischievous tone to the street haggling over prices which had never been there during the old days of desperation.

As he walked and listened, Saliman allowed himself a rare, leisurely moment of envy. It seemed so simple to earn your living that way . . . stock and customers, straightforward transactions where the biggest worry was price-setting and the rent.

How many years had he worked for Jubal now? Did any of these people appreciate or even suspect the amount of work necessary to maintain the crime lord's illusion of omnipresence?

Take this morning's exercise for example. His instructions had been simple enough: Two slaves of a given description, or rather one of a given description and the other a specific, known individual, were to be purchased from a ship where they were being held before that ship set sail. There had been no explanation as to how Jubal knew of their captivity or reason given for their rescue, just the

instruction to effect their release and to deliver them to
Jubal with a minimum of disruption or attention.

It would have been a simple enough matter, if it weren't
for the short deadline for his work. First, there had been a
matter of arranging for operating capital at an hour when
no goldsmith or moneylender was functioning. Then someone had to be sent to fetch a wagon and driver to meet him
at the ship while he prepared for the visit by learning all he
could about the slaver he was to deal with. Though in this
case it had proved unnecessary, the information that the
slaver had a favorite mistress in town could have proved
invaluable if he had proved to be difficult to negotiate
with. A timely kidnapping would have given Saliman all
the leverage he would need to effect the rescue . . . and of
course, that contingency had had to be arranged as well.
The men standing by near the mistress's dwelling would
have to be paid for their time as well as their skills, even
though the latter had not been called on.

Fortunately Saliman's records on the night shift of the
city guard were up to date, though the recent reorganiza-
tion had thrown everything for a cocked hat for a while.
He knew who was on duty, what their patrol patterns
were, who was lax and who was bribable, so the return
journey from the wharf could be routed to best avoid
interference or questions. It might seem a minor thing, but
the recent rash of slaver kidnappings had set the watch on
edge, and Saliman had no desire to purchase the two men
only to be accused of kidnapping them himself.

Yes, it would be nice to be able to do business openly
and simply. Boring perhaps, but nice. Saliman smiled at
the thought, then dismissed it. The truth was, he enjoyed
his work. If anything, his administrative duties had dou-
bled when Jubal moved his organization underground, and

the challenge and excitement generated by the simplest of tasks, like the release of two slaves, was payment in itself . . . though his actual salary was nothing to be ashamed of. Being close to the crime lord meant not only having an overview of everything that happened in town, but actually having a hand in shaping events as well. It was a fascinating job. One Saliman wouldn't give up for the world.

His thoughts amused and occupied him all the way to his destination . . . the delivery entrance of The House of Whips and Chains. This brothel was perhaps the most dubious member of Sanctuary's Street of Red Lanterns, catering to the most bizarre and jaded tastes of a notoriously tasteless town. Even so, it would be strange to have an open wagon pull up to the front door, and as such the use of the delivery door was a must. Even here, or, perhaps, especially here, the streets had eyes and it did not pay to relax one's vigilance.

The thief had been released from his sack and was being held, still bound and gagged, between two retainers. Saliman noticed that the youth's eyes were alert and wary, and assumed that whether it was drugs or seasickness which had caused the earlier dullness, it had since worn off. There was no sign of the brothel's women; caution or the hour confined them to their rooms. Also, there was no sign of the second slave, which he assumed meant that Jubal was currently occupied with the interview. This last assumption, however, turned out to be incorrect.

"He wants you upstairs, third door," one of the retainers greeted him flatly. "You're to take this one with you."

So Jubal had finished with the other slave already and was waiting . . . impatiently from the sounds of it.

Saliman fought back the urge to grimace and simply nodded as he motioned for the thief to precede him up the stairs. Any indication of difficulty or disunity within Jubal's forces had to be hidden from outsiders. He had worked too hard teaching new recruits the necessity of maintaining that illusion to shatter it himself.

His charge paused in front of the indicated door, and he reached past to rap sharply on the door with a knuckle. The particular rhythm he used signaled that he wasn't alone, but when several moments passed without a call to wait, he opened the door and ushered the thief inside.

The room was dark, one of the windowless, possibly soundproof chambers of the house. The only light came from a small brazier filled with glowing embers from which protruded the handle of a branding iron. There were shackles on the wall, and a low sofa where one could recline comfortably while watching the branding process.

"Close the door."

Jubal's voice came from one of the corners the light didn't reach. Saliman obeyed, smiling at his employer's invariable flair for the dramatic.

"Remove his bonds."

Again Saliman moved to comply, this time twirling a blade from its hiding place in his sleeve. He made the move deliberately showy. The thief had a reputation for knives. It wouldn't hurt him to know there were others in Sanctuary who prided themselves in their blade-handling ability. As he reached for the gag, however, the youth beat him to it, ungagging himself with hands that were somehow free from the ropes that had secured them.

Though Saliman showed no reaction, he knew the thief had won this particular round of showing off. So did Shadowspawn, who shot him a mocking glance as he tossed the gag and ropes aside. It seemed doubtful the two would become fast friends.

"Hanse . . . sometimes called Shadowspawn." Jubal said, moving into the light of the brazier. "Do you know who I am, thief?"

The youth folded his arms across his chest, his stance arrogant and rebellious.

"We've never met, but it's easy to figure who you are. You're Jubal, right? You're older than I thought."

Saliman winced at the thief's brazen mockery of Jubal's spell-aged body, but the crime lord seemed to take no offense.

"True, we've never met. In fact, you're one of the few of the local talent who never approached me for work, or at least to sell information. I was always curious as to why."

"I work alone," Hanse shrugged. "Besides, I'm choosy about my friends."

"Not too choosy, if your friends include the likes of Tempus Thales." Jubal retorted, his voice hardening. "And as for being your own man . . ."

He lifted the iron from the brazier.

". . . I fear that came to a halt when the slavers took you. You're mine now. Bought and paid for."

Saliman expected Hanse to flinch, but the thief was uncowed. Though his eyes followed the iron, his voice was firm and confident.

"You aren't going to brand me." he said, more as a statement than a defiant challenge.

"I'm not?"

"You don't have to untie me to brand me." Hanse pointed out. "If anything, the process would be easier if I were still tied. That means you want to talk. All right. Quit waving that iron around and let's talk. What is it you want?"

Jubal stared at the thief for long moments before returning the iron to the brazier. Saliman could understand why.
There was nothing in their record to indicate Hanse pos-
sessed the intelligence he was now displaying. He wondered if this would mean a change in Jubal's plans.

"You've changed, thief," the crime lord said at last.
"What happened while you were gone to change you?"

For the first time since removing his bonds, Shadowspawn
seemed to falter.

"I . . . I'd rather not talk about it."

"Very well," Jubal nodded. "Shall we get down to
business?"

Interesting, Saliman thought. *The thief doesn't fear the
branding iron, but his recent past makes him uncomfortable.* Though Jubal did not look his way or give any other
indication, he knew he was expected to make note of
Shadowspawn's apparent vulnerability and investigate it as
soon as possible.

"How did you know where I was?" Hanse said suddenly.

"I have many sources of information." Jubal waved
deprecatingly. "That particular piece of news came to me
from the S'danzo."

"The S'danzo?" the thief frowned. "I didn't know you
had any friends among the S'danzo."

"I don't," the crime lord acknowledged without rancor.
"But now at least a few of them owe me a favor for
arranging your freedom. No, the information came from
one of *your* friends."

"My friends?"

"Two of them, actually." Jubal added, apparently rel-
ishing the thief's surprise. "One of them, the older, sensed
your danger and went to the younger, the blacksmith's
wife, to divine your specific location. Hers was the added

price of freeing the other slave as well . . . a favor to
another client, I believe. Anyway, realizing time was short,
they passed word to me, asking for my intervention in your
behalf.''

Saliman was listening attentively. This was the first he
knew of the source of this morning's exercise. Learning it
now, he realized why Jubal had been so eager to have this
mission completed, and completed efficiently. He knew a
moment's pride that the crime lord had turned to him as
his first choice for crucial work, then returned to his
analysis.

The S'danzo were tight-knit and mutually supportive.
Jubal had been trying for years to find a chink in their
armor, and now their desperation over the welfare of a
thief had delivered opportunity into his hands. Saliman
wondered briefly of the price exacted for his work. Had
Jubal demanded guarantees and assurances, or had he
risked it all on performing this favor gratis, preferring to
leave the repayment unspecified and therefore open. Probably the latter. Jubal had gained much of his power from
just such favors owed in return for his help at key moments.

"Then I'm free to go?'' Hanse said uncertainly, glanc-
ing again at Saliman.

"I didn't say that.'' Jubal smiled.

"But you said the S'danzo paid for you to have me
freed.''

"What I said was, they asked me to free you from the
slavers. That's been done. However nothing was said about
freeing you from me . . . and I happen to have need of
your services myself.''

"Since when did you need help to steal something,''
Shadowspawn sneered, his old arrogance back.

"I don't, thief. At least, not from the likes of you,''

Jubal replied coldly. "There is, however, a task you can perform for me in return for your complete freedom . . . one involving someone who trusts you."

"I'm a thief, not an assassin," the youth snapped proudly.

The crime lord raised his eyebrows in exaggerated surprise.

"Reluctant to kill, are you? Strange, I don't recall your showing any reluctance the night you helped Tempus kill four of my men."

Even in the brazier's glow Saliman could see the thief blanch.

"I—"

"You *do* remember, don't you? That night outside the Lily Garden? Or perhaps you thought I didn't know about it."

"They attacked us. It was self-defense."

Shadowspawn seemed suddenly aware of the hot iron again.

"They were trying to punish Tempus for murdering their comrades . . . and stop him from continuing his sport of hunting Hawkmasks, of course," Jubal intoned. "I know you had no choice, however. Otherwise I wouldn't have left your killings without response."

He paused to study the thief.

"Now, if I thought you had a hand in freeing Tempus from Kurd's, I might not be so generous in my treatment of you."

Saliman kept a blank expression as he watched the thief try to hide his discomfort. It was clear that Hanse was unsure if Jubal was truly ignorant of his part in Tempus's escape, or if he was simply being toyed with. His fear of the crime lord was great enough, however, that he wouldn't risk Jubal's possible wrath by openly admitting his guilt.

Saliman knew, however, that now that fear was foremost in the thief's mind, they could get down to business.

"That's all behind us now. Rest assured I don't need you to kill anyone." Jubal said smoothly, as if reading Saliman's thoughts. "Actually, all you have to do to win your freedom is to arrange a meeting for me."

"A meeting?"

"Yes. With Prince Kadakithis. I believe he's a friend of yours?"

The thief was clearly off balance now.

"How did you know that?"

Jubal smiled.

"I've been aware of it for some time. I would suggest, however, if you want it kept secret, that you try to keep the Prince from shouting about it in public . . . like, from the top of brick piles?"

Hanse flinched at the memory, but gathered himself to rally back.

"Why do you want to meet with him? I'd have to tell him something."

"Probably not. I believe my name is not exactly unknown to him. Still, if it will ease things, tell him I have a business proposition for him."

"What kind of a proposition?"

Jubal turned back to the brazier and poked at the coals with the iron as he answered.

"There's a civil war coming, thief. Not a local upheaval like we've just survived, an Empire-wide struggle. Even you should be able to see that. This town's only hope of success is to rally behind one leader . . . and right now Kadakithis would seem to be that leader. I plan to offer him my services . . . mine and my organization's. I believe we can aid him as an intelligence network, providing information and, if need be, stilling dissenting voices. I think even Vashanka's priest would admit our value in that capacity.''

The crime lord turned to face the thief.

"All you have to do is arrange the meeting. Unfortunately, my position makes it difficult, if not impossible, to approach him through normal channels. Arrange it, and you may go free."

"What if I agree and just keep going?"

"I'll find you." Jubal said calmly. "More important, until you've discharged your obligation to me, you'll be my slave. Legally, bought and paid for. I don't have to brand you."

The crime lord tossed the iron back into the brazier to illustrate his point. "You'll know it, and I'll know it. I think that knowing you're not your own man, that you belong to me, will mark you more than I could ever do with a branding iron."

Saliman was not so sure, but he had learned to trust Jubal's judgement when it came to people. Watching the thief ponder the proposal, he began to believe anew.

"What if the Prince doesn't agree? He's changed since I've been gone. There's no guarantee I can convince him if he isn't interested in your offer."

"All I ask is that you try." Jubal grimaced. "If he refuses, then I'll let you buy your freedom . . . for five hundred in gold."

Shadowspawn's head came up.

"Five hundred? That's not enough!"

Jubal laughed.

"I should think you'd be more likely to argue the price was too high, especially considering what we paid for you.

Still, if it will make you feel better, I could name a higher figure.''

Shadowspawn shook his head. ''You could double it . . . triple it even and it would be too low.''

''I know.'' Jubal said solemnly. ''The price always sounds low to a slave. It's because he thinks of his worth as a man, while the buyer and seller see him only as merchandise.''

Saliman could see the crime lord's thoughts turning to his own beginnings in the gladiator pens, but then Jubal seemed to shake off the memories as he continued.

''The price stands at five hundred,'' he stated, eyeing the thief. ''Frankly, I'd rather you concentrated on arranging the meeting. *That* is priceless to me.''

''I'll see what I can do. Can I go now?''

''One more thing. While you belong to me, I feel a certain responsibility for your safety. Here.''

The crime lord produced an oilskin-wrapped package from within his tunic and tossed it to Shadowspawn. Opening it, the thief found a familiar assortment of knives and throwing stars.

''I wouldn't ask you to walk the streets of Sanctuary unarmed. You'll probably feel more comfortable with your weapons. In case you're wondering, a man named Tarkle was selling them.''

''I know,'' the thief growled, settling the glittering bits of death in their customary places. ''I recognized his voice when they loaded me on the ship.''

Saliman had to hide his smile. Obviously Jubal had planned this surprise as the climax to the interview . . . a final demonstration of his access to secret information. The thief had already known the secret, but luckily

Shadowspawn was so preoccupied with his knives that he didn't realize how anti-climactic the announcement was.

"Well, whatever you're thinking will have to wait until after you've seen the Prince." Jubal ordered irritably. "I didn't go to all this trouble to lose you in an alley brawl. Remember, for the time being at least, you're not your own man. You're mine."

"Oh, I'll remember. Believe me, I'll remember."

Saliman felt a sudden chill as Shadowspawn met the crime lord's look with a gaze that was not at all subservient.

THE BEST OF FRIENDS

C. J. Cherryh

Morning on the streets of Sanctuary, a cold, knife's edge wind that rattles at shutters prudently closed in the thief-plagued maze, and drizzle comes on that wind, to slick the stones and darken the aged wood and make muck out of the filth that lies in every crack and crevice of the cobbles.

Citizens stir out, nonetheless. A body has to, who wants to eat. Everyone goes cloaked and muffled, from the beggars in their grime-colored rags, to the well-to-do factor on his way to the wharfside warehouses.

Thus Amhan Nas-yeni, an ordinary sort of man, a man with a nobody face and a nobody shock of dark hair beneath the hood, neither tall nor short, stout nor thin. Nas-yeni goes at a moderate pace in these streets, cloaked and muffled, and quite unremarkable among the average Ilsigis of better than average means, merchants, shopkeepers, traders and smiths.

In fact he is a tradesman and still solvent, despite the recent chaos that saw blood, not rainwater, running in the gutters of the town—some might say, *because* of that chaos, which needed supply of weapons and other such illicit things, as well as licit ones, to people who could pay not always with coin, but sometimes in protection, sometimes in elimination of threats, sometimes in liberated goods that had the stamp of Rankene military on them, but there was always a market. There was always a market, that was what Nas-yeni would say. He walked a careful line, did Amhan Nas-yeni, and walked it with, in his own estimation, scrupulous integrity: a man of honor. A man of principles.

A man who loved his son, and who had warned him, at the same time he understood young idealists, and was proud of him.

"Be sensible," he had told his son. "*Trade* is the way to power."

And his son Beruth: "*Trade!* When the Rankene pigs tax us to the bone and confiscate our shipments!"

"Did I say, *compliance?*" he had said. "Did I say, stupidity?" Tapping the side of his head. "Brains, young hothead. Trade is an art of the mind. Trade is an art of compromise—"

"*Compromise!* With Rankan *pigs?*"

"—In which you contrive each time to make a profit. In which you use your *head*, young man."

"When they use the sword. No, papa. Not when they can just take everything. Not when they don't have to play the game. Not with the sword only in *their* hands. You fight your way. I'll fight mine. We're both right."

With that light in his eye and that half-smile that haunted a father's sleep. Like the way he had found him two days later, where the Rankans had thrown the body, out on the rubbish heap where birds, in those dark days, gathered in black, carrion-hunting clouds. Beruth had *had* no eyes,

then. And what else they had done to him before the birds
got to him . . .

Nas-yeni had fought his war of trade then. Had stripped
himself to the bone, not selling, at the last, but giving
away everything that he had to the rebels, paying out coin
and weapons and supply to hire men who would find
Rankans to question, to find out one thing, only one thing:
who.

Who, because the why of it did not matter. He was
Ilsigi. He was an honorable man, the way Ilsigis had been,
before Ilsigis tried to trade with Rankan lords who had a
sword, when they did not. He was of a very old family.
He remembered, as many Ilsigis no longer did, the entire
tale of his ancestors and the worth of them.

He remembered, as even he had forgotten for a while,
until his son reminded him, that blood is worth everything
in the world; and that once that debt is made, only blood
can pay it.

Their names, he had asked of his informants. *Give me
their names*.

And the answer came back, finally: *The Stepsons Critias
and Straton*.

He began then, to learn everything that he could learn
about these two names. He learned their partnership in the
Sacred Band. He learned what this meant. He learned their
warnames and their histories, as much as his informers
could extract from gossip and the talk of Rankan soldiers
in bars and whorehouses.

He wanted more than their deaths. He wanted revenge.
He wanted their ruin, their slow, suffering ruin, of a sort
that would erode the soul, such a soul as such butchers
might have; and he wanted them to fear, at the last, the

way their victims had feared them, with a sickening, hopeless fear.

Therefore he had held his hand from Straton, when his informants told him Straton's soul was already in pawn—to a witch. Therefore he had sweated in agony, seeing the Stepsons ride north and Critias ride with them: therefore he had prayed nightly to the darkest of gods for the saving of one Stepson from war and from the chances of war—and for the weaving of spells about the other, spells that should damn him to hell and bring Critias—the stiff-necked, hard-handed Critias, straight from war and arriving bloody-minded in a town rife with ensorcelments, a town Straton commanded—bring Critias back with a vengeance, oh, yes, the man of war to the man bespelled, his partner, his—lover, doubtless, in the way of Sacred Band partners: Nas-yeni knew every detail he could glean of the Sacred Band, *studied* them, obsessively, the way he had once studied his rivals in business, and studied, most particularly, this Pair, their reputations, their manner, the time of their sleeping and eating and the look on their faces . . . even that, because he had been *near* them, oh, *often*, that he had stood so close to one or the other of them, had brushed against them in crowds, had looked once in Straton's very eyes as they collided, unexpected—

—eyes that looked into my son's eyes, eyes that had no pity, eyes looking out of Hell now, is it, murderer? I could take you. I could slip a knife into you and watch those eyes go, oh, so shocked and frightened. . . .

But far too quick, far, far too quick. Good day to you, Rankan. Good day and gods protect *you, Rankan, against any chance of the streets.*

He had smiled at Straton, friendly as could be. And the Rankan, with whatever burdened his conscience, whatever hate, whatever distrust of Ilsigis who smiled at him, had looked confused and angry that an Ilsigi had touched him.

Perhaps . . . *expecting* that knife in the gut.

Often, on the street, once Straton settled into pattern, in those dark days, when only a fool would observe patterns—but Straton went befuddled in those days, befuddled and more and more hell-ridden—Nas-yeni would smile at him, that same, secret smile that had everything of obsequiousness in it—*Hail, our conqueror. How brave of you, to ride among us, morning and evening, mazy-eyed and bewitched.*

Do you know me yet? His mother always said Beruth had my eyes, my mouth.

But he would not have smiled at you.

His mother died, do you know, in the winter. Took to her bed. Never smiled again. Just died. She took all the drugs I bought, one dose.

I owe you so much, Stepson. Truly I do.

They say the Stepsons are coming back to Sanctuary.

Critias . . . is coming home. What will you say to him, my friend? What will you tell him about this town you rule?

Who will you sleep with, then?

And how will the Riddler deal with you?

Every morning, every evening. One of the crowd.

Part of the crowd when Critias rode in, grim and hard—hard and soldierly, where Straton had grown fey, and strange.

Where Straton served Her who was whispered about only rarely and in the lowest of tones among the few Ilsigis who knew they had a Patron, of sorts.

It confused even Nas-yeni.

But the torment, the absolute hell in Straton's look

nowadays—that satisfied him. So did the rumors of estrangement.

And to help it along, he took to the skills of his youth—set up an archery butt in the warehouse now largely depleted of goods, but enough for a man to live on, who did not plan to live forever.

He had been a damned fine shot, in his youth, in the time that he had spent in the city guard. The hand and the eye remembered. Hate might make the one tremble. Grief might blur the eye. But purpose—that was clear and cold. Critias was back. Straton was in ruin already: one of the Pair was broken, and too difficult to predict.

Eliminate him.

From a rooftop.

In a way that an assassin could escape, and lay guilt upon the other Partner, and fear on all their company. It was what Beruth would have done, it was his kind of vengeance; it had a sharp, keen savor, the drawing of that arrow—blue-fletched, *Jubal's* colors, not because Nas-yeni had any particular grudge against the ex-slaver, but because it might make the maximum of trouble.

And the wind being what it was, and Straton's damned horse in the way—

But it had hit, all the same, and created havoc beyond Nas-yeni's own imagining—delivered Straton wounded, into the hands of enemies who had not handled him gently, by all accounts; and crippled him; while Tempus, displeased with a city block in ruins and with the rise of witchly influences in his ranks, one supposed, demoted him.

And departed, leaving, the gods be thanked, *Critias* in command of a city Straton had lusted after, Straton crippled and drinking himself stuporous night after night in the *Vulgar Unicorn*, Straton with so much witch-sign about him that he was notorious, and even footpads refrained from cutting his throat on his drunken wanderings to and from the barracks or the bars. They refrained because the word was out in the underworld of Sanctuary that this man was *protected,* and that throats would be cut if this man's was.

Things were altogether as Nas-yeni would have them: one enemy in a living hell, banished even from the witch's bed, living because no one was friend enough to kill him; and the other—the other—

There was no more to be done to Straton.

There was Critias . . . safe as yet, newly set into an office that Tempus had given him, perhaps with a sense that here was the only place that Straton might stay alive and Critias the only man who might have a chance to heal him: that much understanding Nas-yeni had of his enemies as he had had of his rivals in trade, canny trader that he had been, and smuggler, and judge of men. It was a fool who failed to see his enemy as man like any man, needing the things a man needed, like companionship, like solace, like—the illusions of these things, where the substance failed. By such things a trader lived and prospered; by such things, the likes of Straton and Critias worked on their victims, breaking their confidence as they broke the body.

By such things a man could unravel another.

A hunter had to *be* his own prey. They were locked together in this hunt, which had achieved a certain intimacy. Nas-yeni who had no family, had two men whose every thought he surmised, whose every move he could now predict; they kept him from loneliness; they kept his heart beating and the blood moving in his veins; they gave him something to think about and to look forward to, something which made him very glad his shots had gone amiss.

First Straton. Now Critias. Critias—who already suffered. He might simply live and watch Critias, watch the slow embitterment of a man left to a town which hated him. But he knew this man like a son. He knew that such embitterment would leach the feeling out of a man like Critias; knew that some morning Straton would simply turn up dead of drink or some mischance no bribe could save him from, and Critias would be sorry and relieved, and the boil would be lanced, that was all, the pain stopped.

That would never do.

A change in fortunes for Critias, the man facing all directions; and absolute hell for Straton, the man who had lost his way. The very plan was an indulgence approaching the sensual for a man who had restrained himself so long, so very long, and nightly prayed for his enemies, that they go on living.

And it was so easy, for a man so like every other man in Sanctuary, to the eyes of the invaders.

Wind and rain spatter at the eaves, rattle the shutters and bring cold into the room where Moria dresses, hastily, in the stink and the squalor of the tenement she shares with Stilcho, late of Ischade's service. A gray, dim light reaches the bed where Stilcho rests, drugged with what krrf she can buy him—sleep, *peace* which she can buy him, who has so little peace nowadays.

He is so handsome, so very beautiful to her whose beauty a mage gave her, whose beauty, Rankene-fair, Haught bespelled with stolen magic; Stilcho's, she had never seen—had been terrified of him, whom Ischade had raised from the dead; she had dreaded the sight of him, shrunk from the chance touch of his hand, which in those days had been chill, had seen only his scars, which the beggar-king had given him, a Stepson, in the long, long night that he had been the beggar-king's prisoner, and they had taken out his right eye, and were about to take the other when Ischade had intervened.

Ischade had claimed him then, since the Stepsons would not have him, a walking dead; and Ischade, whose curse took the life of her lovers, (except Strat, gods only knew why but Moria made guesses) had taken Stilcho in Straton's stead on those terrible nights when the black mood was on her, and she evaded Straton and drove all her servants from her presence—except Stilcho, on whom the curse fell with all its force, who could die, and die, and die, because she had strings on his soul, and could pull it up again from hell—

Moria had seen him on such mornings, had seen his face and shuddered at that look, that bleak terror, that awful intensity with which he would sit and *feel* of things, the table, the texture of the cloth, the flesh of his arm—as if it were precious and all too fragile.

She had heard him scream—had heard him, as no woman should hear a man, break down in tears and plead with Ischade, not again, not again, no more—

She had shuddered at the mere sight of him in those days.

But those arms, however chill, had been there to hold her when her own world came tumbling down. And his goodness, his loyalty, had touched even Ischade's sense of justice: she had brought him all the way *back*. She had set him free—free as a man could be, who had suffered what

he had, and who still waked screaming of nights, seeing
hell, and demons.

Krrf gave him peace. Krrf let him lie safe from his
devils—so, so good to see, his quiet sleep, his face that
was always so pale, at rest, the patched eye and the fall of
dark hair, all that was dark about him: the rest was light,
white-washed in the light that, like the chill wind, came
through the shutter slats.

She tied a ragged brown scarf about her blonde hair.
And from its place in the corner, disguised with clay, she
took a lump that was heavier than any rock ought to be, a
lump that weighed like sin—or pure gold.

She put it in the ratty basket she had, along with some
rags of laundry. She was very careful going out the door,
and left the latchstring inside, so only he could open it.

He would know, she feared, when he woke. The first
thing he would check would be that corner where they hid
the lump she had salvaged from the Peres house. Last
night she had begged him to let her take it to old Gorthis,
who would give her, she argued, fair price for it. He had
fenced for the gangs, back before the war. She *knew*
Gorthis, that he was an honest fence, at least, he gave the
fairest rates in Sanctuary. He need not suspect that it was
Ischade's gold.

No, Stilcho had said, absolute and angry. *No!*

What do you want? she had cried, too loudly, in this
damned tenement where every sound found other ears. Us
to starve?

Better that than some things, he had said, his hands hard
on her shoulders, his voice the lowest of whispers. Moria,
Moria, it's too dangerous, the damned thing's too *big*! It's
too much! Your fence can't afford a lump like that, he
can't pay you, he'll cheat you or he'll rob you, one or the

other, damn it all, Moria, you can't take that thing through the streets!

He was close to panic. His grip hurt her shoulders and the fear in him frightened her, who knew what his panics were like, how bad they were, how unreasoning and how difficult for her to bear, old nightmares, old memories (not so many months ago) of Stilcho's voice shrieking terror through the river house, haunting all their nights. A woman could not take that, in the man she loved. She did not want to remember that. She did not want him to break, who was at once so strong and so fragile.

We'll melt it down, he said.

When? she cried at him, and sucked in her breath and bit her lip. They had *been* over that territory. It was what he always promised whenever she talked about selling it. It took a fire bigger than they could raise in their apartment to melt a lump like that. They could not heat it and hammer it. The walls would carry every sound. The smell would go through the cracks and the gaps. There would be outcries: *fire* was the eternal terror in the tenements, and neighbors would come hammering on the door demanding answers, threatening them with violence, because they already knew that her man was . . . peculiar, and likely a fugitive mage: that was the whisper about him that she had heard, a dangerous kind of whisper, because mages were trouble, and a block of Sanctuary in ashes had proved it to the town at large.

And so, so easily in a place like this, a rumor could get started that would damn them both, and have their apartment broken into.

Or their throats cut.

She would go to Gorthis. He would take the lump and set up an account for her, and there would *be* no money,

except what it took to get a better place to live, and then
the things they needed, and the lease of a shop—a little
shop, that was what she wanted with that gold. A liveli-
hood for herself and her man where he could find the quiet
he needed to forget, and shutters and a stout door she
could bar against the dark, where She walked, and hunted.

Down the stairs, out onto the streets, a woman with a
basket of rags, a woman with a scarf over her head and a
heavy shawl and long skirts to disguise her youth and her
looks.

Uptown, like some cleaning woman going to work, for
some middling-well-to-do family not rich enough for servants. She was legion, in the midtown of Sanctuary: cook
or maid, respectable enough and not soliciting, and not a
mugger in the town would waste time on her, when there
was richer prey abroad.

Straton slid from the saddle and caught himself, hanging
from the bay's stirrup-leather, a little short of impaling
himself on the iron spikes that thrust up through Ischade's
hedge. The bay whickered, swung its head around and
nosed at him with the roughness a big horse could use—
warm, warm, not like Crit said, a dead thing, nor hell-
spawned. *It* loved him. He took it for omen. He clung to
that omen, that Ischade who had withdrawn every sign of
gentleness toward him, did not take the horse back, but
left it with him, left him one gift of hers, at least, which
had no hidden thorn.

He wept against the bay's neck, standing there in the
rain, both of them wet and chilled. He was very drunk.
And he knew that he ought to get back on the horse and
ride, quickly.

But he did not. He pushed himself away from the

warmth of the horse and staggered a step to the gate. The cold of the iron burned his hand. A rose thorn pricked his thumb and he carried his hand unconsciously to his mouth and sucked at the blood that welled up.

The gate swung inward and the way lay open through the yard, the maze of hip-high and scraggly weeds, the thornbushes and black, skeletal trees that all but obscured the little house, the gray stone porch.

He went, staggering a little and desperately trying to balance himself between the drunkenness it needed to come this far and the sobriety he had to muster to deal with her.

The thumb still bled, when he looked at it, and he wiped it on his breeches and looked up again at the door just in front of him, hearing the give of the hinges.

The sight of her hit him in the gut—so beautiful, all dark and light, her black dress blowing in the gusts, her square-cut hair flying like smoke about her face, about dark eyes that seized on his soul and threatened to uproot it.

"Ischade—" His jaw refused to work without his teeth chattering. He was cold through. The wind bit like a knife, here so much in the open, on the high shore of the White Foal. And there was no promise of yielding in the look she gave him. "Ischade, I *hurt*, I hurt so damned bad—" He held his arm, and the pain was there, even through the alcohol, worse, in the rain and the cold; aching so he could not sleep. "You healed the damn horse, can't you help me?"

"There are physicians."

"For Vashanka's *sake*, Ischade—"

"Vashanka didn't help Tempus. I doubt he has power here."

"Damn you!"

"Better men have tried. *Leave*, Strat. *Now*."

He stood there, shivering, his teeth chattering and the pain in his shoulder a dull, bone-deep ache, the way it had been for days and nights of this weather, the way the pain got into bone and brain, and he wished he had the courage to kill himself, but he kept holding out some idiot hope that someone, somewhere made this pain worthwhile. He had had her. He had had Crit. Neither one was acting sane. Neither one had acted sane for months. A man who had been loved once and twice in his life—went on expecting more of it, and believing things could be right again; a man who had seen the two people he most respected—yes, dammit, *respected*, for all she was a damn woman—in the whole universe . . . lose their minds and act like lunatics— kept expecting that they would wake up one morning with their wits about them and come to him and tell him they were sorry.

A man couldn't kill himself, whose world was that badly skewed. A man could not go—wherever he had damned himself to go—with his whole universe gone crazy and right and wrong all tangled; most of all with the faith (still) that if he could just hold on, if he could just beat reason into one of them, that everything would somehow sort itself out.

"Ischade, dammit, I didn't mean what I did! I didn't understand! Ischade, dammit, it's enough, it's porking enough, open the damn door!"

That was his voice, cracking and breaking like a teen-aged boy's. That was himself, on his hands and knees in the wet weeds, because the world had suddenly spun around to the left, and gone black a moment, and he had landed there, and hurt his shoulder in the process. He

nerved himself to push, and got the arm up against him
and one foot and then the other under him, and turned and
walked back to the gate, thinking that was about as far as
he could walk before he fell down and lay there and froze
to death in the rain.

But he did not. He made it to the bay horse, and hung
there against its warmth a while till he could get his breath
back.

"Take *him*, why don't you?" he muttered to the hedge,
the unnatural roses, the witch who had his soul in pawn.
"You've taken everything else, Take *him* and be damned
to you."

If she heard him, in her sorcerous ways of being aware
of everything near the wards, she gave no sign. The bay
horse stood rock-steady for him to mount, and bore him
away, where it chose: he did not care whether it was a
shelter or over the cliffs: let it choose. The White Foal,
beyond the trees, was roiled and muddy, and looked friend-
lier than the town did.

Ischade sat down, at the table in the house that was
somehow larger inside than outside, and which had more
rooms and windows than appeared from outside. She sat in
her cluttered living room, where the cloaks of former
lovers, like torn moths' wings, gave riotous color to the
floor, the couch, the chairs, the bed, cloaks and bright
cloth and here and there a trinket which a careless foot
might tread upon and break . . . of no interest to her these
days, these gray and deadly days.

She rested her elbows on the table and her face within
her hands, and went into that nowhere place which she had
learned to find within herself, as the Stepson Niko had had

it, that inner landscape which in her case was a maze of many doors, each one with a key and a lock.

The hallway was safe. It had turnings and there were dark places, and there were doors that rattled ominously and clamored with lost voices, doors which weakened if she thought of the thing behind them.

So she did not.

But somewhere, somewhere down the hall, there was a door still open. She knew that there was. She sensed it. And it was in that darkness far down the hall, where she did not willingly go. She might go up to that door and try to slip up on it and slam it quickly and lock it. But she was paralyzed with dread of it, that what was inside would remain tranquil for years if she did not attempt it. There would be time. There would be time to gather strength—

There was a room within which was treasure. A blue fragment spun within that room, power, secret power, filched from the ruin of magic in Sanctuary. She had hid it within herself, in that place where no other mage could go without killing her, and she, by the very curse that created her, could not die.

There was that place far away in the dark, where something waited—almost she could see it, red-eyed and smiling at her within that room at the end of the hall.

And there were the doors behind which she had shut away everyone who trusted her. She held those keys. She kept them in the room with the fragment of the Globe of Power.

It was her virtue, her sole virtue, that she listened to their rattling and their clamor at her sanity, when everything in her ached to let them out, to have them with her, vulnerable to that *thing* that waited down there, in the dark.

Especially Straton.

You healed the damn horse, couldn't you help me?

She hurt inside.

Heal him—yes. And prove to him by that, that she had not forsaken him, that there was hope for him and her.

And after that, after that—

She saw him lying still as all her other lovers, by morning light. It was the very fact that he loved her, that would damn him. He could not, now, take his healing as a kindness. No, to him, it would be an absolution. It would bring him to her as he had been—but more insistent, more himself, more violent and more desperate to prove his manhood after what he had suffered—

—and that was the very thing that would kill him. That was the nature of her curse.

The thing in the dark snickered filthily. *It* knew. It was amused by her helplessness, when she was one who held what it wanted.

Go to Randal, she thought. *Seek help in the Mageguild.*

But that would precipitate things for which she was not yet ready. She knew that she was not ready and would not be ready perhaps for years. She was far too unbalanced now. The tides of need and satiation which ruled her with the changing moon—were running too high, too violent. She prowled the Maze and the Downwind and sometimes the high streets near the palace, and dead happened, happened with more frequency than made her feel safe with anything she valued.

She *needed*, that was the unpalatable truth, needed sex the way Strat needed drink, to deal with the dark and the pain.

And she wanted him—so damnably much.

*   *   *

The *thing*—was there again. Stilcho saw it, the red eyes glowing in the murk, the smile like a smug face lit from inside, leaking red light at nostrils and mouth and blazing behind the eyes like hell itself.

It grinned, and the terror of that waked him with a yell that was still dying in his ears as he sat up, sweat-drenched and ashamed and expecting Moria's arms to hold him, Moria's voice to bid him hush, hush, and rest, Moria's lips to kiss him and whisper that he was safe.

"Shut up!" came the yell from somewhere else in the building. "Shut it up, dammit!"

He propped himself against the wall, blinked and shivered in the draft against his bare skin, still krrf-fogged and searching dazedly for Moria.

Not there.

She must have gone out to market.

But they were out of money. Flat broke, except—

Except—

"O *gods*."

He scrambled out of bed. He went to the corner and looked amid the junk and the clutter.

Not there. The gold was gone. So was Moria.

And he knew where.

Gorthis's shop was still shuttered at this hour, but he was stirring about inside by now, Moria knew his habits. The shop was on the lower floor of his apartment, in the building that he owned, and Gorthis, being more than prudent, never left his jewelry downstairs in the shop at night. He packed everything up and brought it upstairs, where a pair of vicious dogs guarded the upstairs halls.

In spite of the fact that no thief in Sanctuary tended to prey on a fence, whose good will was important as sunrise—

such precautions were necessary because there was always
the disgruntled customer.

Or the rival.

Moria seized the bellpull, of the doorbell in the shape of
a smiling Shipri—better, she thought in the hysterical
humor that came of having gotten this far unmolested with
her cargo, that it should be Shalpa, god of thieves. The
bell chimed inside, and she waited, her laundry basket on
the doorstep, herself within the shelter of the alcove, out
of the rain.

The little peephole opened. She stood on tiptoe, and
back a little.

And suddenly remembered—O *fool!*—that she no longer
was dark-haired Moria the thief, Moria the Ilsigi.

It was a beautiful stranger stood on Gorthis's step, her
blonde curls wrapped in rags, but her brows still pale, her
eyes blue, and her complexion whiter and fairer than any
Ilsigi's could be.

"Gorthis," she said, "let me in."

The peephole stayed opened a damned long while longer
than its once-upon-a-time wont. She sensed the consterna-
tion on the other side of the door.

"Who? What do you want?"

"Gorthis, it's Moria. *Moria*. You remember me. I bribed
this mage—"

It was not the truth, but it was close enough to the truth,
and simple enough to explain through a peephole.

The peephole shut. The door opened, on a fat, huge
man who looked more apt to be a blacksmith than a
goldsmith. Not a hair on his head except a tuft above
either ear that stuck out like some brindled monkey's ruff.
He utterly filled the door. His eyes, Ilsigi-dark, were wide
and worried.

"Moria?"

"Makeup," she said, clutching her laundry basket, which had gotten heavier and heavier from block to block. "Com' on. Gorthis, f'gawds'sake—it's *me*. Moria. Mor-am's sister."

He hesitated a moment longer, then backed out of the doorway and held it open for her and her basket, admitting her to the dim interior of counters and barred doors and barred sections: a goldsmith even in this section of town and in these days, had to worry, and Gorthis believed in defense. He always had.

"Shalpa's ass," Moria breathed, setting down the basket and looking open-mouthed at the maze of bars, "whole Rankan *army* couldn't make its way through here."

"Whole Rankan army ner Piffles ner any other damn pack of looters, girl, ain't nobody going to break into *my* place! I been respectable, I been respectable ever since the Troubles started. I ain't doing no more, so you can take yourself and whatever you got there—"

"This ain't no problem, Gorthis, I swear to you it ain't." She bent and dived after the lump in the middle of the laundry, held it up in both her hands, because that was what it took. "This here's *gold*. Gorthis. You don't got to *fence* it, you don't got to tell anybody, you just use it and gimme an account here—*look*, look—" She set down the clay-covered lump and stripped off her headscarf, shaking out blonde curls the sort that Moria of the streets never had had. "It's still Moria," she said in purest Rankene accents, "But I've come up in the world, Gorthis, I *pass*, and I need the money. Do me this favor and I won't forget it when I'm back in society."

"Magery," Gorthis breathed, wide-eyed. "You been witched."

"Expensive magery. And it lasts." She picked up the lump and held it toward him. "Lift it. It's a lot of gold. A *lot* of gold, Gorthis. No plated rock, you can test it. You'll have it. Like I said, all you have to do is pay me out a little at a time, in silver I can spend without answering questions."

"Shalpa and Shipri." Gorthis drew out a handkerchief and mopped his face. "They said it was you uptown. They *said* it was you. Mor-am come in here—trying to pawn this knife. *He* said you'd gone uptown."

"Where *is* my brother?" She did not want to know, she truly did not want to know. He was still Ischade's creature. He must always be, or suffer in terrible pain. But not to know whether he was living or dead—that uncertainty she could not bear.

"Ain't seen him since. I got no idea. Lemme see that thing."

She handed it to him. He hefted it.

"Damn—" he said.

"Told you, that's no rock inside."

He took it over to a work counter, through a barred gateway to a table where a barred shutter gave a little light. She followed, anxious, biting her lip as he brought the lump down hard on the table and shattered the clay around it.

Yellow gold shone in the light, veined with lines of soot.

"This's melted stuff," he said.

"It's not stolen." That was half a lie. She clenched her hands together. "It came from friends. They died in the riots. But I haven't got a place to melt it down. I know you're honest, Gorthis, you always were. You take your old cut, same as you always did, and you pay me out little at a time, isn't that fair?''

"Wait here. I got to get something." Gorthis hurried back past her to the cage door and through it.

He slammed it shut, and Moria stared at him open-mouthed in shock. But Gorthis was a little crazy about security. He always had been. She was willing to think it was that.

Until he turned the key and took it.

"It's *my* damned gold, Gorthis, I'm not going to steal it!"

"You ain't going nowhere," Gorthis said, and went and pulled on the cord that rang a bell somewhere way up on the roof, a thief-bell, that called the watch.

"What are you *doing*?" she yelled at him. She shook the bars of the gate, hopeless, because Gorthis's locks were always sound. "Gorthis, have you lost your mind?"

"I'm respectable," Gorthis said. "I been respectable ever since the Troubles started. I ain't getting into it any more, I got too many uptown clients." Another series of tugs at the bell rope. "Sorry, girl. Truly I am."

"I'll tell them! I'll tell them who you are!"

"Who are they going to believe, huh, girl, when I turn over you *an'* that great lump of gold to the watch? No, missy, this is going to be better fer me than fer you. I *prove* to 'em I changed my ways, that's what this'll do."

"I have friends uptown."

"No, you don't. I know what your *friends* are, girl, the neighbors done talked, the neighbors what got burned out around Peres, uptown. They got a warrant out fer you, hiring mages and all, arson and murder—you know the law doesn't come down on mages, ain't no way the watch is going to arrest *them*, now, is they? But them as *hires* 'em, now, they're *responsible,* ain't they? You go burning the whole town down, come in here with a lump of witched gold—''

''It ain't witched!''

''It come from the burnin'! Ever'thing up there's witched! And I ain't makin' no jewelry out of it and sellin' it to my clients! You're goin' to the watch, girl, an' you can explain to your neighbors 'fore the magistrate what you done up there on the hill, *I* ain't!''

''Let me out of here! Damn you, *damn you, I got friends, Gorthis, I got friends'll fry your insides, you damned snitch! I got* wizard *friends!*''

''No way,'' Gorthis said, pale-faced and sweating, and still ringing the bell for all he was worth. ''No way you got friends like that, missy, or they'd melt that there gold for you and not need no furnace. I ain't no fool! And you're going to hang, that's what's going to happen to *you—*''

An alarm was ringing in midtown, and Crit stopped the gray to listen. Not particularly his business: the watch and the guard responded to that sort of thing, and his own mind was on personal problems—a partner who had had a run-in with the watch last night, and who had been let go because the watch did not know what to do with him—and a Prince-governor whose orders were getting more and more arbitrary—*now* the damned be-curled and perfumed prig wanted a barrel tax and wanted all the taverns in town to pay a head tax . . . per customer. And he was supposed to break the news to Walegrin, whose men were supposed to make the thing work.

An alarm was not the kind of thing the city commander took for a personal responsibility. But he was in a mood to crack heads. He debated it a moment, then, set the horse off at a good clip—no run, counting the slick cobbles, just a businesslike jog that cornered well enough in the twisting streets, with their ghostly drift of cloaked, hooded figures themselves heading toward the trouble—daytime reflexes, the more so that the watch was surely on the way and folk figured there was some kind of entertainment to be had, watching the guard putter about after a thief who had probably run like hell when the bell went, and listening with delicious smugness to the shopkeeper tearing his hair and wailing . . . a mornings's worth of gossip, at least. And more of them would come, when they saw the city commander involved in it.

Damned busybodies.

He had an idea where the bell-ringing was coming from when he found the right street, about the time the bell went silent and he had an idea the watch had gotten there ahead of him. There was a jeweler hereabouts notorious for his eccentricity—and a shady past; and he saw the crowd and the waiting horses that said that matters were tolerably well under control.

He almost turned the gray about to go back about his business, back to his troubles with Strat and with the Prince-governor, figuring there was nothing here that needed intervention.

But the crowd *ohhhed* and *aaaahed* to a great deal of shouting, and pressed close upon the door, where there was evidently something going on. A guardsman was trying to keep spectators out.

Maybe, he thought, someone had cut the jeweler's throat.

But the place was supposed to be a real obstacle course. So the rumor ran. Real crazy man.

Curiosity drew him, since the morning's business was

not that attractive. He nosed the gray on through the crowd, figuring the guard could use a little help—might well be a few neighbors there hoping for free samples, if there had been some fracas inside and some stuff scattered.

"Get out of here!" the beleaguered guard was yelling, shoving with his sheathed sword at a clutch of women who wanted to get their noses in the door. The crowd booed that, and guffawed when a fat man appeared behind the guard and screamed at them to get out of his door.

"What's going on here?" Crit asked the guardsman, forcing the gray into service as a living barrier, and its teeth and the stamp of its feet made a little room.

"Dunno, sir," the guardsman said. "We got a woman and a laundry basket and a damned great lump of gold old Gorthis says is witched and stolen and he locked 'er up and called the watch." The guardsman looked doubtful a second, then: "Woman looks Rankan, sir, and old Gorthis says she's a thief named Moria who lived in the Peres house, and we got a warrant out on her. The corporal don't know. We got a lot of warrants. But she talks uptown."

"Moria. Out of Peres." Crit drew in a deep breath, all at once awake in this slow and nuisanceful morning. He slid down and threw the gray's reins at the guardsman as he ducked under the horse's neck and put his head into the jeweler's shop.

The damn place looked like the city jail, it had so many bars. And in the clutches of a trio of guardsmen was a blonde and distraught young woman, answering questions, shaking her head furiously, no, no, and no.

"Hey," he yelled, interrupting it all. The woman looked at him, and gods, it was for certain Moria, who had hosted the whole Sacred Band at the truce-feast in Peres house.

Before it ended up a pile of blackened sticks and tumbled stone.

"Moria?" he asked. And listened to the whole thing over again, from the jeweler Gorthis shouting in one ear, the guard corporal shouting at Gorthis to shut up, the woman sobbing and shouting that she was innocent, that Gorthis was a crook who wanted her gold, which was *hers*, and Gorthis her enemy who had lured her here with promises of help.

"Gold might be hers," Crit said slowly. "Ease up a little. Let's just all be calm, can we? Ma'am, I think you and the gold *and* Gorthis here better plan to spend the morning uptown and get this straightened out. They say there's a warrant out on you. I don't know about that. I know *I've* got a few questions. Where are you staying?"

The woman's face might have been a waxen mask. An honest woman might have answered. There would not have been that desperate dart of the eyes, like something trapped. Crit had had a lot of experience, judging reactions like that. He pulled out his kit and rolled himself a smoke, giving her time to answer, if she would. Then, finally, lighting the smoke from the lamp by the door:

"Well, sergeant, I think you might as well take the whole damn mess uptown. You can have Gorthis. Woman goes to my office. Gold goes to your captain and it damn well better stay accounted for. Hear?"

"Yessir," the sergeant said, and Crit nodded, puffed on his smoke to calm his nerves and walked as far as the door. He had a rare impulse to chivalry, and turned back to the sergeant.

"*Don't* take her through the streets like that. Put a wrap on her and don't bruise her up any, all right?"

"Yessir."

He walked out, collected his horse and climbed up,
riding out through the crowd, paying no attention to the
shouted questions and the ohhhs and ahhhs and the rumors
flying thick and fast. Up the street, then, where the last
few shyer onlookers stood gawking, and around the corner.

A man fled his path. *There* was one with reason to avoid
him. He was halfway moved to find out why, but the
streets were slick and there was enough commotion hereabouts. The chance of overtaking the man was nil, without risk to the gray, and he was not about to take the
chance. Dawn, and there were still some of the night-
skulkers out, pickpockets, for sure, who worked their best
in circumstances like the press and commotion back there.

Not his business, that. Not a soldier's business at all.

He rode on his way, down the mostly deserted street, at
a walk, already back to the problem of the head tax.

And was halfway startled when a cloaked man came out
of the alley and looked up at him and ran over to him.
"Officer—officer—my son, f'godssakes, my son, they
stabbed my son—"

"Who?" He reined in the gray, which was as like to take
a piece out of the man as not. "How many of them?"
The whole damn district watch was tied down back around
the corner, and a purse-cutting that went to murder was the
way of things in this damn town.

"Come on!" the man cried, running back for the alley—
merchant, to look at him. And distraught.

"Hell!" Crit threw down his smoke, gathered up his
crossbow from the saddle-ties and turned the gray down
the alley after him. He had wanted a head or two to crack.
He was still in the market.

*   *   *

The iron gate flared blue as Stilcho brought up against it and pushed, sweating and gasping and desperate. Witch-fire stung his hands and ached in his bones, but the gate gave to his push, and he waited for no other invitation from the river house. He ran as far as the gray stone steps before slick stone and his exhaustion betrayed him: he sprawled painfully against the edge of the steps and lost his wind, fighting even so to pick himself up.

"Stilcho," Her voice said, and he looked up, heart hammering, at the face that figured in so many of his bad dreams.

"Stilcho?"

He gathered himself up to his knees and to his feet, hanging onto the post which supported the roof. He was taller than She was, if he were not standing beside the porch and She, on it. But Her presence was overwhelming, so that all the warmth of running leached out of him, and all the months of hiding seemed useless. He was back. He had never been free. He had never owned his soul, from the night Ischade drew it back into him.

"The w-watch has M-Moria," he stammered, while the pain in his ribs bent him against the post that was the only thing keeping him on his feet. "They've *arrested* her—"

"For what?" Ischade asked, a soft voice, precise, and cold.

"Th-the—" O gods, there was no lying to Her. There could not be. He tried for breath and knew what bargain he had come to strike, a bargain for what She already owned. "The gold from P-Peres house. They say she stole it."

"She did," Ischade said, that same quiet precision. "From *me*."

He had no answer for that. It was truth. Claiming it was himself, claiming anything but what was—might end everything. "You can help her," he said. "P-Please *h-help* her."

"She left my employ. She stole from me. Why should I intervene?"

"I'll come b-back." His lips stumbled around the words. His soul was cold to the roots, and he met that stare of hers with a vertiginous feeling that it was already sliding away from him. "I'll come back to you."

There was long silence. Then:

"You and Moria," Ischade said. "Love does make fools of us, doesn't it?"

"Please. Get her away from them."

"I thought that *Moria* would come, long since, wanting her fine things and her soft bed. I least of all expected *you*, Stilcho. And for her sake. How touching."

"My lady—"

"I confess I *have* missed you, in more ways and for more reasons than you know." She extended her hand and touched his cheek with the backs of her fingers, a touch which—he could not help it—made him shudder; and She could not but tell that. "A *good* man. And hers. Why, Stilcho? Debt of honor? Or do you love her?"

"I l-l-love her."

"Poor man." She came close and folded her arms about his head, drew it against her breast. Her breath stirred his hair and he felt her gentle kiss, felt the unlikely warmth She gave despite the chill of her hands as She lifted his face. "I will help her. I will take you back. I will keep her with all the fine things she loves. You as well. And I shall be kinder. You know that there are times I cannot be."

"I know that—"

"She will be safe enough. I will send a message uptown. We'll do everything by town law. As the aggrieved party, I *give* her the gold. See? Solved. Come inside and I'll give you the paper with my seal on it. You take it to the Palace and tell them if they have any questions about it, come to me. Come. I shan't bite. You know better than that.''

They had brought the gray horse in from the streets—no one had dared steal it, nor any of its gear; it had wreaked havoc on a storefront and kicked a man in the gut before the watch got a couple of riders to herd it up the street and one of them was horseman enough to talk it calm and get the reins without having his fingers taken off or his horse kicked.

Of Crit there was no sign at all, and Straton found himself coldly, terribly sober, interviewing everyone in the affair, no one of whom knew a damned thing, except the horse might have come from a dozen streets, all of which they were searching door to door; and as many alleys, more likely, all of which they were searching, down to the rubbish heaps and the refuse, looking for the body. Crit's bow was missing, not with the horse and not in any place he would have left it. He must have had it with him. Must have had reason to have it in hand when trouble came on him. So he had not been taken utterly off his guard. And they had still got him. Whoever it was.

There had been some kind of fracas involving a goldsmith and a lot of crowd in that area. Crit had been there. Had found the woman Moria in the middle of it and she was in custody, along with the jeweler and a lump of gold. That, Strat reckoned, had nothing to do with it. Crit had ridden out of there, the guard swore to that, ridden out of there and down the street and vanished somewhere within that district, to judge by where they had first reported the loose horse.

He began to build a scenario in his mind—the crowds, the likelihood of cutpurses and pickpockets, and Crit maybe spotting something—

—running into trouble and ending up just a corpse someone had to get rid of, down some sewer, into some basement, under some rubbish heap: gods, *Crit*, to end like that, in some damned alley, in a damned police action, in something that was not his job, because Crit, being Crit, tended to be all over what he was managing—

—or maybe Crit had seen someone; or someone had seen him, who had a grudge. Gods knew there were people with grudges. He had a vision of blood in the streets again, some new set of crazies with an agenda, murdering any symbol of Authority they could get their sights on. Sanctuary had seen blood and blood and blood, and it had been quiet a while, but the same damned lunatics were still in town, those some other lunatic had not killed.

He felt sick at his stomach, that was what he felt, sick and helpless and scared, because he had shot his mouth off with Crit and done everything wrong he could do—

—he had been stinking *drunk* this morning when Crit had been riding the streets alone, because he had no partner he could rely on any more. And he hated himself. He despised himself. He could not figure out how he had become what he had become. As good as if he had run and left his partner to face his killers alone. That was what he had done. And if men shied off from him this morning and if he could not meet their eyes, there was reason for it.

Oh, *damn*, he wanted his hands on someone.

He wanted Crit alive, he wanted Crit to come walking in

that gate all right and madder than hell; and he would listen to everything Crit had to say and swear that it was right, and go back to him and make it right if Crit would have him, that was what he would do. Crit *needed* him, needed him in the worst way; and Ischade had thrown him out and battered his pride for the last time, he swore she had. It was over. Finished. He had no more intention to go crawling to her a second time.

Gods, if he'd come walking in here—lost his horse, that's all; we'd give him a hard time, he'd curse us to hell, I'd stand there and maybe he'd know without my saying a thing, know what hell I've been through—we could talk, then. Let him swear me to hell and gone, no matter, get him talking and maybe I could talk to him, the way we used to—way we used to be—

A man came up on him, a guard sergeant, to report they had a man in hand, from the gate—"—asking after the woman, the one they arrested, says he can prove whose the gold is—"

He had told them he wanted to know everything about everyone involved. He had sent a man he trusted to ask Moria if there was anything she could tell him, though he doubted it. *This* man was at hand.

Was *Stilcho*. He saw Ischade's former lover, conspicuous in his shabby cloak and in the black patch which covered his missing eye. City guards hastened him along with a firm grip on his arms; and Strat's mind raced wildly, trying to make connections with facts which did not, no matter how he pushed and pulled them, fit any pattern he could understand.

And damn it all, *Ischade* and her household were not what he wanted to deal with now.

Except Stilcho was no longer Ischade's. Nor was Moria.

And somehow, for some terrible reason, they were here, under this wan gray sky, with Crit missing, himself and Stilcho who had met often enough in Ischade's house; and Moria under arrest: that was at least some vestige of connection in events, but it was on the wrong problem, surely it was the wrong problem.

"Stilcho," he said, and did not tell the guards to let him go. One of them handed him the paper.

Ischade's spidery, elaborate hand. Her signet. *To Critias, under the authority of His Imperial Highness Theron, and His Grace Kadakithis. Commander of the City: You have arrested one of my servants for possession of property I gave her, to which she has legal title. The lady Moria is therefore innocent of wrongdoing. I ask for her immediate release and will thank you for your prompt and earnest attention to this matter. Under my personal seal: Ischade, herself.*

Straton read it through twice. *To Critias.*

Critias.

"Let him go," he said sharply, and when the guards did not take their cue: "Leave him!" And waited until the city guard was out of earshot, the paper trembling in his hand. "What's this have to do with Critias?"

"To do with—"

"My partner's missing, dammit, missing while the city guard hauled Moria and that gold out of a jeweler's shop, the last damn place they saw him! Where is he?"

"I don't know," Stilcho said, bewildered-looking, and was not lying. Straton's heart sank, the little that that chance had raised it. "I don't know. Moria got picked up—that's all. Critias was there. I saw him. Corner of Regent Lane and High Street. He was on a gray horse. I didn't want to get picked up too; I ran and he didn't follow. That's the truth, Strat. I was one of you. My oath—it's the truth, it's all I know.''

"Moria know anything?''

Stilcho shook his head. "I don't think so. I was there because she sneaked out with the gold, I knew she was going to get in trouble—'' It was too much truth now. Stilcho let his voice trail off, with that desperate look in his eyes, the look of a man who had committed himself too far to a man no longer in the same game. "It's in the letter. Her seal.''

"Her seal. Dammit to hell, is this *her* game?''

"No! Gods—no, I don't think so.''

She wrote to Critias. She didn't know.

But by the gods, she can find out.

"Sergeant!''

"Sir!''

"Tablet. Fast.'' He grabbed Stilcho by the arm, pulled him close. "I thought you'd left her house. Alive.''

"I'm g-going b-back.'' Stilcho pulled to free the arm, desisted when he did not make it easily. The single eye was desperate, distraught. "N-not easy b-being on the streets.''

"I can slip you into the guard. Call it a favor. You could have come to me. I owe you one.''

"Too l-late.'' There was all hell in that look. "Too late.''

"She's got you.'' *Dead again?* In the chill of the wind, there was no way to tell.

"She's got me. And M-Moria. No help for us. Strat, for godsakes, get Moria *out* of there—if you owe me anything, get her *out* of that hole—''

The sergeant came up with the tablet and a stylus. Straton took it and wrote: *Walegrin*—and a long scratch that stood for all the damned protocols. *Send the woman Moria to the palace guardstation with this messenger and your order to hold her there until I sign the release. Straton, for Critias—* Another long line, for all Crit's authorizations. He slammed his ring into the soft wax of the tablet and shut it. "No damn time for an overseal. Get this to Walegrin at his headquarters and hurry about it."

The sergeant left at a run.

"I'll go with him," Stilcho said, and Strat caught him a second time.

"She's not free."

"Not—"

"If Ischade wants her out, Ischade can find Critias. Come on, man. We're going to go tell her that."

Stilcho said nothing, only came as fast as he could, exhausted as he was.

"Horses," Straton yelled, and the horses were waiting at the gate.

Crit moved, tried to pull himself up from the upside-down position in which he had waked, in which he had already suffered hell, coming to soaking wet and staring upside down into the face of a lunatic with a knife.

He had lost consciousness several times, and vomited his gut out along with a good amount of the water he had swallowed when the Ilsigi who avowed he wanted to kill him slowly had lowered him upside down into a rain barrel and waited till he choked. Again. And again. And again. And in between times had let him down, trussed hand and foot, to lie heaving and puking on the floor of the basement.

He had screamed before his voice went. He was not proud. He had hoped to hell a dozen of his men would be searching by then, would hear the ruckus and come break the door down. But this place, wherever he was, was down deep, lantern-lit, and with some sort of padded baffle all round, so that there was precious little sound going to get up to the streets, if that was even where they were any longer.

This fine, this upstanding citizen with the kid in trouble— had got behind him and hit him with something that stung like hell in the back of his neck and then weakened his knees and dropped him helpless as a baby to the alley cobbles, whereupon this fine citizen had kicked him in the groin, in the gut and in the head, and the light had gone out for he had no idea how long, or through what.

Right now he wanted only to get air past the bubbling of whatever was in his nose and his throat, and upside down, he could not do that, the blood was hammering in his neck and his head and his gut hurt too much to let him get that breath.

The rope paid out suddenly and dropped him onto his arms, his shoulders and the back of his head, driving the breath out of him.

He could not get it in again. He went out.

And came to propped up against something lumpy and solid, and with the self-same lunatic squatting there with a knife in his hands.

"I'm not going to kill you," the man said. "You'd like to know my name, but I'm not going to kill you, not going to give you a thing to give your friends, either. All us Ilsigis look alike—don't we, pig?"

He thought: *I'll remember you, Wriggly*. But he was not about to argue. Never argue with a lunatic with a knife.

"What'll you describe? Medium build. Black hair? Do you a lot of good, pig. I got your partner. Now I have you. Witch has your partner. Maybe the witch can bring back your eyes. Can she? What would your partner pay for that? It might be worth it to me, pig—just knowing that.''

O gods. O gods. We've got trouble, haven't we?

Hell-bent through the streets, too fast, for the weather, but the bay horse made it without slipping and the borrowed sorrel made it, somehow. Strat did not stop to see, reckoning Stilcho would follow as he could.

And this time he pulled up in front of the river house and slid down to drop the bay's reins in front of the hedge, he was cold sober and in a deadly hurry. He shoved at the gate and got a shock, kicked at it then.

''Ischade, dammit! You want that damn girl, you get out here, fast!''

Stilcho rode in behind and slid down, ran up to the gate and got it open—him, it did not shock.

For him, Ischade's door opened, and Ischade came out and stood on her porch, waiting.

''Come on,'' Stilcho said nervously, and grabbed Strat by the arm.

He needed no pull. He all but beat Stilcho to the porch steps; and held Stilcho's distance from her, who stood cloaked and dark and ominously frowning.

''Somebody waylaid my partner,'' Strat said. ''Ischade, I'm asking you—personal favor, if I've got any credit left. Tell me who and where.''

''Where is Moria?''

''Guard custody. She's safe. She'll be fine. I'll let her go when I've got Crit, hear me? You want a favor out of us, we want one out of you. Fair trade.''

Prolonged silence.

''Fair trade,'' he yelled at her. ''Dammit!''

''A remarkable day,'' she said. ''So many people want

favors of me. And magic comes so dear nowadays. You don't want me. You want a fortune-teller. A finder of lost objects. Surely you can find one down at the bazaar with the jugglers and the mimes.''

"Don't put me off, woman, I'm not in the mood for your jokes!"

"You mistake me. Do you want my help?"

"Yes." Breath came short. "Dammit, I have to have it."

She turned her shoulder and the door opened wide. "Come in."

He mounted the steps, Stilcho treading behind him. *Not* like old times in this familiar room that was somehow the same and somehow more chaotic in its disorder and the litter. He was where he would have given a great deal to have been this morning. And now there was ice in his gut, because there was suddenly his partner's life on his hands, and Ischade's temper to deal with, that he had provoked, *he*, when it was Crit's life in the balance.

If Crit was still alive at all.

Ischade took the back of a chair and flung it, shoved the table back, rumpling a litter of cloaks, and simply sat down cross-legged on the floor, hands before her. Her eyes rolled back. Her lips parted.

And a light grew between her hands, spinning and spinning in a way he had seen once and more than once.

Like a small Globe of Power, whirling and staining her hands and her face and all the room with its cold glow.

He hunkered down with his hands clasped against his lips and waited, waited, because what she was doing was not the magic he knew in her, pyromancy and necromancy. This was another thing, a thing that was not supposed to exist.

"I don't find him on the surface," she murmured—no mummery, either; Ischade could talk and wield power at the same time, carry on a running dialogue while doing what would raise a sweat on many a talent in the Mageguild. "There's a far-seer over across town. I'll see. She's erratic. Sometimes she's right."

"For godssake, *find* him!"

"What—" Her eyes snapped shut and open again, present and shocked, as she clapped her hands together and smothered the light.

"Aaah!" Stilcho cried, and held his hands over his eyes.

Straton and Ischade exchanged a look then which understood something Stilcho did not.

"What is it, dammit?"

Ischade bit her lips and drew in her breath. "Nothing. Nothing need concern you." She gathered her skirts to rise. "I will find him. There's nothing I can do from here. We'll have to search out the trail. Stilcho." She gave him her hand, and he helped her to her feet.

"What is it?" Strat asked again.

But Ischade did not answer him. She flung her cloak about her and walked out the door, which had a disconcerting way of opening just when it had to.

He was last out, and it shut behind them with a thump, as the gate swung open. Stilcho's horse shied and pulled at its tether.

The bay simply stood. And when he got there, Ischade was holding the reins.

"I'll ride behind," she said.

Old habits came back. He had his mouth open, and shut it. Useless, with Ischade. One did things her way, or one did not, and they might go to hell for all she cared; he wanted her help in the worst way, with a life at stake.

He rose to the saddle and cleared the stirrup for her. She rose lightly up behind and put her arms about him, too damn familiarly.

"Hyyyyaaa!" he yelled at the bay, and it wheeled about and might have unseated her and him; but not him, and damned well not the likes of Ischade, no such luck.

No chance of falling on the road, slick as the stone was. He laid his heels to the bay, and such was the uncertainty of the misty air and the echo off the buildings, sometimes it seemed like it was only Stilcho's horse striking the cobbles.

"My son," Nas-yeni said. It was safe to tell him that much. There were a lot of sons. There had to have been. "You killed my son. Threw him out like garbage." He sat cross-legged, close to his victim in the lantern light. "You, I'd like to take to the same place when I'm done with you. Maybe I will."

The Stepson never had said much, just took in his breath when Nas-yeni got to work on him, and screamed sometimes, in what voice he had left, but the vomiting had left him with very little voice for screaming. He could still see. Nas-yeni saved the eyes for last. And the tongue, that last of all. Right now it was the fingernails; and Nas-yeni pulled the needle, heated, from the little cooking brazier he had full of coals.

"Come here, Critias. Let's try another one."

Critias spat at him and tried to kick him, but there was panic in his face now, and that kind of hard-breathing sob a man got before he fell apart. Nas-yeni knew. He had practiced, before this.

There was panic in the attempt to scream, too. It was in the pace of things. Nas-yeni had studied these matters. Had done this service for certain of the gangs, who wanted something from one of their own. Rankans he had never touched. He had never risked himself. His mission was too holy, his revenge too important, to risk Rankan trouble. Just internal matters.

Never too hasty. Take one's time. Never let the victim get his defenses together either, or forget there was worse to come.

"He was seventeen, pig."

Slowly, through the afternoon streets, still in drizzling rain, the shops' business slow, the citizens who did find reason to be out on the streets moving about all muffled up in cloaks.

But no few stared at the sight of a Stepson with a black-cloaked woman riding pillion behind him, slowly and deliberately through street and street and street; and a one-eyed man beside them, where Stepsons had searched frantically all day, and rousted citizens and searched warehouses.

Perhaps it was the fey, dire feeling about them, that coursed through Strat's bones and set his teeth on edge.

"Wrong," Stilcho said softly, above the soft clip and clop of hooves on cobbles. "Wrong—"

"Is it me you see?" Ischade whispered. "Or else?"

"I don't know," Stilcho said hollowly, in a voice which itself could raise the hair's at a man's nape.

"Hereabouts," Ischade whispered. "Hereabouts. Steady, Straton. Don't flinch."

He felt something at his back—felt it, like fire and ice, burning through his armor, into his bones. And suddenly the horse whickered and gave a thrust of its hindquarters, skittering forward and taking an undirected turn into an alley, into a maze of balconies and rubbish and discarded barrels. It was crazed. It headed them up a nook and stopped, facing a dead end.

"Here." Ischade said.

"*Where*?" Blank walls surrounded them, windowless, doorless. Strat looked about them in desperation, and twisted about as Ischade slid down.

"The horse knows. It has the scent."

He dismounted and dropped the reins, drawing his sword, looking above them, for some window, any aperture.

The horse pawed the cobbles, put down its head and nosed the rubbish.

Above a hinged iron plate set in the cobbles.

"Damn," Strat said. "*Damn*."

And dropped to his knees and pulled at it with his fingers. It would not move.

"Bolted," he said. "Dammitall!" Desperation welled up in him.

Blue fire ran around the opening, down the hinges, dim in daylight. Metal grated.

"Now," Ischade said.

He pulled and it lifted.

And the sound, the half-human sound that came from somewhere in the depths, ran right through his nerves.

He did not stop. He saw the steps and he went, writhed his way through a hole too small for a man to take easily, down into the echoing dark.

"Stilcho!" he heard Ischade whisper urgently. He heard the slither of someone behind him, but another such moan wrenched at his gut. He felt his way down and down, one hand for the sword, one for the wall, his eyes straining at dark absolute except the little gray light that got through from the open trap above, and that fitful, with his partners leaning over it.

He heard laughter echoing through the vault, soft and awful, coming from everywhere.

And caught himself with his heart in his throat as his foot missed a step and he saved himself at an unexpected landing. There was a chain there. He grasped it and felt it to find the steps, descending again, till he heard the sound in front of him.

He felt ahead of him with his sword, probing the dark till it suddenly touched stone. He felt either side and found nothing, and, with his bare hand, in front of him, and felt a wooden door. He put his ear against it.

And pulled it open, carefully, carefully as dim lamplight spilled against his eye.

". . . friend," he heard.

And a sound hardly human at all.

He saw a light, old columns, watermarked, a pair of figures low to the ground against a mound of dirt. He eased his way in, flexing his hand on his sword-hilt, hardly daring to breathe.

The damned hinge creaked. The man looked around.

"Haiiii!" Strat yelled, for what shock could do, and was halfway across the room before the man jerked Crit up by the hair and brought the point of a dagger right up under Crit's left eye.

"You want him blinded? Drop it! Drop the sword!"

Crit tried to say something. *Fool*, probably. And arched his back and struggled as the knife jabbed.

"Drop it!"

Strat dropped it, and saw the man drop the knife and snatch two-handed at something in the straw beside him, but he was already moving, launched with all his strength and speed across that intervening space—

Crossbow. Crit's. Firing. The bolt tore into him. He spun with it, staggered and kept moving, clawing his way up again, tearing the dagger from his belt, hurling himself and the weapon missilelike against the man with the spent bow.

He hit the man in the gut, he felt that, felt the rush of blood over his hand, the tumble of threshing limbs tangled with his as he went down with the bolt shocked by the fall and the dark closing around him.

"I couldn't stop it," Stilcho said. "I couldn't reach him—"

Ischade held up her hand, dismissal, absolution—whatever Stilcho would accept—and looked down at the carnage that spread blood through the straw.

"Witch—" Crit said, or tried to say, looking at her through the one eye that still would work. It came out a raven's croak. And after so much else, he spat at her.

"Gratitude. Of course." Straton was her concern. She tucked her robes away from the blood that was everywhere and felt of his back and his neck, where a pulse still beat. The bolt had hit high. The bad shoulder. Again.

"Damn you," Crit whispered, "damn you to hell, let him *be*."

She touched Strat's face when Stilcho had turned him over. He was bloody everywhere. He was half-conscious, and he tried to say something, but she touched his lips and his brow and put him to sleep. She did other things too, and bent and kissed him on the brow and on the lips, bloody as he was.

"*Let him be, you damned ghoul!*"

Somewhere Critias had found that much voice, and struggled to an elbow, to try to throw his body into her, if only that.

She whirled and stopped him, her hand on his throat, and flung him back down, spat at again.

But she restrained herself. "He came after you. He came to *me* for you. But you will not remember that." She held him with her eyes only now, cut him free with the knife she drew from the dead man, then put her joined hands to Crit's face, and let the mage-fire flow, mending the eye, the hands, everything that might cripple a man. "Sleep, Critias."

It was part of her curse and her talent, that mesmeric talent that could erase her very passage from a mind, make seeing eyes blind, create elaborate memories that had never been.

Such, largely, had been her affair with Strat . . . until she began to take risks, with Stilcho to die his deaths, assuage her needs, fulfill the curse.

"Come," she said to Stilcho, taking him by the hand. "We have Moria to see to. Crit will take care of things."

And drew Stilcho with her, hesitating at the last, bewildered, surely. But she turned his face to her with a touch of her finger, and erased his memory of this place, before she led him up to the light.

It was luck, surely, that a searcher spotted Strat's bay horse in an alley searchers had been down a dozen times that day, spotted the trap left up, and investigated, all on a hunch that had come on the man even to go *down* that often-searched alley. Crit had run out of strength, dragging Strat's half-conscious weight toward the stairs, collapsing there in the dark with Strat damned near bleeding to death and the stairs yet to go.

After that it was horse litters to get them as far as the guard-barracks infirmary, Crit more exhausted and bruised and with cracked ribs that bandages could help, Strat the worse off of the two of them.

Strat, who had come through for him and done what he had done, before the damned Ilsigi lunatic had had time to carve him up. Strat, who had distracted the killer and taken the bolt, knowing he was going to take it, because that was the only way to get across that distance and knife the bastard that was going to cut Crit's throat.

Strat had had enough strength left in him to cut Crit loose. And then fainted.

Crit ought to have been in his own bed. He was not. He sat by Strat's, just holding onto his arm, thinking, damn, he would go to the witch by riverside, he would go down there and he would beg if that was what it took. The sight of Strat deliberately distracting that bastard, deliberately taking the shot and still having it in him to aim true and hard—would haunt him; like the thing Strat had said when he managed, in his pain, to cut him loose—

"—damn mess, Crit, damn awful mess. How'd you get into this?"

It was Strat the way he had been. Strat before the witch had got him. Strat his partner.

And Strat did much the same thing when finally he came to and found him sitting there, with the candle all but a stub on the bedside table: "What the hell," he said. "I must've made it all right, didn't I?"

THE POWER OF KINGS

Jon DeCles

"I am afraid, my dear, that we are going to get into some trouble over this play," said Glisselrand, picking up another ball of brightly colored yarn and adding its lurid yellow to the dark fuschia with which she had been working all morning. Her knitting was the one evidence of her past that she had not dropped along the way, the closest thing to a regret that she had ever shown in all the years since she had run away from home to become an actress with the travelling players.

"And why should that be, my sweeting?" asked Feltheryn, going over the lines of the play before him, intermittently sipping at the tisane in his cup.

"Well, *you* may have been too busy to listen to gossip, but the thing most discussed in this dreadful town is the possible marriage of Prince Kittycat to the Beysa," Glisselrand replied, her voice just a little more reedy this morning than Feltheryn liked. "Has it not occurred to you that this particular play which Molin Torchholder has commissioned us to perform might be taken as a *political* statement?"

"How so?" asked Feltheryn, devoting only a part of his mind to the conversation.

"It depicts an unsuccessful marriage of state, for one thing," said Glisselrand. "For another, there is that very powerful scene in which the High Priest forces the King to his will. One assumes the words were written originally at a time when the King of some country was overstepping his bounds, and when the magician who wrote it felt it appropriate to bend the will of the monarch to the wisdom of the temple."

"Well, yes," said Feltheryn, looking up at last from the old parchment text of the play. His blue eyes focused on Glisselrand and he was struck, as always, by how beautiful she remained, even at . . .—Certainly more summers than was polite for a man to consider. (At least past fifty.) "But what has that to do with thee and me?"

"Feltheryn, my darling," Glisselrand said patiently, "you know how the plays affect people's minds. Has it not occurred to you that Molin might be attempting to *use* us to get control of the prince?"

"My darling," said Feltheryn, "the plays are magical, there is no doubt about that. But their magic is unpredictable. Surely Molin, as a priest, knows that he cannot depend on a performance of one of our plays to give him any precise results. The changes that occur in people upon seeing our plays are subtle, and like as not they will even go unnoticed. Molin saw the plays in Ranke. He knows they cannot be *used*, I am sure. . . . You must think more kindly of this fine man who has been good enough to arrange a theater for us, hire that charming painter, Lalo, to paint our scenery, and, most important, see that we are all fed until we are established in Sanctuary."

"Perhaps," said Glisselrand after a moment. "But I *do*

wonder at you, even after this many years. You are still such an *innocent*! I wonder how you maintain it.''

This comment left Feltheryn bewildered so he returned to his memorizing of the text; a very normal reaction, as much of what his beloved leading lady said to him was beyond his understanding. In a moment he was absorbed again in the terrible scene in which the king discovers that his new young wife is in love with his son by a previous marriage. Feltheryn moved his hand to his brow and ran his fingers through his bushy white hair in rehearsal of a gesture of anguish. He did not notice Glisselrand's tender smile as she watched him.

The company had lost many of its treasured articles of production in its final days in Ranke, and as *The Power of Kings* was a play replete with royalty, it behooved Feltheryn to replace certain crowns, sceptres, and other paraphernalia of rulership. To this end he headed for the bazaar of Sanctuary, accompanied by Snegelringe, who would play his son Karel in the play (Feltheryn always reserved the parts of kings for himself and left the younger, more romantic parts for his junior) and Lempchin, the boy who acted as factotum to the troupe. They were looking for a blacksmith, but one who had a certain flair and style about his work; for crowns and sceptres were a far cry, artistically, from horseshoes and barrel hoops.

It was perhaps inevitable that they catch the attention of those who frequented the bazaar by day but who made their homes in either the Downwind or the Maze; for after so many years of being a king upon the stage Feltheryn moved with the authority of one, if not the wisdom. Certainly no true king would have been foolish enough to head for the bazaar with only one guard and a clumsy boy for company.

It was luck, and very good luck, that the first to make an attempt upon the old actor's person was not one of Sanctuary's better thieves: otherwise the purse which Molin Torchholder had provided might have been lost. As it was: the apprentice pickpockets crashed into Feltheryn, the "master" of the gang (who had attained at least eighteen years despite his stupidity) rushed in with a knife—and learned quickly that actors must be as good with their swords in reality as upon the stage.

Snegelringe's blade flew from its overly ornamented scabbard, moved in an overly flamboyant arc, and the attacking knife flew from a hand that spurted blood.

The apprentices drew back, their eyes round with surprise as their master clutched his hand and staggered away with a yowl. They had clearly not expected Snegelringe, a paunchy man with a receding hairline, to have any speed of arms.

"Death to all who ride against the King!" proclaimed Lempchin, in a voice that was strong enough but not yet deep enough for the stage. Then the boy spoiled his moment by giggling.

Fortunately the apprentice pickpockets were not versed in the finer points of stage delivery, and they took Lempchin's statement seriously. They ran, scattering as thoroughly as the narrow street would allow.

"Well played, my hearty!" said Feltheryn to Snegelringe. "But *you*, boy, you must learn *never* to break character until the curtain is down! Suppose they had *not* run? Suppose they had taken our defense as a joke?"

"Why then," said Lempchin, "Master Snegelringe would have skewered them all!"

"A pretty move, no doubt," said Feltheryn, and he lowered his deep voice an octave to where it sounded like the dead oracle from *Nodrade*. "But then should we have found ourselves with enemies, and be the target of every friend those fiends ever had. And one dark night when you must walk alone, the sharp blade would cut across your throat!"

The boy gulped.

"And we should have to find another boy to take your place emptying the chamber pots!" added Snegelringe.

Lempchin's discomfort faded and he blushed. He did not really like Snegelringe, Feltheryn knew, but he respected the actor: in fact, he wanted to take his place some day, if he could just learn the lines and arrange an accident.

"Come," said Feltheryn, rumpling the chubby boy's hair. "I see the place Lalo recommended, across the square ahead. While I talk to the blacksmith perhaps you can persuade his wife to read your palm. They say these S'danzo women read the future well, and she may see you upon the boards yet!"

The interview with Dubro, the blacksmith, went well enough, though he apologized for his lack of expertise in fashioning crowns. The huge man was *not* pleased with the way Snegelringe lavished attention on his wife Illyra, but neither did he move to stop it. Feltheryn supposed the fellow would have felt foolish exhibiting jealousy over a pudgy actor with a receding hairline; and he did not feel it appropriate to disabuse the man of his illusions at just this point. Snegelringe's reputation as a ladies' man would spread through Sanctuary soon enough, causing the company problems aplenty. Let that happen later, after people were accustomed to coming to the plays. Then the troupe would be able to weather the criticism of their morals that even a town as corrupt as Sanctuary felt qualified to heap upon mere actors.

As for the wife, Illyra: Feltheryn wondered why it was she dressed as she did, making up her face in such a way that she appeared, to the untrained eye, like a crone. Was it because of the respect accorded to old age? (He knew well that such respect was more often an illusion of the young than a reality. His own years had earned him rather a grudging tolerance than respect. People did not defer to him, they waited for him to die so that they could take his place!) Or did she have some secret distress? She was not responding to Snegelringe's attentions as a woman might usually. The professional mask of a seeress was set well in place, but to Feltheryn's equally professional assessment she seemed mildly puzzled by it all; as if she could not understand *why* Snegelringe was flirting with her. Was it possible she did not know that actors used makeup as skillfully as S'danzo, and for much the same purpose? Was it possible she did not realize that Snegelringe could see beneath her mask to the lovely young woman?

Feltheryn let the puzzle go, another observation of the human condition for his catalogue of character, and finished his business with Dubro.

Lempchin had not found the seeress in a soft enough mood to give him a reading of the cards for free, so the boy begged for a pastry instead, and that led to Snegelringe boxing his ears as they left the bazaar to return to the theater.

The theater itself was still under construction in the shell of a building that had burned during the plague riots. It was located between West Side Street and Processional, near enough to the palace that the prince could come at his convenience yet far enough away for the Rankan lords to retain their feelings of respectability. Molin had at first proposed housing the actors at some distance from the actual playhouse, perhaps in Westside where there was new construction: but Glisselrand had made clear, with her warmest affections, that a woman would feel unsafe going such a great distance alone, and that providing her with a dependable escort would cost Molin much more than was reasonable. She had phrased it in such a way that there was no room, short of acute rudeness, for the priest to suggest she provide her own escort, or do without. Thus the theater included an attached residence which, though small, was better than anything they might find among the workmen's quarters at Shambles Cross.

The Architect of Vashanka had even taken a personal interest in the construction, as if the finishing of the walls on which he had so long labored was somehow not enough to occupy his creativity. He offered plans for a very lavish performing space and was not in the least offended when Feltheryn pointed out to him, with grave discretion, the need for a stage house at the top and dressing rooms below and behind the actual stage; not to mention space in the wings for the storage of properties to be brought on.

The rebuilding had gone on apace and now the structure was beginning to look much the way Ranke's theaters looked. There was a proscenium, a thing never seen outside the capital, boxes for important people who wanted to be seen as much as they wanted to see, and a royal box for those nights when the prince wished to attend a performance. The theater was, after all, a political tool of some import for those, like the late Emperor, who knew how to use it.

It was therefore not as great a surprise as it might have been when Feltheryn entered and found the Beysa Shupansea having tisane with Glisselrand in the foyer, surrounded by several ladies-in-waiting whose raiment was so splendid that it paled only before the Beysa herself.

For a moment Feltheryn was awestruck. The cloth in the Beysa's dress alone could have footed the bill for the whole of the theater. She wore such riches as Ranke never saw, and she wore them well, her breasts thrust out voluptuously and yet with dignity, her head held with a pride that was neither unnatural nor condescending. The gorgeous snake coiling about her throat like a necklace was a priceless piece of theater!

The only woman he had ever seen so queenly was Glisselrand herself, perhaps in the role of Adriana in *Templesmoke*: but of course he would not declare that to the Beysa.

"Does not the day confound the night?" he quoted from *The Archmage* by way of greeting, for he had not yet learned her proper title of address. *"Are not the stars but fragments of the light?"*

The Beysa smiled and the membranes on her eyes nictitated. She knew flattery, instantly understood why he chose to use it at this moment, and decided to accept it graciously.

"I have come to see your theater," Shupansea said. "And perhaps to make my own small contribution to its success, if that would be appropriate and acceptable."

Feltheryn decided he liked her.

"But of course!" he said. "Has my lady shown it to you, or have you waited for my return?"

"Your lady has shown it," said the Beysa, "and we have discussed my gift. She asked only that I accept a few sweets, and this lovely hot tisane she makes, while we awaited your approval."

"If my lady approves it, then so do I," said Feltheryn. "But what is it that you so kindly offer, if I may ask?"

"The Beysa," said Glisselrand (and her voice held the full rich lustre that it always did on stage) "has offered to have the royal box flocked with velvet. Not just the rails but the whole thing, inside and out. I think that is most kind of her, don't you?''

''Not only kind, but generous,'' said Feltheryn. ''May I assume from this that . . .'' (There was nothing for it, he *had* to use *some* title!) ''. . . Your Highness plans to attend our humble offerings?''

''It will be a great treat to see such plays as those the Rankans saw,'' said the Beysa. ''Especially after so long here in Sanctuary. In my homeland there were many spectacles provided to amuse us, and I confess to missing them. I shall be most pleased indeed to come the very night you first perform.''

The irony of her using the past tense when referring to the plays performed in Ranke was not lost on Feltheryn, but he noted it only in passing. An occupied Royal Box inevitably meant a full house!

Later, that night, Feltheryn had second thoughts about presenting *The Power of Kings*. In addition to the King, his son, and the leading lady, the play required a second young male, the son's best friend. It was the most sympathetic part in the play, for the friend, Rorem, died by an assassin's arrow in the last act, even in the midst of swearing his love for the prince, Karel. It was one of the great and moving scenes of the play, and one of the most mystical, for it was never explained. Like the events of real life, nobody ever discovered who killed Rorem, or why.

The problem was that Rounsnouf, the company's comic, was the only person available to play the part; and Rounsnouf had discovered the Vulgar Unicorn.

To be sure, every town had its share of low dives; but the Vulgar Unicorn (Rounsnouf explained as best he could after much too much to drink) was *special!*

"Master Feltheryn, I have *never* seen so many great character studies! The place is a treasure house! I could live there, absorbing the little moves they make, taking in the peculiar touches of their accents! There is a dark-haired boy who is all bluster and covered with knives, yet who possesses a wonderful vulnerability; I would not trust him with a gravestone, yet he appeals to my heart. . . . There was a young woman, clearly of the noblest birth, and yet trained as a gladiator! Can you imagine that? I dared to speak with her, and she told me that she *chose* to learn to fight! So fascinating! Oh, how I wish you would join me there!"

It was not the wine, nor the ale, that thus gave Feltheryn misgivings: it was the seductive quality of observation the tavern offered. While all actors spent much time observing the details of character in their fellow humans, there was something about Rounsnouf that was like a hunger, and that *fed* off other people. He used every observation he made in his brilliant work in the plays, but when one encountered him backstage, or away from the theater, it was always disquieting. Glisselrand said she hated to leave him alone with Lempchin, not because she thought the comic would bugger the boy but because she wondered if she might come home and find him in the stewpot.

"How are you coming with your part?" Feltheryn asked, not valuing the answer of a drunk but trusting to wine to bring out the truth.

"I'll have it by opening," said Rounsnouf. "Never fear! It is only a small part, after all."

"Yes," said Feltheryn, "but it is an important part, and it is not a comedy, it is a tragedy. You have played it before with less than glorious results, I might point out. I would appreciate it if you left off your observations until we have opened, and concentrated on the work at hand. The Vulgar Unicorn will not close nearly as soon as our play will."

Rounsnouf sat down on the floor and folded his short, thick fingers intertwined. He shut his eyes, set too close together, and yawned. Then he scratched his butterball stomach under his motley tunic.

"I suppose you are right," he said, entirely too agreeably. "I would like to be able to deliver Rorem's death speech without laughing. *Oh thou whose blood runs in my veins, more closer yet than any brother. Thou, whose blood I chose against the call of nature . . .*"

He fell back laughing and his legs stretched out so that his feet, too small for his body, wiggled in the air.

"It sounds as if he has to use the outhouse!"

Feltheryn held back his own laugh. Taken out of context, the little comic was right.

"Come, Rounsnouf," Feltheryn said, offering his hand and helping the little man up. "I think that we had best to bed, else wake the house."

"Let me see . . " the comic said as he gained his feet and shook himself. "The boy walked thus . . ."

And without any help he mounted the stairs, his body gliding sleekly in imitation of the shadow-spawned grace of one of the town's most notable thieves.

Feltheryn sat down and considered: Rounsnouf had twice before become so engrossed in his studies that he had completely missed performances. He could not be allowed to do so again, at least not this early in the game. One could not bind him to the theater, nor yet threaten him. He only sulked and gave a bad reading if you did that.

What then?

Feltheryn looked in the purse of gold that Molin had

given him and contemplated the best and most necessary uses the money could be put to. Of these, assuring the performance actually occurred was certainly one of the best, and so he decided upon visiting the Vulgar Unicorn himself.

But early the next morning he entertained a visitor who delayed his visit, a visitor who, of all those denizens of the empire he had entertained, was surely the most entertaining.

He awoke with the feeling that the room was burning. He started to cry out where he lay but immediately stopped. He knew too well that people died from leaping up and breathing in the burning air that accumulated at the top of the room, sometimes not more than a hand's breadth above the sleeping face. He threw one hand out to anchor Glisselrand where she lay next to him, then thrust the other up to see at what level death hovered.

Two surprises greeted his hands. The first was that Glisselrand was not there. The bed was empty but for him. The second was that the air above him was not burning, only warm.

He focused his eyes more clearly, remembering as he always did in the morning that his eyes were not what they once were.

He was not in his room after all, not in his own comfortable bed. He was lying, rather, on a chaise lounge of red-brown satin with a damask coverlet thrown over him. He was still in his long woolen nightshirt, and the lounge was large enough to accommodate two, but that was the only resemblance to the situation in which he had fallen asleep.

He was in a low chamber with a black and white checked marble floor. Thick small carpets were scattered here and there and a huge fireplace blazed brightly not far

away, the source of the heat that had made him think of
fire. The walls of the room were paneled below the wain-
scoting with dark wood, but above they were covered with
damascene silk of a dusky rose color. There were framed
pictures on the walls, but Feltheryn found he could not
look at them directly and see anything. They simply blurred.

A blind servant stood next to the hearth, and across
from the lounge on which he lay was an ornate chair, a
throne really, in which sat someone heavily robed and
hooded, a someone whose eyes could be seen glowing
redly out of the darkness of the hood.

"Master Feltheryn," a voice said amiably from under
the hood. It was a young voice, but he could not tell (and
that bothered him!) whether the voice belonged to a man
or woman. "You are not really here. I trust you realize
that?"

Feltheryn had not, but he nodded in assent since he
seemed to be expected to not only realize it but understand it.

"Very good," the voice said. "I thought an actor would
understand such an illusion. Such a way of communicat-
ing. I am Enas Yorl, a resident of this town who does not
get out much for reasons which I may later choose to
explain. I have chosen to come to you in this manner to
request your help in alleviating my boredom at being so
cooped up within my house."

Now *this* Feltheryn understood. The way the man shadowed his countenance with his hood, the discretion he
showed in conducting the interview, were symptomatic of
many who suffered some deformity.

"You wish me to make some special arrangement at the
theater," Feltheryn said. "Something in the nature of a
draped box, where you may see without being seen; is that
it?"

"Do you then know of me so quickly?" Enas Yorl asked, and his voice began to change, not as to tone but as to timbre. This fascinated Feltheryn greatly, for it did not seem to be a deliberate alteration such as he, himself, would have made.

"No, good sir, only of others who have asked a similar boon. The effects of a pox upon a beautiful lady, the loss of looks that comes from war . . . It is not such an unusual request. In Ranke we reserved a box with curtains specifically for such a need. I think perhaps we might make one here as well, though I had not expected its requirement so soon."

A laugh came from the hood, but even as it bubbled forth the laughing changed, and when next Enas Yorl spoke it was with a rough and guttural tone like that of an experienced soldier. Feltheryn instantly envied the man his remarkable ability!

"You do *not* know of me, that much is plain! And I think that I shall leave it so, for you have made me laugh by your innocence. Soon enough shall you learn. But then again, your assessment of my situation is not incorrect. Return to your rest, Feltheryn Thespian, and consider that you have the best of the bargains a man can make: for you change form at will, and can take off the masks you assume. Now sleep!".

Feltheryn wanted desperately to pursue the conversation and stay in the presence of Enas Yorl, for at that moment he observed that his interviewer was not only seeming to change his form somewhat under the robes, but to change his *mass* as well; and that was a trick he would dearly love to learn. Playing *Roget the Hunchback* was one of the greatest accomplishments of the stage, not because of the powerful emotion of the role but because of the difficulty

of acting while strapped into the elaborate harness that
simulated the deformity. He was about to plead his case
for study with Enas Yorl when darkness intervened and he
was awaking in his own bed, his arm thrown protectively
over his lady and the morning sun pouring through the
casement.

He moved his hand gently back, so as not to disturb her
beauty rest, then climbed out of bed and dressed quietly.

He was in the small kitchen heating water for tisane
when he heard the door of the theater open and close. That
would be Lalo the Limner, come to paint the next set of
flats and the periactois for the *auto-da-fé* in Act Three.

There was certainly nothing more impressive in all the
world than the illusion of fire on stage, and nothing harder
to accomplish. Feltheryn had chosen this time to bring
about the miracle through the use of periactois—three-
sided columns with different paintings on each side—which
could be revolved. There would also be ragged strips of
cloth dyed like flames which Lempchin could waggle furiously by means of strings descending from the flies. The
strings would not be visible, and in the flickering light of
the onstage torches the effect would be terrifying.

The vision so captured Feltheryn's early morning imagination that he quite forgot the kettle of boiling water and
went to get his script and notebook, adding several details
which he thought would improve the stage picture. He
barely noticed when Glisselrand put the pot of tisane and a
clean cup at his elbow, and with it a plate of freshly
scrambled eggs, cheese, sliced bread from the previous
day, and a pot of rare red jelly made from the legendary
oranges of Enlibar; of which they had a dozen left in trade
for seating when they had played *The Steel Skeleton*, a
play which many assumed to have been written by an

Enlibrite wizard, and which the Enlibrites would travel fantastic distances to see.

He was roused from his deep reverie and study of the text when an unfamiliar voice echoed in the theater, followed by Glisselrand's most opulent tones.

"I only came to bring Lalo his midday meal," a woman's voice said. "But I confess I did hope to see if it was you. It's been many years, but how could I forget? While Lalo was working on the painting that won my hand there was nothing for me to do, so I came to see the play. I had seen you do a piece before the tent, so I knew it would be good."

"Why yes," said Glisselrand, and her voice held all the charm and delight that only an actor can know when remembered after twenty years. "What play was it that we did?"

"*The Master Poet*," said the woman, whom Feltheryn now took to be Gilla, Lalo's wife. "It was so personal, at that time, for your situation was much like my own. When I came away I felt as if my whole outlook on life had changed. People looked so different! I felt so differently!"

Feltheryn smiled to himself. Yes, the plays worked their magic in strange and subtle ways. And that play was a comedy of love, a comedy of love between the generations. But even then he had chosen to play the older man, the lovable shoemaker who could have the young girl, but who chose wisely to let her love the younger man, the man of her own generation.

"I am so pleased that you remember my performance," said Glisselrand, and Feltheryn knew that it was true. He tried to hark back in his mind to that distant day, to remember some trace that would lead him down the path to a sensual recall of time and place, but it was hopeless.

He had done *The Master Poet* so many times that one performance blended into another. The sunlight falling on flowers that his mental search prompted could have been in any of a hundred small towns. The play was too universal to attach itself to time and place. Only the first time he had done it was clear in his memory, and then he had not played the older man, but Dainis, the apprentice who danced and fought . . .

The King recalled him to the page and Glisselrand and Lalo and Gilla faded into the paint of the periactois like soft music played behind the potted palms in the Emperor's palace. His hand shot out into the air, retreated, his lips moved, and anyone watching might have thought him in the grip of some seizure as he moved in slight indications of the broad gestures he would use upon the stage.

It was much later when he came to the realization that he was eating his supper, not his breakfast, and that he had been absorbed for the whole of the day. He carefully set the script aside, finished the boiled turnip with butter that was the last of the food on his plate, and washed it down with the watered wine that Glisselrand had provided. He was not up to the full strength stuff anymore. Then he stood and stretched his very tall frame, forcing air back into the stagnant blood. It was, he considered, time to visit the Vulgar Unicorn.

Snegelringe and Rounsnouf were already there, drinking at a table in the company of a handsome young man with shoulder-length glossy black hair, a man dressed far too fine for the likes of this low dive, Feltheryn observed as he entered unobtrusively and looked over the place.

And yet, low though the dive was, it was not without merit. He thought of the many taverns he had entered over the years and the general lack of lustre they displayed, and he decided that perhaps Rounsnouf was right, the place was a treasure house. There was a certain dark color that crackled with hidden decisions, a subdued excitement that spoke of desperation. He spied out the barkeep and headed across the room, then dodged deftly as a scrawny, heavy-lidded man who feigned sleep at one of the tables tried to trip him without seeming to.

"It would seem that Hakiem does not like you," the big man behind the bar said.

Feltheryn had assumed his dodge deft enough that no-body would notice the interchange, but that was clearly not the case. The eyes of thieves, he reminded himself, were trained in much the same techniques as those of actors, to see and learn what was not always apparent.

"Now why should that be?" he asked, drawing out a small coin and putting in down.

"He views you as competition, King of Players," said the barkeep. "He is a storyteller in the streets. What will you drink?"

"Half water, half wine," said Feltheryn. "That is fool-ish of him, for he will be able to tell a thousand tales to each play I perform. And the stories we offer are different."

"Half *water*?" the barkeep asked, and his look was of the greatest contempt.

Feltheryn drew himself up tall, taller than the barkeep though not so broad or strong: taller than anyone in the room, though probably thinner than anyone as well.

"I am an old man, in case you have not noticed," he said with dignity. "My body does not move as quickly as it once did, nor do my guts digest as well. I will pay you as if the whole cup were wine."

That settled the matter and the barkeep gave him what he wanted.

"I will pay for something else as well," he said after he had taken a drink. "Something within your proper duties but which might be distasteful without the gold."

"And what is that?" asked the barkeep suspiciously.

"By now you know Rounsnouf, my comedian," Feltheryn said, gesturing toward the table where his actors were so engrossed that they had not noted his entry. "I fear that he knows this place better now than he ought, at least for the welfare of my plays. I will pay you a fit sum if on certain nights, when we are to perform, you will forbid him entry until the play is done."

"And what's to stop him drinking elsewhere?"

"It is not the drink he values in this place, it's the people. I do not think he will find such a ripe assortment elsewhere in Sanctuary, and if he knows that he can come here *but* for play nights, I do not think he will feel abused."

The barkeep named a price, Feltheryn dickered it down (though it was within reason) and the bargain was struck.

"But you must tell him what you've done," the barkeep concluded.

"Just so," said Feltheryn, finishing his drink and gesturing for another.

His cup refilled, he made his way across the room, avoiding the table of Hakiem, and joined the party. Rounsnouf and Snegelringe introduced him to their new friend, Hort, then they all swapped stories and poems for a while. Feltheryn did not tell Rounsnouf what he had done until the next morning, when the little comedian took it in stride.

"Would that the gods," he said in acceptance, "were so steady of will as a director!"

*   *   *

The final piece of planning involved extra bodies, for *The Power of Kings* was a spectacle play and the effect of spectacle was achieved largely through filling the stage with elegantly clothed people. Feltheryn had taught many a young actor the importance of a walk-on role by citing the case of the handmaiden in *The Murder of Queen Ranceta*, a part which gave the young woman playing it but a moment on stage but without which the play could not exist. (It was the handmaiden who delivered the tray with the fatal flagon of poisoned wine, and without the poisoning there *was* no play!) Now the question was where to hire attractive young women to don the robes of court ladies, and where to hire young men to wear the garb of court gentlemen.

Feltheryn asked Lalo, who certainly should be able to ferret out beauty if anyone could, and Lalo asked his wife Gilla, for he was not confident in the enterprise. Gilla suggested that Feltheryn talk to Myrtis, the proprietrix of the Aphrodisia House, with the admonition that the women who worked there were above average in looks for their trade; and a vote of confidence in their honesty to their employer. Feltheryn did as Gilla bid and was delighted to find that Myrtis could not only supply him with lovely ladies but knew where to hire young men just as pretty and reliable to wear the beautiful clothes he promised.

It was not long before the theater neared completion, before the sets were painted and dried, before Glisselrand had brought in seamstresses to help her finish the arduous task of building the last of the costumes. Actual rehearsals got under way, the piecemeal chunks of the drama were glued together into scenes, then acts, then the ladies and gentlemen of the evening were called in (by day, so that they could continue to work nights until the opening) and the grand sweep of the drama was stitched in its final glorious pattern.

Feltheryn ceased to sleep much, for even after so many years an opening night excited him. He ran lines in his mind constantly, missed, re-ran them. He worried over the success of his new theater, he worried over the nuance of each line in the play, he worried over things that a week before would have flowed by him like mist in the night. He took to dressing in a shabby cloak and wandering the streets, hunched over so that his height would not mark him, and listening to the crowds.

Were they talking about the theater? About the play?

If not, something must be done.

He longed for the days when the mere fact that he and Glisselrand slept together without benefit of marriage was sufficient to titillate the masses. In *those* days there had been no difficulty in drawing a crowd. The pride of the youthful Rankan Empire had filled the streets of Ranke with pleasure seekers, and the craving of a young empire for respectability had made scandal easy.

Scandal in Sanctuary would be hard work, he thought.

The theater was decorated within with banners and garlands of flowers made of gayly colored silk, and the night before opening they decorated the outside as well. It must be a festive occasion, and it was to be such a novelty in Sanctuary that all kinds of people offered help. Molin came by and asked that they move virtually everything movable, to make sure it would work. Myrtis stopped in—at an hour unknown to a woman of her profession—and assured Glisselrand that she and her ladies would be bringing trays of sweetmeats for opening night. A wagon pulled up and unloaded several barrels of excellent wine, courtesy of the as yet unseen prince. It seemed as if nothing could go wrong.

Feltheryn retired that night with only the slightest anxiety, and sank immediately into a sleep filled with flaming vistas, tragic emotions, and thunderous applause.

The actors slept late the morning of the opening, as was usual. Days of rehearsal had now to be traded for nights of performance, and the energy required for such was enormous, particularly of people who had reached the ages Feltheryn and Glisselrand had. Lempchin brought them breakfast in bed, a tradition which they indulged despite the cleaning which the kitchen would require after the boy's attempt at cooking.

Snegelringe came in and Feltheryn complimented him on his performance at the dress rehearsal: "I think you have the role at last," he said. "The way you walked was *perfect!* Just the right balance of nobility and indolence for Karel."

"I was pleased with that myself," said Snegelringe. "Actually, I owe it totally to Rounsnouf and his fascination with that tavern. I was casting about for a model and one of his friends, a dark young woman who fights as a gladiator, told me she could show me a man very much like Karel if I would attend her. I did, and we rode to a brief hunt. Out on the hills she pointed out some noble dandy and his guards, and even from the distance I could see that he was what I wanted for the part."

"Who was he?" Feltheryn asked, sipping at the tea which Lempchin had made too strong. He much preferred tisane.

"I've no idea," said Snegelringe. "I asked her, but she

laughed and said it were better I did not know, for he was not the kind of man I would enjoy knowing.''

Feltheryn furrowed his brow. It was not likely to be a source of difficulty, but he preferred to know from what hand all the cards in the game had been dealt.

"Will she be coming to the play?''

"She says she would not miss it for the world; especially once I had told her Prince Kadakithis and the Beysa would be there in the newly flocked box. She said she would be bringing several other ladies as well.''

"Ah, good,'' said Feltheryn. "The more nobility the merrier!''

"The house will glitter like Midwinter Festival in Ranke,'' said Glisselrand nostalgically, and Feltheryn detected just the slightest regret in her voice. It *had* been good in Ranke with the Emperor's support.

She threw the covers back dramatically and sat up in the bed.

"And *I*,'' she announced, "must glitter twice as bright! *Lempchin!* Go out to the herbalist and get me a box of henna, my hair is beginning to show grey!''

That buzzing, casual time before the opening passed, the afternoon when there was nothing to do but a thousand tiny things that had to wait, then had to be *done*. The blue hour came, the stars began to prick the sky, and Lempchin lit oil lamps on the front of the theater. The inner doors were closed and the outer doors were opened, and Lempchin prepared to sell admittance.

Feltheryn headed for his dressing room, stage left, and prepared to put on his makeup. He did not need as much as he once had. Now the job was to make him seem young enough for the part of the king. Once it had been a task to make him seem *old* enough.

He was part way through when he heard the voice of Hort outside his door, and with it that of Rounsnouf.

"But you could *wait*," Hort said. "He will still be there later!"

"I could, but I won't!" said Rounsnouf, and the voices moved past the door to Feltheryn's dressing room, toward the back entrance of the theater.

Feltheryn felt a moment of panic, dropped the sponge with which he had been applying rouge, and leaped to his feet. He hurried out into the passage, but it was too late. The door was closing and Rounsnouf and the storyteller were gone!

"Shipri's Dugs!" Feltheryn swore, and his voice carried like Vashanka's thunder. The door to the dressing room next to his own opened and Snegelringe looked out, his facing looking oddly pale with only the base applied, and no eye or lip color.

"Hold the house!" Feltheryn instructed. "Rounsnouf has fled, and I must chase him!"

"To the Vulgar Unicorn?" Snegelringe inquired.

"If so, I'll have the hide of the barkeep. I *paid* him to be sure the curtain was on time!"

He went back into his dressing room, wiped the makeup from his face with a wet towel, then pulled on a tunic. Just to be sure he would be taken seriously he added the belt with the King's sword. He threw a short cloak over the tunic against the chill, then he left the theater. No matter that the sword was cheap iron, a hand on the hilt was all it usually took!

He glanced up the alley from the stage door as he went and noted that people were already arriving. He would have Rounsnouf's skin for this escapade, and possibly a bit from Hort as well!

He rushed through the gathering darkness, still running lines in his mind for the second scene of the first act. In a matter of minutes he was at the Maze, then within it. He was so angry that he barely noticed the patter of feet that fell in behind him, forced them in fact from his attention until they speeded up: until it was apparent that they were running after him, close and with intent.

The skill most necessary to an actor upon the stage is the ability to adjust rapidly to changing circumstances. If a door sticks one must be ready to make it appear a part of the play. If a sword sticks in its scabbard one must be ready to dodge a choreographed blow and keep the action flowing while one gets it free. It was not so much self-preservation as stagecraft that made Feltheryn whirl upon his assailants at the last moment and slide his sword free, raising it over his shoulder in the menacing stance of a broadswordsman ready for the downstroke.

The shadows before him skidded to a halt. There were five of them (poor odds) and he recognized them at once as the pickpockets who had tried for his purse that first day in the bazaar. Wicked sharp steel glinted in the scant starlight, definitely better weapons than the fake sword he wielded.

The tallest one, the boy whom Snegelringe had wounded, gave a laugh.

"King indeed!" came the young voice. "Nothing but an old player! One with too much gold on his person at that! And this time with no pudgy sidekick to defend him!"

The youth was right, Feltheryn observed, but his words showed inaccurate judgement.

"The gold is all spent," he said, keeping his voice

carefully level and below the middle force. "As to the rest: I am old, but not without skills."

"Skills to be tried!" snarled the boy, and they all came at him.

"*Die then!*" Feltheryn cried, and this time he let forth the full power of his voice, a voice trained to reach at least the third balcony of the largest theater in Ranke. And as he spoke (for he did not have to shout to be heard from one end of the Maze to the other) he brought the iron sword down with his full strength and speed, straight at his opponent's head.

One knife caught in his cloak as he swirled it with his left hand. Another thrust between his ribs, under his descending right arm; but its force was not sufficient to go all the way in, so startled were the thieves by the force of his voice. Two of the boys jumped back, terrified. The leader, primed on his pride, managed to avoid the iron blade descending toward his head, but not quite enough. The edge was not terribly sharp but it was moving fast enough to break his collarbone where it struck, even as his blade sliced across Feltheryn's belly, drawing blood but not managing to gut him.

It was not unlike the fight in *Rakesblade,* and Feltheryn, barely feeling the wounds in the excitement of a performance, delivered his lines with force enough to rattle their teeth:

"*Is this your best, you unborn whoreson snakes?*
Is magick then your honorless defense?
See too my holy blade I can enchaunt.
So that its light your rude entrapment breaks!"

The fact that they were *not* using magic against him quite escaped their attention at that moment, for the sword in Feltheryn's hand began to glow a bluish white, spilling its weird light into the shadows and illuminating the scene dramatically. They had no idea that the light from the blade was all there was to the magic of the spell contained in the play. They only knew that their leader was once more screaming in agony and that the man before them was *much* taller than he had seemed a moment before: that he seemed unharmed by their attack, and that they were not winning.

"Gralis, *forget* him!" cried one of the boys to their leader, and then they all bolted, leaving the wounded Gralis to fend for himself.

Felthryn stepped forward, brandishing the glowing sword at his agonized enemy.

"*Go thou into darkness!*" he commanded, from later in the same play. "*Take demons now for playmates if you will, and leave forever, these the lands of light!*"

Through the pain in his ruined shoulder the boy heard these words and, harking back to the terrors that had so recently reigned in Sanctuary, he lost control of his bladder even as he turned and staggered away, doing his best to run.

Feltheryn stood triumphant, the light blazing from the sword in an unnaturally quiet and empty street. He watched the horrified and incompetent thief disappear into the shadows, then he realized that something was wrong.

There was no applause!

The light of the sword fizzled out as if it had been doused with a bucket of winter cold water, and the pain hit Feltheryn where the two blades had cut him. He shook himself, took a deep breath, then thrust the stage sword back into its stage scabbard. He felt the wound across his belly and determined that it was not going to be fatal, then checked the piercing between his ribs. *That* was more serious, and would require a chirurgeon: after the performance.

He turned and headed for the Vulgar Unicorn, his anger returning full force.

—But he was not prepared for what awaited him when he slammed open the door and raked the brown darkness with his steel-blue gaze.

Rounsnouf and Hort were two of three sitting at a table engaged in animated conversation while the barkeep—a barkeep different from the one Feltheryn had bribed—poured dark beer in their mugs.

The barkeep registered a look not much different from that of any other man faced with trouble, but it was the third patron at Rounsnouf's table who captured and held Feltheryn's attention. A daemon! They were drinking with a gray-skinned, wart-faced, wall-eyed daemon!

"Oh dear," said Rounsnouf. "I believe I've upset my director."

"Lady of Stars!" exclaimed the young storyteller. "You're wounded!"

"*Not so much in the flesh as in my heart!*" Feltheryn proclaimed, a quote from the play he should now be ready to begin.

"I would not have come just *now* . . ." Rounsnouf said lamely, and he gestured to the daemon.

"Snapper Jo's fault?" the daemon queried. "Just a little drink with friends. Very *human* thing to do!"

"*To the Theater!*" Feltheryn proclaimed. And if the habitués of the Vulgar Unicorn had been familiar with the whole corpus of the sacred plays they would have seen in the fire of his eyes the conjuration of most ancient deities from the most ancient dramas.

They were not, but nobody argued.

Still, the night's difficulties were unended.

Bandages, ointments to kill the pain, makeup, costume,

light calisthenics to fill his blood with air to support his voice; all these were accomplished, and the curtain went up. From the wings Feltheryn listened to the love scene in the garden between Snegelringe and Glisselrand, running his lines and clearing his mind of all the nonsense that had slowed him. It was past, after all, and only the play now existed.

The scene drew to a close and the curtain was drawn, then he and Rounsnouf and Lempchin, with the aid of the roaring boys provided by Myrtis, pulled the ropes, moved the panels, and in general changed the scene to that of the King's study. He took his place on the stage, seated at the King's great desk, and the curtain went up.

Feltheryn came alive.

There was an audience and he could feel it, feel every living being as a presence, their eyes upon him, their breathing slowed, their minds involved—their emotions guided as they submitted themselves, for the duration, to the magic of the show. He began the monologue in which the King voiced his doubts, then Glisselrand entered and he began the part of the play that was his personal favorite, for it said, better than any words of his own could ever hope to say, what he felt about her:

"*How shall I call you then?*

Like some great bird, that though she be my slave can yet take wing?

Like some famed horse, that though I hold the reins can race the wind?

I call you love, and hold you in my arms, and yet you overpower me.

I call you wife, and you must call me lord; and yet I worship at your shrine!"

He ceased to exist as a separate person and *became* the

tragic king, a man doomed by circumstance to destroy all that he loved in life, rescued from the ultimate humiliation only by the intervention of supernatural forces at the end: forces beyond his comprehension.

The scene changed again and the pain hit him, then he launched back into his performance and it was gone. Only when the first act was complete did he really understand that he was seriously wounded. Instead of going out to the little secret passage behind the lobby (Molin had included it without question) to listen to the public reaction to the play, Feltheryn stayed in his dressing room, resting for the forceful and terrible interview with the High Priest, preparing for the cold and terrible act of burning his enemies at the stake, the *auto-da-fé* that was the play's most stunning spectacle.

By the end, however, as the story ground to its inevitable conclusion with the ghostly figure of the King's dead father dragging his grandson Karel into the tomb, the pain was pushing past all Feltheryn's defenses. And there was something else, something that had tugged at him increasingly throughout. As the curtain fell and he dropped the character from him like a discarded robe, he placed it.

There was no applause.

No more applause than there had been in the alley earlier. Instead there was a curious buzz, something between anger and amusement, partaking of both; as if the audience didn't know what to do.

He had felt it, had known with the back of his mind that something was wrong, but he had been too much at odds with the pain to pay attention. Now his mind focused on it with a clarity like sunlight on springwater.

He started to go through the curtains for a bow, if not to

receive applause then to gauge the danger, but Glisselrand took his arm and stopped him.

"I think not," she said, and he saw that there were lines in her face that age had not put there.

"What's wrong?" he asked.

"I don't quite know," she replied, "but I think we shall find out. The Prince and the Beysa have sent word that they are coming backstage. Let's get to the green room."

They had taken the precaution of providing their own greens for the opening, so by the time Prince Kadakithis and the Beysa Shupansea swept in, Feltheryn and Glisselrand were seated behind a desk amidst baskets of flowers and fruit with potted palms to either side. It had not been easy to find potted palms in Sanctuary, but they had grown used to them in Ranke and they felt it would identify them positively with the capital in its days of glory.

The effort was apparently wasted.

"How *dare* you!" accused the prince, and Feltheryn instantly knew what it was that he had dared, though just how and why he did not know.

Prince Kadakithis was clearly the young nobleman on whom Snegelringe had modeled his walk and manner! It must have appeared that the whole play was directly aimed at him, a warning or an insult or . . .

"Oh *look*!" said Snegelringe, entering on the arm of a beautiful young woman and accompanied by several more. "Here's the young man you pointed out to me! Kind Sir, you cannot know how grateful—"

Snegelringe stopped.

The whole world seemed to stop for a moment as one of the ladies in the pudgy actor's retinue stepped forward.

"*Daphne!*" Prince Kadakithis exclaimed.

"My husband!" said Princess Daphne, and the look she

gave him could have frozen the oceans all the way to the Beysa's homeland. "I heard that you had made a gracious contribution to the evening, so how could I do less?"

She stepped past him and drew out a small velvet bag which she dropped on the table in front of Glisselrand with just enough force to indicate that it contained metal: from the sound of it, gold. Then she looked back at the prince.

"I hope that you enjoyed the evening as much as I did. For now you must excuse me. I have an appointment with Master Rounsnouf, the estimable actor. Then Masters Snegelringe and Rounsnouf and I will be going to the Vulgar Unicorn. It is amazing how much of Sanctuary I never used to see!"

She swept from the room, followed by the other women who had come in with her.

Snegelringe, perceiving that he had been duped, stood motionless while the full import of his actions crashed down on him. "I . . ." he started, but then he stopped, clearly unable to formulate an appropriate apology.

The Beysa laughed.

"Master Snegelringe," she said, "your imitation of the prince was most enlightening. Only less so than the reason for it which we have just had revealed. But perhaps you might choose another model for the performance you will give tommorow night."

"Unless," said Feltheryn, the plot of the play before him coming clear, "Your Highness would consent to see it in another light!"

The Prince and the Beysa turned to him and Glisselrand clutched his hand.

"While it is true," he continued, "that the role of Karel is tragic, it is also noble. Karel, like His Highness, spends

much of his time in a backward land; so much so that he
comes to love its people, even to the point of standing up
for them against his father, the King.''

A different tension now came into the room, for the
relationship between Prince Kadakithis and his half-brother
the late emperor, was well known.

''If it were spoken in the palace that the Prince was
pleased with our seeing him in such an heroic light, tonight's performance could not be taken as an insult by
anyone, no matter how it was instigated. In fact, I doubt
anyone would believe that it was anything but the best
compliment we poor players could offer. More, it is known
that Your Highness has supported our efforts, so it might
seem that it was with Your Highness' compliance that we
performed the play thus.''

He did not dare say further. The seeds of the idea were
planted, it would be up to them to keep them watered. The
magic in the plays was subtle, but it *might* be sufficient to
transform the image of the Prince from that of a ''kittycat''
into that of a tiger.

The Prince and the Beysa looked at one another. The
Beysa's snake slid out of hiding in her sleeve.

Molin Torchholder stalked into the room, his face full of
the lightning of the god he worshipped, but before he
could speak the Beysa turned to Glisselrand.

''Turn out the pouch the Princess Daphne gave you,''
she instructed.

''*Daphne?*'' echoed Molin, clearly outraged.

Glisselrand did as she was bid and dumped the sizable
pile of gold coins onto the table.

The Beysa eyed the coins, then reached down to her
dress and plucked off several large jewels. Smiling, she
placed them on the table next to the gold.

"I believe your next play should be *The Queen of Tarts*," she said with consummate modesty, considering that the play was accounted too lascivious to play in many towns. "In case you do not remember, it is the one about the noblewoman who sells herself in the market-place. I have never seen it, but here, far away from home, I believe I can risk it. These jewels should serve in earnest of the costs."

"Oh, Your *Highness*," said Glisselrand, looking at the jewels. "We could not *possibly* accept such a gracious donation . . ."

—*Now what was she saying?* Feltheryn wondered; for at that moment the pain between his ribs began to blot out his thoughts and he was sure that he must immediately slip from consciousness. The Prince and the Beysa might be nobility, but opening night was over and he needed a physician—

"Not unless," Glisselrand continued, "Your Highness would accept a small *token* of our thanks."

Feltheryn understood and plunged back to consciousness, but he was not quick enough. Before he could inter-vene Glisselrand had pulled out the object she had been knitting, a multicolored tea cozy that would have put the S'danzo to shame for its garishness, and she was proffer-ing it proudly to the Beysa.

RED LIGHT, LOVE LIGHT

Chris Morris

Sunset gilded Sanctuary's domes and spires as Shawme, the new girl at Myrtis's Aphrodisia House, sat upright in her backroom bed. Fists clenched, she took deep breaths, shaking off her bad dream.

Her blue eyes wide, she stared hungrily out the window, at the sunset to which she woke, at the window frame itself, at the whitewashed walls of her little room. The room was plain by Aphrodisia House standards, but not by Shawme's. The room had a real window with glass panes; it had a feather bed and clean sheets; it had a writing desk *cum* dressing table on which were such luxuries as pots of body paint and makeup, kohl and powdered cowrie shell, even a hair brush made from boar bristles, and a bone comb; it had a closet with clothes in it—clean clothes, free from holes, dresses of fine sheer silk and even a coat to keep out the spring chill.

It was a room of unimaginable luxury, high above the street, not like the room in the dream from which Shawme had awakened to flee. In the dream, she'd been back in her old Ratfall burrow, shared with five other orphans, fighting over the raw and bony thigh of a dead cat they'd found in the street. In that dream, the other kids had teased her that all of *this* was a dream. They'd been sure there was no room for her in the Aphrodisia House, no job among the perfumed women of the evening, no marvelous future unrolling day by day.

In the dream, Shawme had been back in Ratfall where no one had a future and no one had a past, not a chance or a hope. Except Zip. And Zip didn't pay any mind to the youngsters. You couldn't matter to Zip until you weren't a kid anymore . . . until the PFLS found a use for you.

Shawme unballed her clenched fists and rubbed her eyes with her hands. As the dream's terror fled, joy filled her and crested into exultation. She was really here! She'd made it out of Ratfall!

So all of this was true and real—the down coverlet she pulled up against her naked shoulders, the lavender-scented oil lamp ready to light by her bed as night came on, the beautiful sunset—because even in Sanctuary, the night could be beautiful when you were safe inside the walls of a fine house instead of lurking cold and vulnerable on the streets.

And it was all real because of Zip. Zip had noticed her, all right, when she'd come to him with the treasures she'd found on the Downwind beach. Zip had looked at her with focused eyes for the first time and Shawme's heart skipped a beat. You couldn't do any better than Zip. Zip was the fantasy lover of all the young girls in Ratfall and half of Downwind. Zip's power could shield you, Zip's connections could get you anything, even *out*.

In front of Zip, Shawme had bitten her lip and pretended she wasn't about to swoon. She had to be grown up and impress the PFLS leader for her plan to work. The PFLS—

Popular Front for the Liberation of Sanctuary—was working with uptowners now. Zip's connections were legend in the shanty towns. She'd smiled bravely and said, "I found something—things you'd want. I'll give them, for a price."

And he'd let her show him, let her tell him, what she'd found—a bronze rod that turned noble metal to dross, an amulet of uncertain value, a rusted knife whose edge could be coaxed to life. There's been one other thing she hadn't shown him, but that was her secret, still.

And the PFLS leader had seemed to be impressed, and said, "What's your name, girl, and what do you want for these?"

She'd replied, as cool as if she dealt with handsome rebel leaders every day, "I want out of Ratfall. I want a room in the Aphrodisia House. I want to be one of Lady Myrtis's girls and meet a noble lord and marry well." Her chin was high, to show she knew the ways of the world and the implications of what she was saying. As she spoke, she ran spread hands down her bodice and over her hips as she'd seen a whore do once, when she was uptown in the Maze where men could afford to buy a woman's favors and women sold themselves for money rather than having to give themselves for survival.

Zip's eyes had narrowed, his mouth had twitched. He'd stroked his stubbled chin and gazed ruminatively at the treasures she'd found. Then finally he looked up from under his black sweatband and said, "That's what you want, I'll see what I can do. But leave these with me, or somebody might take them from you and you'll have nothing to trade but what you started with."

She'd been suddenly uncomfortable under his stare, a different look than he'd had on him before. It seemed to go right through her clothes and she thought, terrified for an instant so that she'd begun to shake, he was going to ask her to demonstrate her expertise, such charms as could qualify a girl for Myrtis's, the finest house in all of Sanctuary's red-light district.

If he had asked, all chance of Shawme's escape to luxury and bright tomorrows would have been dashed on the spot, for Shawme had no idea what a man like Zip would want from a woman, let alone a professional woman.

In point of fact, Shawme had no idea what to do with a man, except run from them and throw whatever you could at them if they got too close. If you didn't do that and they grabbed you, the next thing you knew you were battered, bleeding and pregnant.

But it wasn't that way for the uptown women of the Aphrodisia House, and ever since she'd found that out, Shawme had wanted to go there.

So when Zip's voice deepened, she was terrified. If he found out she knew nothing about the job she'd demanded in exchange for the treasures she had, he'd never help her. And if she ever was to let Zip do what men did to women, she'd have to know what she was doing. Or else he'd laugh.

Men always laughed at virgins.

Shawme's virginity was still a problem now, after a week at Myrtis's. She'd meant to tell Myrtis, when the time was right. But the time had never been right. Zip had gotten her the interview, and sent her uptown with an escort. She hadn't returned to Ratfall again, not for the whole two weeks since then.

She'd been taught to bathe herself, to deal with her moon flow, to make herself soft and beautiful, to keep from getting pregnant. But she'd been taught nothing of how to rid herself of the awful curse of virginity. Or of how to please a man.

All the other girls—older girls, poised girls, wise girls
with gold rings in their ears and gemstones in their noses—
assumed she knew her trade. They were arch and competi-
tive, and their gossip had teeth. If they found out, she'd be
driven from here, back down to Ratfall. Like in her dream.

But no one had found out, and Shawme was going to
go downstairs this evening, for the first time. Tonight, she
would be among those in the great salon, posturing and
fanning themselves, luring men upstairs.

Tonight, Shawme would become the woman she was
pretending to be. She'd lied about her age, said she was
eighteen, when she was years younger. But no one had
noticed. All the other girls were too busy counting conquests. *Who* came to see you mattered most here. Who
came more than once, who became your regular, who your
regular knew and what kind of gifts he brought you. It
was a different world.

And she was on its threshold. Her heart calmed, she
stretched in her bed, watching the sunset slink into dusk,
the colors no more beautiful than the garments the girls
downstairs wore. Myrtis had given her the smallest room,
the plainest clothes, the lowest percentage, but only because Shawme was the new girl.

"Except for Zip, you wouldn't have this bed at all,"
Myrtis had told her, not unkindly. "We've got a waiting
list down to the White Foal Bridge. You'll have to make
your way here, make friends, develop regulars. Then you'll
have your own money, and we'll settle up what I've
advanced you against a piece of your gross."

Shawme hadn't even known what a "piece of your
gross" was, until she'd gotten up yesterday early and
snuck out of the house to meet Merricat at Promise Park.

Merricat was Shawme's only uptown friend, a girl apprenticing at the Mageguild because of her shadowy, powerful aunt up north. The two girls had met on the beach one day, and been fast friends ever since.

When they'd met, Merricat had been crying as she beachcombed, and Shawme had drawn her knife, ready to protect the other girl if she could. Merricat's tears, it turned out, were tears of unrequited love for Randal, the powerful mage who served the Stepsons.

So they'd had something in common, both girls unnoticed by the men of their dreams. Merricat had confided all about Randal, and Shawme had told of her hopeless love for Zip.

Then together they'd concocted this scheme, that was supposed to make Zip notice Shawme, come to the Aphrodisia House some day and sweep her off her feet. "*After*," Merricat had said wisely, with a nod of her prim little chin, "you have mastered the womanly arts better than anyone else. To make Randal love *me*, I must become a wondrous adept."

Merricat had given Shawme a spell to hide her virginity yesterday, given it with a frown: "I'm not very good at this—yet," she'd cautioned. "So be careful."

Merricat was shorter, rounder, and fairer than Shawme, with a plump face and button eyes and all the softness of good breeding. Yesterday when they met, Merricat had had her peregrine, Dika, with her, the gift her aunt had sent to qualify Merricat for Mageguild apprenticeship in the first place.

"I trust you," Shawme had replied, rubbing her tanned arms because suddenly she didn't.

"Trust Dika, it's his doing. Lightning and thunder, I hope it works." Merricat was suddenly solemn. She leaned forward on the park bench: "And you'll tell me, promise.

What it's like. Who it is . . . everything. Or I'll curse you. You wouldn't want that.''

As long as Dika didn't curse her too, it probably wouldn't hurt worse than growing up in Ratfall, Shawme thought. Out loud she said, ''Of course, as soon as . . . it . . . happens, I'll put the lantern in my window. But won't you know, by magical means?''

Merricat lived in constant fear of being found wanting, of failing in her apprenticeship. ''I should know,'' she said, her full lower lip beginning to tremble, ''but I probably won't. I'm not good enough, Shawme,'' she said, a whine edging her tone. ''I'll never—''

''Shush, bitch,'' said Shawme sharply, and then regretted the gutter talk up here where words meant different things. Shawme took Merricat's fine, soft hand and squeezed it hard before letting go. ''You're better than you think. Dika knows it. He's not flying away.''

Merricat reached up, onto her shoulder to stroke the peregrine who perched there. The bird cocked its head at Shawme and opened and closed its beak once as if in agreement.

''He's right, Merricat. Got to go before I miss breakfast.''

''And I miss bedcheck. Good luck with Zip.''

''Good luck with Randal.''

So the two friends had parted, Shawme armed with a root of dried mandrake on a thong that was supposed to keep her secret safe from discovery.

Keep it safe, tonight. Tonight she would lie abed with her first man. She rubbed her tawny arms, stroking the fine sun-paled hair on them. She hoped he would be beautiful, bold and not too old. She wanted him to be just like Zip, with a full head of hair and a lithe young body, with high cheekbones and the fire of revolution in his eyes . . .

But he could as easily be a fat, greasy-lipped merchant from the Street of Weavers, or a drover from Caravan Square. There were no gods left alive in the part of Ratfall that had spawned Shawme from the chance meeting of an Ilsig matron and a soldier who, from Shawme's blue eyes, was probably Rankan.

No gods to pray to, but prayers aplenty. Shawme closed her eyes and chanted, "Red light, love light, first light I see tonight. Wish I may, wish I might, have the boy I love tonight."

Quick as a spooked cat, she opened her eyes and there, out the window, she saw the first lights flare along the town's skyline. Against the torpid blue of early evening, they seemed like an omen. Zip would come, she was sure of it. Come to make sure that Shawme had a customer on her first night at Myrtis's. Come to make a woman of her.

Sliding out from under her coverlet, she clutched the mandrake root around her neck on its thong. Thanks be to Merricat's magic, everything would be all right . . . *if* she could just decide whether to wear her blue dress, or her red one.

For a girl who'd never before owned even one dress, but only cast-off shirts and trousers, beggar's rags, choosing between two new and filmy dresses with low cut bodices and gilded laces was no small challenge. When she'd donned the blue one and was padding down the Aphrodisia House's stairs, male laughter was already rising over the raucous strains of music from the downstairs saloon.

And tucked beneath that dress, tightly bound with a scarf to her thigh, was the other thing she'd found on the beach that night, the weapon she hadn't shown to Zip, the weird artifact from the sea that Merricat had squinted at, frowned over, and told Shawme that she'd better keep.

The guard was changing in Sanctuary, and nowhere were the winds of chaos more keenly felt than in the Mageguild.

Even Merricat, who hadn't been an apprentice very long before pillars of fire uptown had signalled the coming of the New Era, knew that. She could see it in the faces of the adepts, in the hunched shoulders of the handsome, mysterious and nameless First Hazard.

She could feel it in her classroom sessions when a real mage was teaching, as Randal was this evening. Usually, when Randal taught the gathered apprentices, Merricat found herself daydreaming. She'd watch Randal's freckled face and envision it gazing fondly on her ih some secluded bower to which he'd whisked her for private lessons. She'd stare at his prodigious ears and taste what it would be like to nibble them. She'd meditate on the strong arms of the warrior-mage in his adept's robes and wonder what it would be like to feel them around her.

But not tonight. Tonight even Randal—who always made Merricat feel calm and safe and less afraid of being exposed as an untalented imposter among the students—even Randal seemed tense and wan.

The lesson was in progress, though, and Merricat tried hard to concentrate.

". . . go to your trances, and then we'll start adventuring up among the planes. On each plane we visit, you'll have time to look around, meet denizens. When you meet a denizen, be sure to remember its name. The eventual object of this lesson," Randal said in a sharp voice that forced Merricat's attention away from daydreams, away from schemes to get Randal alone on pretext of discussing Shawme's plight, away from everything . . .

". . . the object is, eventually, to reach the twelfth plane, where you will encounter a spirit guide, a connection to help you negotiate among netherworld powers. This is magic of the most potent sort, magic of the kind that will stay with you lifelong and determine even your after-life. It has nothing to do with mundane spells failing, with irate harridans complaining about inefficacious love potions—"

The score of students tittered.

Randal continued. "This is profound business. Some of you will make this journey slowly, in stages. Some will only partly complete it during this term. But to be truly an adept, you must in your lifetime journey to the twelfth plane, conquer all that stands in your way to do so, and there meet your guide face to face. Your guide is your representative where feet cannot tread. It is privy to knowl-edge you otherwise cannot tap, to power you'll never wield on your own."

A hush fell over the students. Randal's voice had deep-ened even further. In his fighter's tunic and dark pants, he was the picture of a field mage, so much more suited to this lesson than some soft adept in a festooned robe of power. When Randal leaned forward, his neck outthrust, his eyes raking their ranks, no one even shifted in surprise at the words he spoke next.

"Class," Randal said in a suddenly softened voice that signalled his most intense concern for their welfare. "This is a lesson not without its dangers. Afterwards, there will be no teasing among you, no bravado from those who proceed faster toward those who go slowly. All of you are about to risk your sanity and mortal persons among the planes. Go cautiously, go with determination, and go with my blessing.'' He straightened up.

A murmur ran through the students.

When it subsided, Randal said, "And now, if you'll all put your feet flat on the floor, hands flat on your thighs, I'm going to guide your trances."

As Randal ran through the relaxation litany, Merricat let his voice be her beacon. When he instructed her right hand to rise, of its own accord, from her lap and hover before her face, it seemed that her hand was indeed weightless. And when he told her to open her eyes and behold the manna of her person, she was unsurprised to see a green nimbus surrounding her fingers, to see the bones beneath the skin, and to see blue lightning spurting from her fingertips.

When she was instructed to close her eyes again, they closed without her volition. When she was told that her hand would now fall to her thigh and when it did, she would open her eyes and see the first plane around her, she was not afraid.

Until her hand hit her thigh. Then Merricat was plunged into vertigo and if she could, she would have grabbed onto her chair. But she could not. Her body was under Randal's control, not her own. When the snap of his fingers caused her eyes to open, she beheld a landscape windwhipped and strange, stretching forever in all directions, where hills had crests like frozen waves and trees were perfect spheres. Beneath those trees were others and she knew (without knowing how she knew) that some of those others were her fellow students.

She knew because she was under one such tree and beside her were creatures part human, part not. One creature came toward her in wide strides, staring at her through one burning round eye, cocking the head of a falcon and saying through the beak of a bird: "Welcome, Merricat, to the first plane. What is it you seek here?"

"Knowledge," said Merricat as she'd been coached in Randal's lesson. "Friends. Power of mind."

The beak of the bird grew large and from it came the words, "There are no friends for you on the first plane, as there are no friends for you at Aphrodisia House. You must seek higher. Here, as there, you will find only tools."

"Give me one, then," she heard her own voice say, and was appalled at her temerity.

The bird head nodded and the bird beak came close.

She wanted to shy away from the sharp beak but she could not. Her palm extended and the beak neared the soft offering of her flesh. And into her palm it dropped an insect, like a wasp. The insect tickled her palm and on her flesh, with many legs, it danced. And as it danced, a wasp's nest came into being and into it, the wasp soon crawled.

Then Merricat's hand became very heavy and the next thing she knew, it had fallen to her lap, for Randal's voice was saying, ". . . at the count of three, your spirit will return to your body and your eyes will open and you will be in your seat beside your fellow students."

It was as if the adept spoke only to her. She listened only to his voice as again dizziness overcame her. She was flying through clouds of many colors, among ancient seas, and farther.

When she found her body, she felt absolutely sucked into it and her spirit came to rest in its prison with a thud that was her hand hitting her thigh.

Her eyes opened. She blinked. The students around her were all pale-faced, white-lipped, and silent. No one looked at anyone else. But Merricat looked at her hand on her thigh.

In the palm of her hand was a red blotch about the size of the small wasp's nest. The hair rose all over her body. Surely this must mean something, or else she'd done it all wrong . . . What connection could the first plane have to Shawme's plight and the thing she'd told her friend to keep secret?

She was shaking, trembling all over. Her skin was blotchy, red and fishy white.

She didn't hear the rest of the lesson, she just heard Randal's voice, the only comfort in her universe which now was no comfort at all.

She had to tell the adept what she'd done, how she'd failed, and find out what the omen meant. She had to.

When the class filed out, her throat constricted: what if Randal left before the last of the students were gone? She couldn't chase him down the halls, or sortie to his private chamber where real magic was always under way. She just couldn't.

But Randal was surrounded by other questioners, excited voices asking about what they'd seen on the first plane. Merricat waited until all but two of them were gone and then walked slowly up the row toward the front of the study hall.

As she did, she felt the mage's eyes on her. And met them to see concern there, and recognition.

For what she was sure was the first time, Randal had noticed her—not just because she was giving a dinner menu to the First Hazard and he happened to be in the room, either. But noticed her with his whole attention.

If she hadn't been so frightened, she'd have blushed red as a beet. As it was, her gait stiffened and her steps slowed.

Then Merricat stopped. She held back, watching, miserable. She didn't have the courage to walk brassily up to the mage, who was pestered with unending questions from other students. No matter the meaning of the omen, she'd go to Shawme by herself. They'd figure it out together. She couldn't, just couldn't, bother Randal with her insignificant problems, not when the whole Mageguild was reeling from the magical recession taking place in Sanctuary; not while teaching a new generation must seem so futile . . .

Randal winked at her. Her hand flew to her mouth. She must have imagined it. Two students were much closer than she, prattling away. She clutched her tablet, on which she'd taken not a single note tonight, to her bosom.

He winked again, and she heard him say to the two fawning apprentices, "You two compare experiences, it will do you both good. Right now, I have an appointment with this young lady, whom I can't keep waiting any longer. Go practice first plane access. Tomorrow we do the second plane. Go on, now."

Both students looked over their shoulders at her with resentful, jealous eyes that changed visibly when they saw what "young lady" Randal meant. She glimpsed surprise and a new respect and something nastier in their backward glances as they left, whispering together.

With their passing, she and Randal were alone. She drew back a step. He didn't follow but stood unmoving, hands hooked in his fighter's belt, a slow smile on his freckled face.

He was so bold, so handsome, so brave. He was the Stepsons' chosen mage, a fighting magician who'd battled in the Wizard Wars. He was the most romantic single figure in the beleaguered Sanctuary Mageguild and Merricat wished miserably that she could disappear, sink through the floorboards, and be gone.

What did he care of her troubles, her doubts, her questions? She wished Dika was here, a comforting weight on her shoulder. Sometimes Dika seemed to speak for her, lend her courage. But not tonight. Falcons weren't welcome in Mageguild study halls.

Neither was she. It was obvious that the keen eyes of Randal were reading her soul. She trembled, went up on tiptoes, and eyed the doors through which the others had gone. Still time to run.

"Well, Merricat, how was your trip to the first plane?" said Randal gently as at last he came toward her.

He knew her name! She could hardly believe it. She said hastily, "Well, it's fine, there was a blird who spook weirds to me, and round trees." Damned and tongue-tied, she wanted to die. She closed her eyes.

And heard a voice so close she nearly fainted, "I saw something or other of that, I must admit. Would you like to talk about it over a drink?" and felt the mage touch her arm lightly, oh so lightly.

Saw something? What a mage he was! Talk about it over a *drink*? She took deep breaths and opened her eyes and said fervently, "Oh yes you, bless!" And, mortified, put her hand to her mouth again. If she could just calm down, her words wouldn't get scrambled. *Blird who spooked weirds.* She cringed inwardly.

The mage's fingers covered hers and drew her hand away from her lips. Then he was examining her palm, where the wasp nest's mark still could be seen.

When he looked up, his brow was furrowed. "What's here means more to me than you'd understand. It would be a favor if you'd share your experience with me, and anything else that might be relevant that's happened to you lately. Wasps and I have a . . . special understanding.''

The hand that wasn't holding Merricat's went to his waist, where a wavy sword, short and foreign-looking, hung in a tooled scabbard.

Miserably, afraid to trust her traitorous voice, Merricat nodded. How to tell him about it all? About the wasp on the first plane, and the weapon her friend Shawme had found, that silver tube that shot tiny wasplike pieces of metal when you blew through it—the weapon Merricat was certain that Dika had wanted Shawme to keep?

In fact, how to tell Randal anything at all, with her tongue tied in knots and her heart pounding? How indeed, while she was sure to the very depths of her soul that she'd done something wrong in helping Shawme, and in coming to the Mageguild, and in falling hopelessly in love with the famed and fearsome mage Randal in the first place?

Shawme was trembling uncontrollably and afraid someone would notice her, making herself small in a corner among the other girls in Myrtis's saloon.

And someone had. One of the musicians, a percussionist who pounded drums and shook bells and crashed cymbals, kept watching her as he played.

The attention of the musician made things worse. As did every man who came ducking in through Myrtis's beaded curtains, who stalked around the room, drink and smoke in hand, and touched this girl or that before making up his mind and escorting his chosen up the back stairs to the girls' room.

Worse, because none of them so much as ogled Shawme. She might as well have stayed upstairs. Worse too, be-

cause if a man did approach her, she was sure she'd break
and run. Unless, of course, that man was Zip.

After a while she closed her eyes, secure in her corner
with stout red-frescoed walls against her back, certain
she'd get through this whole night unnoticed. As much
trouble as that might cause with Myrtis, she knew she
could handle that. Other girls must have failed to make
conquests on their first night here. Most of those who'd
gone upstairs already, went with men they obviously knew
quite well, men who took them boldly in strong arms and
crushed silken bodies against armored chests with no
preamble.

Shawme didn't know anyone like those soldiers, any
more than she knew the sort of brocaded nobles who came
in groups of twos and threes, smelling of perfume like the
women, and gathered up giggling ladies by the armload.

The only man who noticed her was the musician, a
youngster with barely a beard and naked, sweaty arms.
Her sort. From undistinguished beginnings. Eking out a
living among his betters and here to please. The more he
watched her, the more Shawme felt a kinship. She began
wondering if, when his music was done, the youth would
come toward her.

But it didn't work out that way.

She was studying the frescoes in the salon through a
growing fog of smoke, finally realizing how instructive
they were to an ignorant girl. On them men were portrayed
doing what she'd seen dogs do in the street. And women
knelt before them, doing mysterious things that involved
kissing. Shawme was trying to guess at what that would
be like, feeling her mouth grow dry and her heart pound as
each successive man took someone else and the crowd of
women thinned while she tried not to notice and prayed

that Myrtis wouldn't come down tonight to find Shawme the only unclaimed girl, the only one who hadn't made a copper's worth of profit for the house . . .

So she didn't notice the newcomers until the beaded curtain rattled, and then she quickly lowered her eyes.

Three men had come in together, laughing, arm in arm, with a fourth behind them, taciturn. The three were military men, highly ranked since they'd been allowed to wear their weapons in here. The fourth was armed as well, and unsmiling. His glance caught hers before she looked away.

In front of Shawme's corner was a couch on which three older girls reclined, each showing thigh or bare perfumed shoulder or a hint of rosy breast. The three jolly soldiers, unmistakably a little drunk, came their way. The tallest one was blond with braids in his hair and a goblet in his hand.

He stared directly at Shawme for three heartbeats, and on the fourth her heart threatened to stop entirely. That look was a look of recognition, but she couldn't remember ever meeting such a soldier. She was sure he was coming for her.

She shrank back in the corner, trying to push her way through the frescoed walls; trying to get breath into her lungs, enough breath for flight if he held out a hand to her as she'd seen men do here.

She would run right past him, duck under his arm and fly out through the curtained doorway, into the street, back to Ratfall. She'd run and run until her heart burst.

But the blond man looked away then, at the girls on the couch between Shawme and his soldier friends, and held out a hand to one of them, who squealed, "Oh, Walegrin, you're looking fit tonight," and giggled.

In relief, Shawme squeezed her eyes shut. In that solitary darkness, her relief was eaten up by chagrin. Then came embarrassment and mortification, shame and despair. No man was going to choose her. She was going to fail. All the other girls would laugh at her.

She thought to herself, Perhaps it's the mandrake. Perhaps it's ugly. Perhaps it's working too well and keeping the men away. So she reached up behind her neck, eyes still shut, and undid the thong that held it there.

When the thong came undone, she opened her eyes and surreptitiously pulled the mandrake from between her breasts, hiding it behind her, under the cushions of the bench against the wall.

When she straightened up, a shadow fell on her. She looked up. And up. Standing directly in front of her was the fourth man, the one who'd come in alone.

She thought wildly, He's not here for me, he's going to ask one of the girls on the couch. But all of them were gone. While she'd had her eyes shut, they'd left with the blond soldier and his friends.

There was no one else in this corner, darkened by the big man's shadow, but Shawme. She craned her neck, unable to rise as a girl should, her knees like water.

He seemed gigantic, all dark cloth and leather. She looked up past his weapons belt at eye level, and could hardly see his face, just the dark shadow of new beard and a hand that came suddenly toward her.

"Young lady," his deep voice said, "what's you're name?"

"Sh-Shawme," she quavered and hated herself. His hand was waiting. Somehow, she lifted hers. Then, with his help, she was standing.

"Your room, if you please," said his voice and still she had no clear impression of his face. Her gaze was level with his broad chest, and his eyes beat down on her with such fire in them—as only those of Dika the peregrine had ever done before.

Too late to run, the deed all but done, she remembered her training: "A drink, kind sir, or something stronger?" Drugs were purveyed at Myrtis's—drugs to embolden, drugs to give stamina, drugs to make up for whatever needed making up for, so Myrtis had told her.

"I'm known as Shepherd, little lamb," he said and she knew from that he wanted no drink or anything at all but her.

At the last minute, while his hand inexorably drew her from the corner toward the stairs, she remembered the charm that Merricat had given her, her mandrake root, without which this man was soon going to know she was a virgin.

Anguished, she halted, their arms stretched out between them, without the strength to pull away. His big head turned questioningly and she saw his profile for the first time: a grown man's profile, hard and seasoned, a bold nose and lips trying hard not to laugh above a stubbled chin. This was a stark man, a man from whom you ran on the streets because such men took what they wanted. There was no fooling such a man as he.

"I—I forgot something, left something on the bench."

"You don't need that, not with me," he said with such authority that Shawme could do nothing but obey the pressure of his tug, which pulled her in and under the circle of his arm.

Up the stairs they went, the big man's right arm crooked around her neck, her right hand pressed against her collarbone by his grip, his fingers against her throat. She hadn't remembered the stairs being so many, or the trek to her backroom bed so long. His breath in her hair was hot and the things he said were a matter of tone, not words.

The tone said, You're mine, I'm in control. Relax and you'll be fine. The words said whatever Shepherd thought she should hear, but she heard only an end to her childhood in them.

It didn't matter what the words were; it didn't matter that she took moisture from his lips to wet her own. It didn't matter that he wasn't Zip, even. It only mattered that she not fail, that he not be angry when her virgin blood was spilled, when her lack of expertise was on display.

When they got to her room, Shepherd wanted no help with his leathers or his weapons. Help with his boots was something any fool could give. And then he helped her, wordless and with a strange look on a face that seemed unaccustomed to humor or kindness but displayed both in red-brown, fiery eyes, eyes so much like Dika's . . .

When it became clear to him that she was unworthy of the job she held, ignorant and ill-prepared, an imposter, she was sure he'd leave her, go straight to Myrtis and complain. But he did none of those.

He treated her like fragile glass, like the musicians below in the salon treated their instruments. And soon enough she was learning, under his hands, why the other girls went to work smiling each evening.

She learned enough so that, when the moment came for her skirts to come off, she was forgetful of everything: what he must soon find out, how disappointment and disgust would oversweep him, even of what form his wrath might take.

And then it happened. Shepherd sat back on her bed, his diaphragm with its line of dark hair quivering, and said,

"Take that off!" His voice was very harsh. "Put it on the table. Now!"

"It?" She was breathless, her voice a fear-constricted squeak. How could she take off her virginity? How could he even see it? He'd just this moment glimpsed her unclothed form.

Then she followed the big man's pointing finger, and relief flooded her. The silver tube was what he meant. The sea-gift, the one Merricat had advised her to keep. "This?" she said with fake aplomb. "I always wear it."

"Not with me, you don't." He rose up, off the bed, and she saw his body start to change. Chest heaving, she blurted, "Please, don't go. I'll take it off."

Hands on hips, he waited until she had. Then he took her in his arms and, his lips against her breast, said, "The rest of it, I can handle. Just trust me, lamb."

And somehow, she whispered to him, "But I don't know . . . I've never . . . I don't have anything to offer you, no tricks, no skill—"

"You have something none of those others could offer, lamb," he replied in a rumble that made her legs weak. "Something only you can give. And for it, I'm going to give you a lesson in love as has never been taught in Sanctuary."

And then she knew that Shepherd knew, somehow, and that he wasn't going to be angry no matter if she bled all night. What she didn't know, until he tapped her on the mouth with a reddened finger, was that it didn't have to hurt to become a woman.

Anymore than she'd known anything about the joys of womanhood that lay beyond her body's barrier, all of which the man called Shepherd showed her before, while she dozed, he slipped away, leaving a piece of gold upon her pillow.

"Wake up, wake up!" said Merricat, shaking Shawme's shoulder. Behind Merricat, Randal hovered in the doorway, with Myrtis beside her. And Myrtis was wringing her veiny hands, saying, ". . . this is highly irregular, mage, and the least you can do for me, since I allowed it, is make our weather-control spell your first priority."

"Later, Madame," said Randal. "Now leave us, if you please."

Shawme was rubbing her eyes and stretching widely, still unaware that there was a man in the open doorway behind Merricat.

"Merri!" Shawme smiled with delight. "What are you doing here? Never mind, I've got so much to tell—" Shawme saw Randal and stopped speaking. She pulled her coverlet up around her neck and hunched in her bed.

"Shawme, this is important," Merricat said quickly in a low voice. "That's Randal the mage. He wants to talk to you. About *that*." Merricat pointed to the silver tube on the table beside Shawme's bed.

"That?" Puzzlement crossed Shawme's face. "It doesn't matter. Thank you for the mandrake, Merricat. Thank Dika. I had the most wonderful—"

Randal crossed the room in quick strides. "Pardon the intrusion, miss, but did you—?" Randal stopped and looked at Merricat imploringly.

"Shawme," Merricat demanded, leaning over the other girl stiff-armed and reaching for something glinting gold on the pillow with her other hand. "Does this mean what I think?" She fingered the gold soldat.

"Oh, yes, and it was wonderful! I can't tell you how wond—"

Merricat's face fell; she blinked back tears. If it hadn't happened yet, Randal had promised that he'd sponsor Shawme for Mageguild apprenticeship, to get her out of Aphrodisia House. Now . . . Merricat turned an imploring face to Randal. "Too late," she whispered.

"I thought it might be," said Randal, and Merricat saw Shawme's eyes dart from face to face as the others spoke. "Shawme, if you will cede this instrument," he ignored the coin that Merricat held, and tapped the table on which the silver tube rested, "to the Mageguild, you'll have my undying gratitude, enough money to move out of here into your own house, and favors to be claimed from Merricat and myself whenever you need them. Such favors as a mage can grant."

"What? Why? I—"

Merricat sat back, beaming now, looking fondly upon her friend, who was saved after all by the fine auspices of Randal, the most wonderful mage who ever lived.

Randal replied, "It's too long to explain. I have an affinity for wasps, let's say. So does Merricat. This washed up on the beach, I was told?" The mage stood over her, beginning to voice his questions.

Shawme nodded and answered every one, while Merricat held her friend's hand, until Randal asked, "And will you tell me who you went with tonight? Who came up here with you, and what happened then?"

Shawme's jaw set. Her eyes seemed to go cold. She said, "You want the pea-shooter, take it. My client didn't like it anyway."

"And your client . . . ?" Randal blushed and Merricat thrilled with love. "Did he, ah, was there blood spilled here tonight?" Randal pressed.

"What *is* this?" Shawme demanded, bolt upright now. "You *told* him, Merricat! How could you? It was our secret. Get out of—"

"Shawme, I had to; it's important. Did it happen, the spilling of blood?" Merricat's grip tightened on Shawme as the other girl tried to shake it off.

"Of course it did, and it was wonderful!" Shawme's anger blazed. "Now get out of here, Merricat. I'm never going to forgive you for this. My business, bitch, is with this here mage, not the likes of you."

Merricat stood up uncertainly, head hanging. Randal put a comforting hand on her arm, a reassuring touch that told Merricat she'd done the right thing, no matter what Shawme thought.

Randal stepped forward then, saying to both girls, "Shawme, Merricat, friends are too few to fall out over something like this. Shawme, Merricat was brave and tireless in your behalf. Merricat, your friend needs your understanding. Blood shed in this way, right now in Sanctuary, *is* important. All of what I've promised you, Shawme, is still yours—money, favors for the asking—even if you won't answer me. But as a favor to me, we need to know if the man who gave you this coin is anyone *we* know, whether he's friendly or inimical to us."

Shawme blinked like a startled alleycat. Merricat was afraid her friend would ask Randal just who the mage meant by "we," but Shawme didn't.

She didn't say anything at all. She threw back the coverlet hiding her nakedness and vaulted from the bed. There, on the linen, was proof of the act, and of Shawme's boldness.

Merricat's friend reached languorously for her robe, head high, a proud look on her face. And Merricat was beginning to think it must have been Zip who'd come to Shawme and made her a woman when the Ratfall girl said, "He calls himself the Shepherd, or something like that," and, shrugging into her robe, snatched the gold coin from Merricat's fingers. "He gave me this, and more." Her eyes burned.

Merricat got up from the bed and backed right into Randal, her own body feeling wooden and numb. Peering into the mage's face desperately, Merricat strove for comfort and found none.

Randal shook his head infinitesimally as Shawme flounced by, announcing her intention of "going back downstairs, where there's food and drink for celebration."

Left alone in the courtesan's room, Randal said only, "*Shepherd*, by the Writ." He sighed deeply. "The only good in this came from you, Merricat. And will have to come from you, henceforth. You must help your friend, even if she doesn't understand anything about why you're doing it. And you'll need all your powers, as well as my help. Are you up to it?"

Powers. Merricat had no powers, but Randal did. And Shawme needed her. The blood spilled tonight was spilled in sacrifice, an Ilsigi rite that Shawme hadn't understood, but was now inextricably bound up in. And in a way, it was all Merricat's fault.

She saw Randal pick up the silver tube and fondle it, then look back at her and offer his arm.

She'd done *something* right. "Of course I'll help Shawme. Even if I didn't want to, an apprentice always obeys the Adept who is her instructor. Have no fear, dear Mage. I shall do whatever you say."

And she took Randal's offered arm and let him escort her out of the Aphrodisia House and back to the Mageguild, where she belonged.

A STICKY BUSINESS

C. S. Williams

The Serpentine is a partially cobbled street that zigzags its way like a snake through the Maze. At one end stands the sleaziest, skungiest, most disreputable dive in all of Sanctuary: Sly's Place. Since Sly's death several years ago no one knows who owns the place, but it is run by a huge man in a mailed vest. His name is Ahdio. His origin is questionable, but in this neighborhood so is everyone else's.

To the right of Sly's Place is a dark, narrow, dirty, uninviting lane known as Odd Birt's Dodge. Nobody lives there, or will admit they do. The wider street to the left of Sly's is the Street of Tanners. The stench there on a hot day can make even a Downwinder nauseous.

Three blocks down Tanners is the location of Zandulas's Tannery. Zandulas is a friendly enough fellow, if he would ever bathe.

Zandulas's supplies Chollandar's Glue Shop next door. The proprietor, called Cholly by his friends, makes the finest glues and pastes in town. He uses only the best ingredients: tree sap, inedible fish, hooves and unusable hides, flour, acids and other compounds from the chemists, and people.

Each night in Thieves' World people meet violent ends. Some die by accident, others by "accident," others by design. Most are left where they lie or dropped in some dark alley. Many of them have led useless lives and belong to a social class deemed worthless. No matter what his life had been, in death no man is worthless to the gluemaker. Under license from the Governor he and an apprentice go out with a wagon every morning and pick up the remains from the previous night's mayhem as a social service. Cholly will not, however, pick up a corpse that has apparently died of disease. Those he leaves for the Charnel House wagon.

For a substantial fee he also makes house calls.

The bodies are stripped and dismembered and the goods sorted. Scalps go to a wigmaker, clothes and leather goods and weapons to used goods dealers in those items, gold teeth and jewelry to jewelers. The rendered tallow is ladled off and sold to a soapmaker. The bones are dried and used to help fuel the fires under the great iron pots. Yet all these are bonuses, for the primary product is glue. Nothing is ever wasted at Chollandar's.

Cholly awoke from an elbow nudged into his amply padded ribs. He grumbled and rolled over, snuggling deeper beneath the woolen blanket. The elbow returned with greater force.

"Get up. It's time you left for work."

"Yes, Pet," he groaned.

A small tortoise-shell calico named Crumpet was sitting on his hip, purring loudly. She was a smearing of orange and black with a white chin, feet, and belly. The gluemaker often called her—lovingly—the ugliest cat in Sanctuary. He picked her up and gently placed her at the foot of the bed before crawling out from beneath the covers.

He pulled on a faded black tunic and belted it with his weapons belt. On the belt were a dagger, an Ilbarsi knife, and the axe he used for dismembering corpses and chopping firewood. Onto bare legs he drew soft-soled knee boots. A knife was sheathed in the top of the right one. Finally he wriggled into his vest, heavy leather covered with iron rings, and slid his wax-boiled vambraces onto his forearms. He did all of this in the dark so Ineedra could go back to sleep. He kissed her and went downstairs to the kitchen.

"Oh, all right, nuisance," he gently chided the cat rubbing against his leg and purring. "You know, most cats have to find their own food."

He fed the puss some chopped meat and fixed himself a thick slice of hard sausage and a wedge of cheese between two pieces of black bread. He washed it down with watered wine. Crumpet finished eating before he did and began preening herself, ignoring him with that aloofness only felines are capable of.

It was a miserable morning. Usually Cholly took his time to walk to the shop, but not in this downpour. The cobblestones were slippery and unpaved streets were slimy bogs. Twice he had to backtrack and take a different street. At least his greased boots and oilcloth cloak kept him relatively dry.

He opened the big brass lock and replaced the key in his pouch. The front portion of the shop consisted of row upon row of shelves full of clay jars, each jar marked with a symbol that told him what compound the pot contained. At the rear, in front of a curtained doorway, stood a large wooden counter.

He slapped his hand onto the counter and was answered by a yelp. "Aram, get up. It's time to get started. Go wake up Sambar."

A tall, lanky youth of perhaps sixteen years crawled sleepily out from beneath the counter, yawning widely. He stood and stretched, scratched, and ran one hand through a shaggy mop of blond curls.

"Morning, master," he yawned.

Aram went through the curtained doorway and crossed the brick floor of the rendering room with its four huge iron pots, firewood and dry bones in the rack, and shelves and bins of ingredients. On one side was a butcher's beam and a water pump. A second curtained door, wider than the first, opened onto the stable.

Enkidu and Eshi, two grays with hooves the size of dinner plates, were in their stalls. In one corner of Enkidu's stall a pudgy boy with olive skin snored beneath a coarse wool blanket.

"Get up, Lazybones. Old Baldpate's here. Rise and shine," Aram announced, giving the fourteen-year-old a kick.

"Already?" Sambar stood and shook the straw from his blanket, folded it, and hung it across the stall divider. Satisfied, he brushed the straw from his tunic and began picking pieces from his blue-black straight hair.

By the time the boys had had a bite of bread and cheese and gotten the horses harnessed, the rising sun had barely lightened the tenebrous clouds to putrescent gray. Thunder rumbled like an empty barrel rolling down a cobbled street. Instead of forked streaks, lightning flashed in weak patches scattered randomly on the face of the thunderhead. The

White Foal would overflow again and uncover the trench graves of the unnamed flood and fire victims.

Rain cascaded off their oilskins in icy torrents. Enkidu was prancing, ignoring the weather and enjoying his work. Eshi sulked, wanting to return to her nice warm dry stable. Aram was walking ahead because visibility was so poor. They had just turned onto Odd Birt's Dodge.

"I see one, back of Sly's."

Gray water splashed at every step of Aram's greased buskins.

"Father Ils' beard! He's still bleeding!"

"Can we help him? Is he still alive?"

"No, Cholly. His head's nearly cut off."

"Do you see anybody? The killer may still be around close."

Aram drew his dagger. Cholly climbed down from the driver's seat and unsheathed the Ilbarsi long knife. There was no one to be found. The door to Sly's Place was securely barred and a search of the area revealed no one hiding. No one had gone past them.

"I don't understand. It would take a magician to get out of here without us seeing him," Aram said.

"Anything is possible," Cholly replied.

Aram jumped down and ran to open the stable doors, jumping over the bigger puddles. The double doors swung open easily. Cholly backed the wagon inside. Aram unhitched the team, wiped them down, covered them with dry blankets, and gave them food and water. Only then did he stop to remove his rain gear. He replaced his wet leather gloves and apron with dry ones.

Cholly was smoking a pipe while he inspected the pots Sambar had been left to clean and fill. It was a minor vice, but one to which his wife objected, ". . . because it stinks up the entire house. Even my hair smells like smoke."

There was nothing in Sanctuary that he feared, that he was not married to. Neither wizard nor demon, man nor god, living or dead. When the night was filled with the undead of Ischade and Roxane, he had dispatched several of the poor wights, beheading them so they might return to the hell they had been called back from.

Not all of them were eager to go. One, a former Stepson, had argued for over an hour that it was not dead. It even had the gall to draw a shortsword and threaten the gluemaker. Fortunately the expression "the quick and the dead" was inappropriate. Cholly hacked the zombie to pieces with his axe to prove his point. Sure enough, the Stepson was dead.

Over a dozen bodies were stacked in the wagon. Five had come from Red Lanterns or nearby, indicating it had been a busy night. Three bodies were female. One had even been pretty, in a cheap way.

"You see," Sambar chided while he and Aram began unloading the wagon, "this is what happens to people who spend all their money at the Slippery Lily."

"I hope they had at least finished their business and were leaving. It would be a shame to die without gettin' what they came there for," Aram chuckled.

"One of these Moonday mornings you may come in with the load as a client, not a passenger."

"I can take care of myself."

"The least you'll get is Eshi's measles."

"I haven't had a dose yet. Besides, it isn't fattening like your candy. In another year your taste will run to sweets of another sort. Mark my words."

*   *   *

"Idiot!" Markmor shrieked. "Fool of a fool!"

The young man with flowing silver hair trembled at the tirade, staring at the floor lest the most powerful mage in Sanctuary look him in the eye. Until a few years ago the apprentice wizard's father, Mizraith, had been the chief of those mages not bound by the Rankan Mageguild's hazardous rites. Markmor had been a brash upstart, scarcely more than a child by sorcerous or any other standards. Yet he had slain Mizraith fairly in a wizard's duel and thereby proved himself supreme among those who held to the magical traditions of Ilsig. He'd had to lie low a while— feigning death, abandoning his skein of spells lest he be drawn into the mage-killing and god-killing that had beset Sanctuary these last few years. But he'd survived, and returned, and meant to recapture everything he'd lost, with interest.

"Th-there wasn't time, Master," Marype stammered. "I was just slitting the messenger's throat when I heard horses. I vanished for just a moment, hoping whoever it was would pass by. When I returned the body was gone."

"All you had to do was take the amulet and run. You didn't even have to kill him. A blow on the head would have done the job. How could it be so difficult?"

Markmor's robes of shiny vermilion silk brushed the polished marble floor as he paced angrily. His short hair and pointed beard were as black as his soul. Beneath a single shaggy brow his amethyst eyes were blazing with rage.

Several moments of threatening silence passed before he continued, "Do you have any idea how valuable that bauble is? Not only to me, but to all of us who stand outside the Guild? Much less what could happen if it ever reaches the first Hazard as it was supposed to? Do you see

the danger your bungling has placed us in? Do you? Do
you?''

"I think so, Master." Marype cringed.

"No, that's your trouble, Marype. You *don't* think. If
you had you wouldn't have left the amulet behind. There
are times when I wonder why I took you into my service. I
really do.

"Now tell me again—from the beginning—exactly what
happened. If the person who has the amulet has not yet
discovered its powers we may not be too late."

"I had been following him from bar to bar. By Argash's
bloody nails that man could drink! Eventually he wandered
down the Serpentine to Sly's Place, but it was closed.
Despite all I had seen him drink he wasn't staggering, so I
hung back at a short distance to await an opportunity. As
luck would have it . . . AAAHCHOOO!—Sorry, I may
have caught a cold in the rain last night—he stopped to
relieve himself. I transported myself to a spot right behind
him. Even as I slashed his throat I heard the clatter of
hoofbeats and at least two men talking. They sounded very
close, and coming closer. I knew that the amulet would
have made escape impossible, so I gambled that the amulet
would look too cheap to be worth stealing. I vanished for
just a moment. When I returned the entire body was
gone."

"Did you see anyone about? Anyone at all?"

"It was pouring. Even the beggars were hiding somewhere. He was gone without a trace. I searched and
searched. AACHOO!"

"Marype, you surprise me. You really do. You left the
amulet on him in the hopes it would look too worthless to
steal. Correct? Every child knows that Mazers and Down-
winders steal anything that is not nailed down too securely

to pry up. If you didn't have your father's talent in your blood I wouldn't put up with you. Such talent deserves training, but you severely try my patience.

"Still, all is not lost. Perhaps we can scry its location."

The day's first customer was small, with delicate bones and a slender figure. Her face was veiled and a scarf almost hid her mane of chestnut hair. Although she dressed as a lady's maid, her bearing was more suited to giving orders than taking them. She looked around nervously, making sure no other customer was about. At last: "You are Chollandar?"

He nodded. "How may this humble gluemaker serve you, Milady?"

"I was told you will pick up . . . uh-uh-uh . . . ''

"Raw materials, Ma'am. Raw materials. For a fee we will pick up that which you no longer desire, and turn it into a variety of useful products. We do stipulate, however, that the goods must be ready to use without further treatment. Do you understand?"

"Yes. You mentioned a fee. You will do it, then?"

"Certainly, Beautiful Lady. For ten soldats we will remove your raw materials from any address you name— which we promptly forget. For this reason we ask for advance payment. Otherwise we might remember and send a bill. Does this pose some problem?"

To his surprise she did not haggle.

I should've asked for more, he thought.

She gave him the address and turned to leave.

"A moment, Milady."

Cholly held out a clay jar. She looked at him in puzzlement, then took the jar.

"This is a glue shop. If you leave with one of my jars

anyone who sees you will see why you have come and notice nothing else.''

Her veiled face whitened. ''I hadn't thought of that.''

''By the way, this variety is made especially for porcelain and ceramics. It does wonders on broken dishes.''

After she had hurried away, the clay jar held where it could be seen, Sambar came through the curtained doorway. ''Master, why do you always insist that the pickup be dead? Wouldn't they pay more if you did it for them?''

''They would, but I will not take blood money. See, I deal in death every day without adding to it. If people want to kill each other, I can't stop 'em. But I'll be damned if I'll do it for 'em.''

With the work on the city walls and the repairs from the aftermath of the witches' fire and flood, business was brisk. Kadakithis's workmen had bought an entire wagonload of mixed varieties. The new tax was at least being spent for the purpose it was collected for, rather than lining the Prince-Governor's purse.

Privately Cholly had no use for magicians, but that did not prevent him from doing business with them. One came in seeking a human skull. Another, a lanky fellow with graying hair and beard and an unusually dynamic voice, came seeking fingerbones. These gentlemen never knew that their treasures came from his fuel pile of dried leftover bones.

A third aspiring thaumaturge sought a hand of glory. Cholly went back into the rendering room once more. There was a thunking sound. A moment later he returned with a severed human left hand.

One last minor magician—the truly powerful ones needed no such props—requested an entire human skin. He was sent next door. Zandulas would pay him a referral fee later.

When business slowed down enough for him to check on the boys, Cholly saw that that had been busy indeed. The bodies had all been stripped and the belongings sorted into neat piles, according to type. The smallest pile by far was money. They were honest enough lads, but he knew they kept a few coppers, even as he had done when he was apprenticed to old Shi Han Two-Fingers.

He sent Sambar to the front counter while he and Aram scalped, bled, and dismembered the remaining corpses. Once the bodies and the proper additives were mixed into the scalding water to his satisfaction he told Aram, "When you get time, take those barrels of tallow across the alley to Reh Shing the Soapmaker. It's time I started my rounds."

Chollandar scratched the back of his neck. For a moment it itched like someone was staring at him.

He always began his trading at Shamara's Wig Shop. In her youth Shamara had been striking. Her present beauty was of a different sort, a warmth that radiated from her sweet soul. They dickered for a bit, Shamara fingering the scalps for quality and texture. At last they settled upon three silver bits, eight coppers, and a kiss.

"The things I do for business," Shamara laughed before pressing her lips beneath his moustache. There was no lustful passion there, but there was something undefinable. "Enough. You make me feel like a girl, and I've survived that nonsense already."

He whistled a happy tune all the way to Marc's Weapons Shop. Most of Marc's goods were shoddy, but so were the weapons Cholly sold him. The really good stuff he sold separately. Some special blades he kept for himself.

Even so, he sometimes ran across an interesting piece in Marc's stock.

Cholly regularly had lunch with Furtwan Coinpinch while Hazen, Furtwan's nephew, watched the shop and kept an eye on the gluemaker's wagon. Today they decided on beef, so they found themselves a quiet table at the Man in Motley, where a joint was always skewered to the carving board.

"Anything interesting happen last night?" Furtwan asked between swallows of True Brew.

Cholly did not answer right away. He felt the feeling return that he was being watched. By whom and for what reason he had no idea. He scratched his neck again.

No one seemed to be looking in his direction, but he knew damned well someone was spying on him. The itch was stronger. He slid his right hand under the table, pretending to scratch his bare calf. He assured himself the extra knife was in place in his boot. Good.

The two men gossiped spiritedly for an hour. When Cholly left the shop the itch returned. If anything, it was stronger. The most unsettling part was that he could spot no sign of anyone following him, yet he knew they were there. But who? And why?

He missed the friendly greetings he used to get from Ganner, Lalo's son who was slain by the mobs in the False Plague riots. He had enjoyed the brief chats they used to have. Instead of Ganner it was Herwick himself who met him at the door. The jeweler still wore the symbolic torn collar and black armband of mourning.

"Good to see you, Cholly. Are you here to buy or sell? I believe Ineedra has a birthday coming up. Next week maybe?"

"Next Eshday. The trouble is she still hasn't given me a

hint what she wants like she usually does, or else for once she's been so subtle I missed it.''

"You can't go wrong with good jewelry. I've got some nice new pieces. Take a look. I could make you such a deal . . .''

"Not today, I've got a few days yet in case she drops a hint. In the meantime I did bring you a few trinkets to examine.''

He fished a folded square of cloth from his tunic. Unfolding it upon the counter, he displayed a jumble of glittering ornaments. Most were cheap junk, worth a copper or two apiece. A few were good quality paste and worth a bit more. Two pins were set in real gold and sparkling gemstones. Finally there was a solid gold pendant covered with strange markings.

"Where did you get this? I've never seen this type of workmanship before. Most unusual. And raw gold! I can't read it; it isn't Rankan or Ilsigi. It isn't Beysib—I've had too many Fisheyes in here not to recognize it when I see it. If it was older I might guess it might be Enlibaran.''

"Now that I've had a good look at it, I think I'll keep it for the time being. It's sort of interesting. Can you think of anybody who might be able to tell me what it says?''

"Try Synab. If anyone can tell you, he can.''

His next stop was Synab's artifact and curio shop just down the street. The daub of blue paint smeared on the door meant the owner was paying protection to someone. Cholly himself had never paid anyone for "protection" and he vowed he never would. A bell jingled when he entered.

The white-haired man in green linen said, "I haven't seen you lately. I trust you have something of interest for me?''

"Maybe. I found this medallion in this morning's goods. Can you decipher the writing?"

The little man's bushy eyebrows raised. His sallow face turned ashen. His gnarled hands trembled, dropping the bauble onto the counter as if it had suddenly become hot.

After a moment he said, "Do me a favor, Cholly. Go. Get that thing out of here. Please."

"Why? Mother Bey's balls, man, at least tell me what's wrong."

"I guess I owe you that much. I can't read it, but I've seen enough relics to recognize it. There is one word here I do know: the name *Theba*."

"Isn't she some sort of death goddess?"

"Yes. Anything connected with her has to mean trouble. If I were you, I'd get rid of it as quickly as I could."

Cholly thanked him and left.

His unseen stalker was still there. The tingle was so strong it was becoming painful. Hopefully whoever it was would not make his move until after Cholly reached Renn, his banker.

Renn was one of the few men in Sanctuary he completely trusted. Due to the armed men at the door and some less obvious defenses, no one had ever robbed Renn's bank and lived to reach the door. Thieves had gotten the message and stayed away.

The gluemaker deposited most of his cash and got a receipt, keeping out enough to pay the boys, take Ineedra out to a nice dinner, and enough left over to go to the games at Land's End and have a few coppers to bet. Compared to what he had been carrying it was spare change. Unfortunately his tracker didn't seem interested in money.

Upon his return to the Street of Money the feeling

intensified. Damn! He wished whoever it was would make his move. This cat-and-mouse ploy was making him angry. Maybe he could shake them up a bit.

He turned Enkidu and Eshi onto Olive Branch, sped down to Saddlers and turned left, leaping off the wagon as soon as he thought his pursuer could not see him for a moment. He stepped through the doorway of a tack shop and waited.

Two thugs came running around the corner. One was of average size; the other was short and round, like a beer keg with legs. They were trotting to keep the wagon in sight.

For a middle-aged fat man in a ring-mailed vest, he moved quietly. And quickly. Any sound made by his soft-soled knee boots was masked by the din of street noises: beggars asking alms, shopkeepers and customers haggling, the clop of horseshoes on cobblestones, children shouting and playing.

The shorter man was lagging a few steps behind his partner, panting. He never heard anything suspicious.

The taller man glanced over his shoulder in time to see the barrel-man topple from the flat of Cholly's axe. Before he could break away a large hand extending from a wax-boiled vambrace had grabbed a handful of his tunic and slammed him against a brick wall, driving the air from his lungs. His head bounced against the bricks, painfully but not far. He became acutely aware of the axe haft pressed against his throat when he struggled to inhale. A melon-sized knee pressing into his stones also caught his attention.

Cholly's normally merry hazel eyes were narrow slits of cold green. His voice was calm, even, almost a whisper.

"Why are you following me?"

"I wasn't. (Cough)"

Cholly lowered his knee slightly, then snapped it upward "Don't lie to me or you'll sing soprano. Let's start again. You were about to tell me why you followed me."

Tears filled the tall man's eyes. "I swear I wasn't following you."

He would've screamed when the knee drove into his crotch if it weren't for the wooden haft flattening his gullet.

"Let's try again, shall we? I ask you a question, you answer it. Honestly. For the last time, why were you tailing me?"

"All right," he whimpered. "We was paid a silver bit apiece to rob you." Tears rolled down his dirty unshaven cheeks.

"Fool. If it was money you wanted you would have jumped me before I reached my banker. You didn't make your move, although you've been chasing me all afternoon. So what are you after that is worth dying for?"

"The medallion."

"What makes it so valuable?" Cholly demanded.

"Don't know. He didn't tell us. He just paid us to get it."

"Who paid you?"

"He didn't give us a name. He was dressed in magician's robes."

"What did he look like?"

"Silver hair—"

The knife just missed Cholly's ear before burying itself in the tall man's eye. Blood and clear liquid gushed out of the wound. The dying man jerked once and went limp. Cholly released his hold. The body slid down the wall, the stubby knife handle still protruding from the eye socket.

The barrel-man was just vanishing into an alley.

"I should've hit him harder," the gluemaker muttered.

He gave a shrill whistle and Enkidu and Eshi backed up. Business was business. He loaded the dead man into his wagon and covered him with canvas. No one thought it unusual for him to be picking up somebody this early. There were accident victims all the time. It was common practice to mind one's own business.

Babbo shifted his weight from foot to foot while wringing his unwashed hands. His gaze never left the floor. The room was cool, but the hireling's stained homespun tunic was damp with sweat.

"What in the Shadowed One's name are you saying? How could he get away? There were two of you! Both armed! Do you mean to tell me two of the best muggers in the Maze were bested by a bald old shopkeeper?" Marype raged.

"He was good," Babbo said defensively. "Dorien was one of the best men I knew in a brawl. When I came to—I never heard him coming before he busted my head—he had poor Dorien pinned against the wall with an axe handle and a knee pushing Dor's balls up to his belly button. Believe me, the man is good. How do you think he got that old? Only way I could shut Dor up was to spike 'im."

"Why didn't you knife the gluemaker instead?"

"Look, I didn't have a lot of time, you know? I wasn't in no shape to tangle with the man. Maybe I just throwed amongst 'em and ran. Besides, you're the magician: why didn't you do something? Turn fatso into something?"

"As long as he has the amulet, magic doesn't work on him. Why else would I hire you two bunglers?"

"Big hotshot magician," Babbo retorted. "You can't

do the job with your spells, so you hire us. Then you got
the balls to come down on me 'cause I didn't get him
neither. Far as I'm concerned you can go diddle yourself.
See ya around, Cotton-top,'' he snorted, his fear replaced
by contempt.

It was crowded in the stands Lowan Vigeles had built at
his Land's End estate and the stone benches were uncomfortable. The spectators had already swilled down enough
Red Gold to be rowdy. Zandulas and Cholly were hooting
and hollering with the rest. The early rounds had been
condemned criminals pitted against each other. Not much
skill there; mostly brute strength. Chollandar preferred the
chariot races.

He was picking them well. The fourth race had just
ended, and for the third time he was collecting his winnings. Zandulas, who was zero for four, got to his feet
with a sour grin.

"I'm getting a brew before the final heat. Want one?"

"No thanks, Zan. Want me to place any bets for you?"

"Neh. Oh all right. If I'm not back in time, just put two
coppers on whoever you pick."

Cholly's favorite driver was Borak. Behind his three
chestnut geldings Borak's long oily whip moved like a
living creature, while he used the bladed wheel hubs better
than most men wield a sword.

The other drivers in today's final race were Magyar
driving whites, Atticus with dappled grays, and Crispen
with a second team of whites. No second-raters there.

Everywhere were shouts of "Six coppers on Atticus,"
"Two on Magyar," "Four on Atticus," "Eight on
Crispen."

Caught up in the betting, Cholly shouted, "Two silver on Borak!"

"Take 'em all. I'll cover the balance," Zandulas whispered, returning. "I'd have taken Atticus, but then I haven't been right all afternoon and you're on a hot streak. I just hope it holds."

The big money bets were in the box seats, stacks of golden soldats. The difference was that those in the boxes could usually afford to lose. The simple townsfolk in the cheap seats were hard pressed if they lost a handful of coppers.

The tingle was back. Someone was watching him again.

Four teams entered the track, having drawn lots for position. Cholly frowned. Borak was on the outside. Next to Borak came Crispen, then Magyar, and finally Atticus at the advantageous inside spot. The games master dipped the flag and they were off. Horses crowded each other. Sharpened steel zinged each time the wheels whirred close together. Crispen forced Borak into the wall, but the wily veteran kept control. Dust flew as his blades gouged the masonry. To even the score he flicked his whip, welting the closest white racer's hindquarters. The horse broke stride. It took only a moment to get back in sync, but that was enough.

Cholly looked around. Was that a flash of silver hair in the crowd behind him? Maybe it was a woman who had joined in the fad. Maybe not. His left hand rested upon the hilt of the Ilbarsi knife.

A white stallion screamed when it was hit by a blade, chewing his rear leg off at the gaskin. The crowd roared. The animal's fall yanked the singletree to one side, causing the rest of the team to wheel, overturning the chariot.

Magyar's hand was caught in the reins and he was dragged along beneath.

The silver hair was out of sight, but not gone. Cholly could feel it.

Zandulas was shouting, "Did you see that?"

By the last lap Borak was ahead of Atticus by half a length. Crispen had gotten tangled in Magyar's wreck and lost too much time to make it up.

"Collect my winnings," he told Zandulas.

"Why? Where're you going?"

"Must be the Red Gold. I'm not feeling so good," Cholly lied.

He could hear the crowd shouting Borak's name as he hurried down the steps. A knife darted at him but was deflected by the iron and leather vest he wore. He was lucky, and knew it.

Once out of the estate, Cholly ran as fast as his thick legs could carry him through the construction gangs working on the walls, through a gap in the emerging wall itself, then darted down twisting alleys and taking random turns. Few others knew the streets as well as this man who traveled them each morning. Soon he would reach the docks. He saw no sign of pursuit, but the feeling remained.

The Winebarrel catered to fishermen. Most of the clientele knew Cholly. They bought glue from him to use on their boats. He, in turn, or his apprentices, bought unsold or inedible fish from them. He was made welcome.

Of all the folk in Sanctuary, only the fishers had truly accepted the Beysib—at least the Setmur clan of Beysib—because the newcomers were hard workers, honest and good sailors. Inside the net-hung walls of the Winebarrel, all seamen were brothers, comrades-in-arms in the endless battle to eke a living from the merciless sea.

It was not surprising then that the one-armed Ilsigi should be sharing his table with a small, quiet fish-eyed man. Cholly walked over and joined them. For a moment the tingle was gone, or else so weak he did not notice it.

Omat, the Ilsigi fisherman, gestured with his glass. "You're getting thinner on top and thicker in the middle. And you look like you could use a drink. Pull up a stool and let me buy you one. You know Monkel Setmur, don't you? Monkel, Cholly here makes the best damned glue you can buy—"

"—Or get in trade. What fisherman doesn't know Cholly?" the small man said, smiling sincerely and extending his hand. "What brings you to the Winebarrel?"

"I'm in a real fix. Somebody's trying to kill me. I found this medallion in the stuff I took in this morning. Ever since then, someone's been on my tail. Two gutter rats tried to waylay me, but I caught 'em off guard. I conked one on the head and put the other up against the wall. That's how I found out the connection with the medallion I'd found, and that they'd been hired by a wizard-type with silver hair. But, I hadn't hit the first one hard enough, and he knifed his partner through the eye before I got any more.

"Just a little while ago I was out at Land's End. I saw someone with silver hair in the crowd near me, so I decided to get out of there. He followed me long enough to throw a knife, only he didn't take this vest into account."

"Can we do anything to help, Cholly?" Omat asked.

"Run me around to White Foal Bridge by water. That should get him off me for a while."

"I could use a bit of fresh air. Coming with us, Monkel?"

The little fellow nodded.

*   *   *

The dying sun was streaking the western sky with its blood when Cholly parted the thirty-one cords with their thirty-one knots.

"You're early today," Ahdio commented. "Anything wrong? You look upset."

"You might say that. I need a brew—the good stuff. Say, what happened to Cleya? I see the pretty one is back. Jodeera? Isn't that her name?"

Ahdio looked down into the other man's eyes—not too far down, for he was only an inch or so taller—and paled slightly.

"What did you say? That's Cleya right there."

"Quit kidding. I'm looking right at her."

Ahdio stood silent for a moment then said, "Would you mind stepping into the back with me a moment where we can talk?"

The two men walked back to the stockroom. Ahdio closed the door and turned to face Cholly. He looked worried.

"How did you know?"

"Know what?"

"That Cleya and Jodeera are the same."

"Oh, come on. Cleya is a sweet girl, but she is skinny and sort of homely, like a stray cat. Not that I don't like her, but she isn't even in the same league with that lovely creature."

"They are the same. I'm going to trust you because I like you. See, when Jodeera first came to work here there was trouble. Remember?"

The gluemaker nodded, paying close attention.

"It wasn't her fault she was so pretty, but it did make the boys rowdy, trying to outdo each other. I didn't want to send her away. I love her. What could I do? I had a spell put on her to hide her beauty from all eyes but mine. How'd you see through it?''

"Maybe this had something to do with it.'' He fished the gold medallion from inside his tunic.

"Take it off. I'll hold it. You go back and look. Tell me if you see Cleya or Jodeera.''

He returned a moment later. "Cleya. It was the medallion.''

"Where did you get it?''

Cholly told his story again. Ahdio stroked his chin glaring from his friend, to the medallion then at the door to the taproom. "You got trouble here,'' he said, returning the medallion. "Bad cess. Look, I have this old war buddy named Strick. He's a magician. Hold on, he's not like the ones you've seen. He's strictly a white mage . . . literally can't use his powers for evil. Take my word, he's one of the good guys. Tell him I sent you.''

"Where do I find him?''

"You mean to tell me you lost him again?!'' Markmor screamed, his face almost as livid as his robes.

"I almost got him at Land's End. How was I to know the knife would bounce off his vest?'' Marype cowered.

"Then what happened?''

"I followed him to the docks. It wasn't easy. He must know every twist and turn of every alley in town. He went into a place called the Winebarrel, and when he came out he was with two other men. One was a fish-face, and the other had one arm. They got into a boat and rowed away. I had to be careful. People tend to notice when you appear and disappear in public. Besides, as long as he has the amulet not even you can trace him by magic.''

"You insolent pup, you brainless piece of dung, do you

dare to question my powers?'' the would-be greatest magician in Sanctuary roared.

Marype cringed even more. ''I don't doubt your power,
Master, but did not you yourself tell me that the gods
themselves have no power over the one who wields the
talisman?''

''Precisely, imbecile. That is how we shall find him.''

''I don't understand.''

''I didn't think you would. By Argash, if I want something done right, I'd best do it myself. Pay attention and
you may learn something. First we cast the Net of All-
Seeing over the city in the name of Father Ils.''

''What good will that do, Master? We still can't see
him.''

''Sometimes I wonder why I even bother with you. Tell
me, do you ever use your head for something besides
growing hair? Think! With this spell we can see the entire
city at once *except for one blind spot*. Wherever that blind
spot is, there we shall find the one who has the medallion.''

He was bigger than Ahdio, but only slightly so. He
moved like a swordsman, keeping his weight evenly distributed and his gaze unfixed, looking at nothing yet seeing
everything. It seemed odd that he wore no weapon, not
even a dagger. He was dressed all in blue from boots to
skull cap.

''My niece says that you would not tell her your problem. You would tell her only that Ahdio sent you. You
confuse me. I see a spell about you that is not a spell,
something that is not magic yet very powerful. Is this the
problem you wish to consult me about?''

Cholly removed the chain from his neck and handed the
medallion to Strick.

"I am a simple gluemaker. Each morning my apprentice and I take a wagon through town to pick up the bodies left from the night before. I make glue from them. It's all legal; I have a charter giving me the right to pick them up and dispose of them for the city. This medallion was on one of the ones we took in this morning. Since then I have had two attempts on my life, I have been followed every step I take, and I have discovered that when I wear it I can see through a magic spell. What I want to know is: just what is it, really?"

Strick handed back the medallion. "Do you know of the goddess Theba? According to legend she declared that nothing, not even gods, should be immortal. Gods, you see, live on many planes at once. If they die they still live on all the other planes. That's what happened to Vashanka—gone from here, but not dead. Now it seems Theba was ambitious and didn't want to pursue her rivals through the infinite planes, so one night she called down a star from the sky. It fell like a blazing comet, and in its heart was a lump of unearthly gold. Theba took the white hot nugget in her bare hands, she shaped the medallion, then inscribed it with her fingernail, and quenched it in the blood of a virgin."

"Sounds like a real sweetheart."

"That, says legend, is how the Spell of No Spells was cast, a spell that cancels all magic. Perhaps antimagic is the proper term. Its power nullifies all spells and powers. It is the supreme defense against magic. There is one catch. It also cancels any magic the wearer possesses. Spells, blessings, curses; all are useless."

"Let me see if I can take it from there. Immortality is a supernatural gift, right? So, if a god had the medallion,

he's no longer a god; he's mortal, and can die like anybody else. Right?"

"Yes, but even Theba was appalled when She felt her
rival die the one, true death. She threw Her trinket away,
and it fell into mortal hands. Most mages—including
myself—want nothing to do with it: Its risks outweigh any
possible rewards. But there are always a few like Theba,
caught in the blind throes of ambition, greed or jealousy.

"Be careful, Cholly. At least one mage, maybe more,
wants Theba's medallion and knows you have it. Because
of what it is, because of what he *is* to want it in the first
place, and because as long as you wear it no one can tell for
certain if you're a powerful wizard or an ordinary gluemaker—because of these, you're a marked man, my friend."

"Thanks for the information. How much do I owe
you?"

"Nothing. I could not help you with your problem, and
I charge only for services rendered."

"Well, I feel I owe you something for telling me about
the talisman. I'll tell you what: the next time you need to
mend anything, send word to me what you are working
on, and I'll send over the right compound for the job with
my compliments. How about that?"

"You are a fair man, gluemaker. I have enjoyed meeting you, and I hope you solve your problem."

Cholly stopped by the shop and paid the boys their
weekly bit of copper. Sambar would spend all his at the
bakery and sweets shop. Give him another year or two and
he'd be paying for sweets of the same sort as Aram. Father
Ils but that lad was randy! It was only blind luck the boy
hadn't yet contracted a dose. Ah, youth!

Before he left in his best clothes Aram said, "Some

fellow was in here looking for you. The first time was the middle of the afternoon, then he came back a little while ago. He didn't say what he wanted, just that he wanted to speak to you. Special pickup, I guess.''

"Did he leave a name? What did he look like?''

"No name, but he's easy to recognize. He's got all this silvery hair and he dresses like a magician. Know him?''

"In a way. I think I've seen him. How would you like a bit of extra pocket money?''

Aram's eyes lit up.

"Go run ahead to Ahdio, at Sly's Place, and tell him I'm going to need his backroom for a while. And tell him to ask his friend Strick to join us. Do that and I'll give you an extra week's pay.''

Aram was gone like an arrow. Cholly walked down the rows and picked out jars of glue and solvent. From beneath the counter he took a satchel of several brushes.

He hoped this wouldn't take long. He was already late, and Ineedra would have his head on a salver. He'd better take her to Hari's or the Golden Oasis to unruffle her feathers once this business was over with.

Ahdio didn't recognize any of the trio who strutted into the crowded tavern, and he usually remembered faces. One of them, the youngest, did have a flowing silver mane, so these must be the ones he was watching for.

The squat, broad red-faced one asked Throde, "Hey, Gimp! You seen Cholly da Gluemaker in here? We was s'posed to meet up wit' 'im.''

"Not that I recall, but we've been pretty busy. Ask Ahdio,'' Throde replied, nodding at the mountainous man in the mail vest. He smiled and hobbled away to deliver his tray of beers, giving Ahdio a wink in passing.

Again it was the toadish one who spoke. "You Ahdio?"

Ahdio smiled. "What will you have, gentlemen?"

"You seen Cholly da Gluemaker? We'll make it worth ya while. We got bidness wit' 'im, see?" said the red-faced man, bouncing a coin on his palm.

Ahdio held out his hand. "Maybe."

The man tossed the coin onto Ahdio's broad palm. Ahdio neither spoke nor moved his hand until several copper coins were stacked there.

"He's in the back room. Follow me."

Cholly was watching the door. He noticed the argent hair at once, then he stared at the others. The dark one in red damask silk was the obvious leader, a man accustomed to power as his due.

"What the hell is *that*?" he wondered, seeing the last of the trio enter through the doorway.

It was shaped sort of like one of the rendering pots in the shop, squat and rotund with thick stubby legs ending in horned, splayed, webbed three-toed feet. It had ears like a donkey, little beady rat's eyes, and a wide froggish mouth full of long yellow-green teeth. Its thick muscular arms hung down so low its knobby knuckles dragged the ground. Its matted, scraggly feathers were the color of iron rust. Topping it all off was something resembling a coxcomb. It had no head or neck per se.

It was ugly.

He gestured for the two men to sit opposite him in the booth. He asked Ahdio to bring a chair and three large beers for his guests.

"Nothing personal, you understand. I'd just rather not sit where I'm hemmed in. We haven't been introduced.

My name is Chollandar. And you?'' He spoke to the black-bearded man.

"No offense taken. I am called Markmor. This young fool is my apprentice, Marype.''

"Does the demon have a name?''

"I'd forgotten you can see his true form. I'm afraid I can't tell you his real name. He does answer, however, to 'Rubigo.' ''

"Rubigo it is then.'' He took a sip of his Baladach wine.

"How much will you take for it?'' Marype asked.

Markmor glared at him. Rubigo snickered at such a breach of manners. Even he knew better.

"I never discuss business until after a sociable drink. I wouldn't think of doing business with a man who won't have a friendly drink with me first. You seem to have some breeding, Markmor. Surely you understand. Perhaps in time your impatient apprentice will learn. If he's like my two, it may take a while.''

After what seemed an eternity with the demon standing sullenly by the door, Ahdio returned with a chair. Throde followed with a serving tray. Upon the tray were three pitcher-sized tankards holding perhaps a half gallon of Red Gold each, possibly more. Rubigo plopped down and hoisted a pewter tankard, chugging it into his mouth with hedonistic glee. Throde set the tray down and left.

Cholly sipped his wine and asked, "Is beer all right? It's the best brand he carries. I forgot to ask.''

"This is fine,'' Markmor answered, taking a tankard in both hands. Marype did likewise.

Rubigo drained his in one long, gurgling, slurping pull. When he went to set the tankard down he made a startling discovery—the tankard was stuck to his lips and hands. He squealed in anger. When he tried to rise he found his feathers glued to the chair.

Markmor and Marype realized the trap too late. They too were stuck. Their mouths and hands stuck to the tankards and their robes stuck to the booth. Even their shoes were stuck to the floor. The master wizard's eyes seemed twin flames of amethyst. A growl of rage rumbled in his throat.

There was a puff of sulfurous smoke and Rubigo's tankard clattered onto the wooden floor. An instant later the smoke cleared, revealing the demon standing in the center of the room.

"Nice try, Fat Man. Too bad you didn't know us demons could jump planes just by thinkin' 'bout it. *Hawhaw!* Didn't nobody never tell ya not to go messin' wit' us? Now you gonna die, boy."

"Are you sure? It seems to me that as long as I have the Theban Talisman you can't touch me. Suppose I used this axe of mine on you. How do you know it wouldn't kill you?"

Rubigo paused a moment. Cholly eased out of his chair and slid his dismembering axe from its iron ring on his belt. He drew the Ilbarsi knife with his left hand. He waited, smiling.

"One way to find out," Rubigo growled, swinging a long arm around to slash at Cholly with green adamantine claws. The hand had three webbed fingers plus a thumb. Cholly ducked easily. The demon was slow. Cholly hacked with the axe.

Rubigo's hand fell to the floor. For a moment it lay wriggling. It vanished. The demon's wrist stopped oozing brackish fluid from the severed stump because the hand was back. He had an ugly laugh.

Uh-oh, Chollander thought.

Chortling and drooling, Rubigo circled, intending to play with Cholly for a while before killing him. He lashed out with either hand, his claws raking the air around Cholly but not making contact. The gluemaker stayed calm, ducking and blocking, chopping and slashing at every opening. Once he darted in and managed to plant the axe deeply into Rubigo's chest, only to see the wound heal as soon as he removed the weapon.

Markmor and Marype watched every move of man and monster over the tankard rims.

The hellspawn was wearing the gluemaker down. He was untouched, but he was getting tired and winded. Sweat trickled into his eyes and the salt stung. He slid the Ilbarsi knife into its sheath and shifted the axe to a two-handed grip. He blinked and continued to block and counter and attack. He knew he would have to change tactics before exhaustion caused him to err.

Damn, he thought. *I've given him enough blows to kill a squad of men, but his fiendish magic heals him every time. If he was mortal I could take him apart.*

Cholly smiled.

Changing back to a one-hand grip on the axe, he used his free hand to reach for the talisman. Yanking the chain over his head he said, "That's enough. This is what you're after. Take it. I can't fight any more. Just take the damned thing and leave me alone. I know when I'm beat."

"That's more like it, Fatso. Youse is good, butcha ain't no match for da ol' demon. Now gimme."

He caught the medallion in the palm of his webbed hand. Now he was going to kill the fat bald man, since there was nothing to restrain him. He looked over to the wizard and apprentice wizard, holding the bauble aloft and smiling. He looked back just in time to catch a sparkle of light reflecting from the gleaming blade descending. Realization flashed in his beady little eyes just before they rolled back into his head.

Cholly picked up the medallion from the lifeless fingers, returning it back around his neck. Next he placed a foot upon the fiend's face and worked his axe free from the skull. Slipping the haft through its ring, he sat back down at the table.

"That was thirsty work." He drew his long knife and placed it between himself and the magicians. He poured himself another goblet of wine and sipped it. He paused long enough to get out his pipe, fill it, and light it from the candle on the table.

He took his time, seemingly ignoring the two prisoners. He would take a puff or two, blow a few smoke rings, and sip at his wine. All the while he kept smiling, sometimes idly playing with the Ilbarsi blade.

"What am I going to do with you?" he said, breaking the tense silence. "If I let you go we'll be right back where we started, except I'll know who you are. I've got better things to do than play hide-and-seek with your hired flunkies and conjurings. I have to work for my living.

"Have you ever seen glue being made? We start with a body. First we strip it naked and inspect for obvious disease. Next we lop off the hands and cut the throat and hang the body head-down to drain the blood. Are you following this? Oh yes, if the client has a nice head of hair—yours would fetch a pretty price, Marype—we scalp it before we hang it up."

He paused to pour himself another serving of wine. Markmor looked nervous and Marype was quite pale.

"Then we hack off the arms and legs and dump 'em in a

big kettle of scalding water and render them down. We sell the fat to make soap, and dry the bones for firewood.''

Markmor looked nauseous and Marype's countenance was paler than his hair.

Cholly sipped at his wine, inwardly smiling at achieving the desired reaction. He continued, ''Look at it from my point of view. The only way to be sure I'm safe is to get rid of you. My way you can not only remain dead, but serve a useful purpose. I guess you know I don't like magicians much.

''On the other hand, I could spare your lives. The problem is: how do I know you won't attack me again? I suppose I could chop off your hands and cut out your tongues. Feet too, so you can't learn to use them for hands like a beggar I once saw. The eyes, naturally would have to go. Can either of you wiggle your ears? No? I'll leave them, then.''

Markmor stared at the man, unsure whether he was bluffing. If it were the other way around he knew what he would do.

A combination of beer and fear finally took its toll upon Marype's bladder. Markmor turned to glance at his apprentice with disgust.

Setting down his goblet, Cholly smiled. ''Look on the bright side. You'll get to wear the Theban Talisman—for a few minutes at least. Isn't that what you wanted? Look at it from my point of view. Silverlocks here—acting on your behalf—has tried to kill me already. He did kill the fellow who had it before me. This chunk of gold is too powerful to give to the likes of you, and at the same time I have a living to make. I have to have some assurance you won't bother me again.''

Cholly knocked the dottle from his pipe, refilled it, and

took another light from the candle while Markmor reflected upon what he had said.

"Nature calls," he told his prisoners. "I'll be back in a minute. Don't go anywhere," he snickered, sliding out of the booth. He sheathed the Ilbarsi knife and stepped across Rubigo's carcass.

Cholly returned several minutes later. Behind him came the big bartender, and behind him a bearded man even bigger, carrying a staff. The last man, largest of the three, was dressed in blue and seemed to radiate power.

The wizards were trying unsuccessfully to escape.

"Nicely done, Cholly. What are you going to do with them?" Strick asked, chuckling.

"I haven't figured that one out yet. I can't let them go, but I'd rather not kill them unless I have to. Any ideas?"

"There are a couple of things that could work. First, to a mage knowing someone's true name gives you power over him."

"That's why he wouldn't tell me the demon's name."

"Right. Second, there is only one oath he cannot break: one sworn on his powers. All you have to do is make him tell you his true name and make him swear by it and on his powers to leave you alone. If he breaks that vow, at the very least his powers shall be forfeit for eternity."

Markmor stared at the stranger. Only a magician could have spoken so certainly, yet this man was not known to him. He knew the few remaining Ilsigi mages, and the ones in the Mageguild, and the outsiders like Enas Yorl and Ischade. Whoever this upstart was, there would be a score to settle later.

Ahdio spoke up. "How do you know if he is telling the truth? Wouldn't it be more likely he'd lie?"

"A good point, my friend. I can be of some assistance

there. This staff I carry is not just a walking stick. It is a Staff of Truth. Whoever touches it may not lie and live.''

Cholly puffed at his pipe, weighing the idea. Finally he asked, ''What will it be, gentlemen? Will you take a vow to stop seeking the medallion and to leave me in peace?''

Strick touched the staff to Markmor's head. He nodded. When it touched Marype's head he too nodded. Markmor growled into his tankard.

''I'm going to free Markmor first. This will taste awful, and it will sting, but it will free your lips in a couple of minutes.''

Cholly reached under the table and withdrew a leather satchel. From it he removed a stoppered bottle and a brush. He kept brushing the liquid from the bottle onto the sorcerer's lips until they were freed from the tankard. The Staff of Truth rested upon his head.

''Faugh! What was that unholy liquid?'' he sputtered.

''Trade secret. Just be glad it worked. Are you ready to give me your name?''

''Yes, damn you.'' Markmor gave his secret name.

''Now, do you swear, upon that name you have just spoken and by your powers, to never again seek the Theban Talisman and to leave me and mine forever in peace?''

''I so swear.''

''Say it, all of it.''

He said his name once more and swore on it and his powers.

Marype was more difficult, mainly because he had drained his tankard and was not entirely sober.

Finally Markmor growled, ''Oh, for Anen's sake, take his bloody oath so we can get the hell out of here!''

Cholly freed the younger man and received his vow and name.

"May we leave now?" Markmor asked impatiently.

"In a minute. I just thought you ought to know that if your fair-haired boy there had simply come to me this morning and made me a reasonable cash offer before I found out what it could do, you could have bought the talisman outright. Too bad you didn't try straight dealing, because when somebody tries to push me around I have this tendency to push back. You can go."

Markmor's face was almost as scarlet as his silks. "You mean you never made the man an offer?! You mindless dungheap, where was your brain? You were dealing with a *businessman*. What do you think he does? He buys and sells things, that's what he does. At times like this I could almost justify destroying you, talented or not. Brain damaged is what you are. Brain damaged . . ."

He was still ranting as he and Marype faded from view, leaving their clothing still glued to the booth.

Tears were trickling down Ahdio's red cheeks and Strick was gasping for breath. Three big bellies jiggled with uncontrollable laughter.

Ahdio was able to speak first. "I haven't laughed so hard in ages. Did you see the look on his face when he found out he could've bought it for a few soldats?"

"Yes, and when he sobers up the silver-haired one is going to catch seventeen hells," Strick added.

"Couldn't happen to a nicer fellow," Cholly giggled.

"I have a special bottle of wine I've been saving for a special occasion. Share it with me. This calls for a celebration," Ahdio declared.

Strick asked Cholly, "If they hadn't agreed, would you have killed them?"

"No, but there was no way they could know that. I let them worry once I brought up the possibility. As soon as

Markmor put himself in my place he was convinced I would kill them both. It's only human to think other people would act the same way you would in the same situation. Since Markmor would kill me without a second thought, of course he believed I would do it, just more reluctantly. After all, he had already seen me split his pet demon's skull.''

"So it was all a bluff," Strick marvelled. "What if he called you on it?"

"I'd have waited him out. He wasn't going anywhere. Sooner or later he would have to give in. That's lot of beer in those mugs," Cholly chuckled.

"Remind me never to gamble with you."

Three large bellies began shaking with laughter.

Eventually the gluemaker asked, "Is that Staff of Truth for real, or was it a bluff too?"

"Does it matter? Markmor believed it was real."

"How am I going to clean up this mess?" Ahdio wondered aloud.

"There's several bottles of solvent in my satchel. We can toss the demon out the back door and I'll pick him up in the morning. I wonder how good a glue he'll make.''

THE PROMISE OF HEAVEN

Robin Wayne Bailey

Tiana struck a brazen pose, turning her back to the small bust of the Rankan goddess Sabellia on its stone pedestal. The full moon shone overhead through a break in the trees, filling the small garden niche with a sublime light that revealed her full, pale breasts as they strained against the too-tight fabric of her green dress; a light bright enough, she also hoped, to lend luster to her deep green eyes so carefully kohlled and her lovely red tresses.

She rumpled her hair with one hand and thrust her hip a bit further to the side, feeling the perfect vixen. She stretched, lifting her arms until the material of her bodice threatened to rip. She faked a yawn and dared another glance down the white-pebbled pathway that snaked through the Promise.

The man still stood there. She knew he'd seen her. What was wrong with him, anyway? Didn't he like women? Maybe he was one of those Stepsons, there were a few left in town; that would be just her luck.

She stepped back into the niche out of his sight and bit a fingernail. Perhaps she should have chosen a darker spot tonight. With the moon so full maybe he could see how faded her dress really was, how the rose in her cheeks was only rouge, how skinny and bone-rough she'd become, despite the size of her juggies. Curse the fates that had brought her to this miserable town, and curse the lying, womanizing stonemason who had lured her here with his promises and sweet words, only to throw her into the streets the moment he found someone prettier.

She had no experience at this kind of work. She had to eat, though, and desperation emboldened her. This stranger down the path seemed to be the only man in the park tonight. He'd better have coins, though. Just last evening some wine-soaked fool had offered her a bundle of smelly hides for her service. What was she supposed to do with hides?

Tiana stepped onto the path again. The pebbles were smooth and cold under her bare feet. The air felt crisp; she would have to earn enough for shoes and a cloak, and soon. Food, too. She couldn't afford to let this man get away. Feigning an expression of boredom she rubbed her right breast, teasing the nipple. Then, she looked down the path.

Damn, damn, damn! He was gone! Into the bushes with some other woman? Her shoulders slumped, and tears welled in the corners of her eyes. She looked down at her toes, pushed a few of the milky stones around. Hadn't he liked her looks? Maybe she'd acted a little too whorish.

But gods, she was *so* hungry! How did the other women in the park do it? What was the knack she lacked? A whole week in this sad, silly place, and she had yet to break into the ranks of the professionals!

Tiana squeezed her stomach, trying to ease the emptiness as she leaned against Sabellia's pedestal and slowly sank down to sit on the grass at its base. Pressing her back to the fluted stone, she drew her knees close and hugged them.

She feared the night. The quiet solitude seemed like a menacing thing. The darkness engulfed her, swallowed her in a black maw, chewed and choked her down all in a preternatural silence. Even the gods whose busts and statues lined the walkways held their tongues in this unfortunate park.

She looked up into Sabellia's face. The moon itself seemed a weak and helpless emberglow in the vaster dark.

Tiana felt small and alone. She wanted to go home, but that, too, took money. She thought again of her stonemason lover who had lured her so far from Ranke. He had treated her kindly and promised her heaven.

Well, he'd given it to her. That was what the locals called this park where she now tried to ply her charms: the Promise of Heaven.

She rested her head back against the pedestal and at last let go the tears she'd held in check for so long. Each one seemed a precious thing to her, a fragment of her heart. She caught one on her finger and held it up to see. It gleamed like a tiny crystalline moon, a very piece of her goddess.

Even through her fear she felt the shadow fall over her. She sniffed once, then quickly wiped the moisture from her face, giving no thought to the rouge and kohl that turn to a smear. She scrambled to her feet as fast as her dress allowed and faked her best smile.

It was the same man. Same height and build, same dark garments. The moon touched his features. He was young, she thought. Only a little older than herself. Not bad looking, either, despite a peculiar edge, a hardness, in his gaze. She took a deep breath, swelling her favorite assets.

Then, suddenly she dropped her pose and brightened. "I know you," she said. "You came down with the workers' caravan—"

"I need you," he interrupted throatily.

She met his gaze. He had beautiful eyes full of warmth and charm. "Of course," she answered, remembering why she was there, why he was there. Yet, there was more hope in her voice than seduction. She thought briefly of the meal she would buy come morning, and maybe an apartment. She hated sleeping in the alleys, constantly afraid. All she had to do was please him, and that shouldn't be hard to do.

He had such beautiful eyes!

"Come with me," he said softly, holding out a hand.

She took it. His touch warmed her; his hand felt soft and uncalloused. That puzzled her. If he was one of the workers sent to rebuild the wall around Sanctuary his hand should have been rough. Yet, it pleased her that it wasn't, and she pushed that concern aside. There was something else she was supposed to think about, something she should say. What was it?

"The cost . . ." she hesitated awkwardly, unsure of the usual charge. "I mean, well, a sheboozh?" Oh, damn, she thought. That's far too much for a common street whore. A whole gold coin!

But he moved his other hand close to her face. She caught just the flash of the requested payment before he made a fist and the money disappeared.

Tiana couldn't believe her good fortune. Gold and beautiful eyes. The gods were with her this night after all. He really did have the most incredible gaze, full of oceans and full of darkness, full of promises.

"Come with me," he said again. His voice was the high wind, and when he spoke no more she still heard his words. He was the sound of the night.

She looked into his eyes. Hand in hand, they stepped from Sabellia's garden niche and onto the pathway. Out of respect for the silence that shrouded the park the gravel refused to crunch beneath their tread.

Unable to help herself, Tiana smiled.

The moonlight continued to shine on the small bust in the Promise of Heaven.

Over the rest of Sanctuary, Darkness began to chew.

The full moon poured its radiance perfectly through the skylight above Sabellia's altar, lending an opalescent sheen to the graceful sculpture of the goddess. Her flawless marble features shimmered as the smoke of incense swirled upward from a score of braziers set in the floor at the hem of her skirts. It rose higher and higher like a wizard-weather mist, caressed her sensuous curves, curled toward the silver disc and out into the night.

Dayrne looked up, seeking Sabellia's shadowed gaze. He knew she was with him, present in this first full moonlight of autumn as it illumined her altar. He felt her power, felt her touch upon his heart.

"Cheyne," he murmured as he knelt. "My Cheyne." He prayed no other words aloud. He didn't need to. Sabellia knew him well. The goddess had set her mark upon his soul.

He reached inside his tunic and extracted a small bundle of white silk. Carefully, he unrolled it. Several strands of fine blond hair gleamed in the moonlight. A silver thread bound them into a delicate lock. How long had he carried

them in secret, those hairs stolen from her brush? Three
years? Four?

He laid his small offering on Sabellia's altar. It was not
a gift of great value, but it was very dear to him. The
goddess asked no more.

Dayrne bowed his head. But suddenly prayers would not
come.

Where had she gone, his Cheyne? Why hadn't she waited
for him to return with the One Hundred? He closed his
eyes; it was easy to picture her face when he closed his
eyes. In the silent sanctity of the Rankan temple he
whispered her name.

Chenaya.

But in his heart he called her *Cheyne*. It was one of the
names the gladiators had given her in the Rankan arenas.
Hard as metal they had said of her. That wasn't true. She
was tough, yes, but he had seen the softness buried deep in
her soul, the piece of her she kept hidden from the world
and from her father.

She was a child, sometimes. A spoiled child. Yet he
loved her. *Cheyne,* he thought. *My Chain. Chain that
binds me beyond reason.* He shook his head in a moment
that was a mixture of pity and joy. *Let me never be free.*
He looked up at Sabellia's face. She seemed almost to
mock him as she peered down through the swirling incense, and he knew that was one prayer the goddess had
already answered.

But where had Chenaya gone?

He thought again of that strange portrait hanging in her
room. The power of it was startling, but though he ad-
mired the artistry, each time he looked upon it a subtle fear
tingled through his spine. Unmistakably, it was Lalo's
work. But when had she posed for it? Lowan Vigeles said

she had brought it home one night, shut herself in her room until dawn, and departed with the morning, saying nothing to anyone. Not even her father knew more.

Dayrne suspected, however, that Rashan did. The old priest had made a habit lately of going to Cheyne's room and staring at the portrait with that queer smile of his, peering through half-closed lids at Chenaya's face and the resplendent sun that framed her, seemed to caress her, an effect that went far beyond mere paint and craftsmanship. Her hair flew into fire and light; her eyes shone like tiny suns. Chenaya was beautiful beyond any woman he had ever known, but not even she was so glorious as Lalo had rendered her.

Strange as those things were, though, there was something else that stirred terror into his blood. The painting radiated a tangible warmth.

Could it be true what Rashan claimed? Was his Cheyne truly the Daughter of the Sun? Or was it all some trick?

He turned his gaze back to Sabellia, who governed matters of the heart. If Cheyne was a goddess or some avatar of Father Savankala, then what hope could there be for any love between them?

He touched the few strands of hair he had placed on the altar. They belonged to the goddess now. He bowed his head, uttered one last prayer, and slowly rose to his feet.

The Temple of the Rankan Gods was quiet and dark. He shook his head, feeling shame for his people. The construction of the temple had never quite been completed. The outer shrines with altars for Savankala, Sabellia, and Vashanka had been finished, but many of the inner ritual chambers and priests' quarters were still in various stages of completion. There should have been a festival in Sabellia's honor this night of nights. Rashan had elected, instead, to take his priests and hold the ceremonies at the smaller, private temple at Land's End which was not only completed, but sanctified. It didn't seem proper to Dayrne, though. That temple was Savankala's hallowed ground. This hour should belong only to Sabellia.

Well, he was just a gladiator. What did he know of priestly affairs?

He walked through the temple, his sandals ringing softly on the smooth stone floor. Lonely, troubled, he made his way outside, down the high steps, and into the avenue.

The street appeared empty. It would be foolish, though, to rely on appearances. Even with the street gangs smashed, there was still danger in the Sanctuary nights. There were too damn many alleys and shadows in this town. Sanctuary. He smirked, considering the name. As if a man was safe from anything at this end of the empire.

He wrapped a lightweight cloak about his shoulders and moved soundlessly down the street. Like the rest of Sanctuary's citizens he, too, knew how to turn invisible, to become a shade or wraith, as he wandered the darkness of Uptown. Cheyne would have mocked and teased him. She would have strode brazenly down the center of the road. Unlike his mistress, though, Dayrne had no taste for confrontations.

He bit his lip and cursed her silently for leaving him behind. *Where the hell are you, Chenaya,* he wondered bitterly. Then, thinking of Lalo's painting, *Who the hell are you?*

Worry and confusion gnawed at his insides. *Rashan,* he thought, furrowing his brow. He owed himself a long talk with that sunstruck priest.

                    *   *   *

Daphne worked the training machine with only the moon and a single torch to see by. She leaped and dodged as four spinning wooden arms swung at her head and knees. Sweat gleamed on her body, ran in free rivulets down her throat and chest, down her arms into the hand that held an immense sword. Once, the sword had been too heavy for her. No longer.

For a time her mind was utterly free, devoid of thought or concern. The smooth working of muscle, the stretch of tendon, the pulse of her blood, the heat in her flesh—these were the only things that existed for her. She breathed the cool air of night, felt the crunch of sand beneath her sandals, listened to the rhythmic *whoosh* of the whirling machine. Nothing else mattered for her.

But when the arms began to slow she stepped clear and drew a deep, frustrated breath. Then, she leaned on her sword and looked around, strangely aware of the silence and her aloneness. She would not have called it loneliness.

A few lamps burned in the windows of the estate. In the opposite direction a few more lights showed distantly where the new barracks had been built at the easternmost wall of Land's End. Beyond the wall the sky glowed redly with the bonfires that Rashan and his priests had made, where they celebrated by Chenaya's temple on the shores of the Red Foal.

She was alone as usual, on the outside looking in again. But it didn't bother her. Practice was what mattered, and training and hard work. Dayrne would be angry if he knew she was out here so late, but she didn't care. He was only her trainer, nothing more. He'd made that abundantly clear. Her hand clenched and unclenched on the hilt of her sword, though, when she thought of him.

She didn't care, she didn't care at all. But she raised her

weapon suddenly and carved a great chunk out of one of the machine's arms. The breath hissed from her as she struck. Then, she stood for a moment and trembled. It was not Dayrne, she told herself. It had nothing to do with him.

It was that damned husband of hers.

Kadakithis had summoned her to the palace again. Again, he had begged her for a divorce. *Begged!* A prince of Ranke! No matter that divorce was forbidden among the Royal Family. Hell, he'd practically crawled on his knees to convince her.

What had she ever seen in that man that had made her consent to marriage? It certainly hadn't been his thin, spindly body or his face with a chin that could stitch sailcloth, or that armor-piercing nose. It certainly hadn't been the execrable poetry he once had written, or his mediocre talent on the harp.

It sure as the gods hadn't been his fidelity. Why, the bastard had stocked his larder with fresh meat almost before their wedding bed had cooled. And when the Raggah kidnapped and sold her into slavery, did Kadakithis come to rescue her? Hell and damnation, no! He'd curled up, instead, with his pet fish, and left that task to Chenaya.

She carved two more chunks from the training machine, uttering a curse with each stroke. *Damn it, Chenaya!* (Thunk!) *Why didn't you take me,* (Thunk!) *with you, damn it!*

It didn't matter that Dayrne loved Chenaya, it really didn't. She missed the blonde-haired little bitch. With all the new faces around Land's End, all the recruits for Lowan's new school, Daphne wished for someone to talk to. Chenaya was always best for that, though they usually only traded insults and catty comments. Still, there was a communion in that. Chenaya understood her, and as much as anyone could, she thought she understood Chenaya. Everyone else was too much in awe of Lowan's daughter. But not Daphne. Too often they'd looked each other straight in the eye and muttered, "slut," or some such.

That made her smile.

That business with Zip, though, that hadn't gone down well for Chenaya. She suspected that in the process of ridding Sanctuary of that verminous street gang (laughingly called the Popular Front for the Liberation of Sanctuary) Chenaya had lost part of her heart to the cutthroat little back-stabber who called himself its leader. Just like her, Daphne thought, to ignore a real man like Dayrne who cared for her and to fall for a piece of puke.

Still, it was a damn good thing Chenaya had left town so soon after the palace ambush. If she knew that Zip had been set free, or that her own husband, that splinter of manhood, had elevated him to a position of authority . . . Hell, even she burned when she thought about that.

How, she wondered, could Shupansea allow it? If she'd hated that carp-face before, Daphne had nothing but contempt remaining for the Beysa. Her own people had suffered worst of all at Zip's hands. Daphne remembered the massacre of so many Beysib near the Vulgar Unicorn. Why didn't Shupansea? Wasn't she the real ruler of this city? How could she allow Zip to live when Chenaya had practically poured his blood into a cup for her to drink?

Daphne leaned on the machine and stared toward the red haze that flickered against the vast eastern darkness. The noise of Rashan's celebration barely touched her ears.

Only days after that incident Chenaya had vanished. Reyk, her falcon, rattled listlessly in his cage. Her father, Lowan, rattled around the halls and corridors of Land's

End, himself, like a caged bird, fretting in his own quiet way.

Fortunately, he had matters to occupy his mind: the arrival of one hundred of the empire's finest gladiators, the opening of his new school, the construction of suitable barracks on the estate's northeast section, with lumber transported all the way from Bhokar. And there were his plans for the upcoming Festival of Man. All that kept him from worrying too much about his daughter, and it gave him no time at all to visit the palace.

But Daphne had been to the palace on three occasions of late. It galled her to listen to Molin Torchholder and Tempus's crag-browed flunky—What was his name, anyway? Shit or Spit or something like that—muttering about Chenaya's treachery and Chenaya's scheming and Chenaya's this or that.

Not that the two had seen her. Woe to any woman raised in a royal household that never learned to listen at a keyhole or from behind an arras, or that never learned to carry on one conversation while overhearing another. Daphne had learned a lot on her three visits, and she swore to learn more when she answered Kadakithis's latest summons.

Divorce was all he had on his mind these days.

Treachery. That's all Daphne had on hers. There was another traitor that everyone seemed to conveniently overlook, a man who'd befriended Chenaya, pretended to love her. He'd helped her shape the trap that had netted Zip that night, and he'd killed piffles right at her mistress's side.

Then, he'd let Zip go, freed the piece of offal that—more than any man in the world—he had reason to hate, cause to kill.

It made Daphne mad.

She reached out and gave the uppermost arm of the

machine a push to set it spinning. Gears began to whir, moving the lower arms in a timed counter-rhythm. Daphne gripped her sword tightly, barely repressing a curse. She prepared to leap into her practice again, then stopped. As a perverse afterthought, she extinguished her torch in the sand.

She would try it without the light. She didn't need it anymore, she was sure. She was better than her trainer realized, and getting better still. She listened to the gears, to the *whoosh* of the arms. It was more of a challenge this way, but not much more. The moon was too full.

Leap and dodge, leap and dodge.

For a time, she abandoned thoughts of treachery and vengeance and found calmness in the smooth mindlessness of motion.

But only for a time.

Dayrne crept across the Governor's Walk and proceeded up the Avenue of Temples. Though a few lights burned in the windows of some of the greater edifices he walked the streets alone. Or, if he was not alone, then whoever else walked abroad moved as silently as he. In Sanctuary, he was willing to concede that possibility.

He had planned to go straight home to Land's End. There was so much to do these days with the One Hundred to organize and train. They were good men. He'd personally handpicked every one of them. Their first task upon arriving in Sanctuary had been to construct their own barracks with the lumber Dayrne had purchased in Bhokar. That done, he'd given them one day of rest in honor of Sabellia's celebration. Tomorrow morning would be their first full workouts. He would supervise the session himself.

Tonight, however, he wanted a good sleep.

Nevertheless, he slowed when he approached the eastern entrance to the Promise of Heaven. Two stone pedestals high as his waist stood on either side of the wide white-pebbled pathway. He hesitated, then moved toward them and frowned. In Sabellia's blessed light he spied a flat black stone upon the left post. Such stones washed up only on the banks of the White Foal on the farther side of town.

It was a signal. He palmed the small bit of rock and walked stealthily down the graveled path. He had gone less than ten paces when the smell of a very cheap, but very potent, perfume brought him to a cautious halt.

A woman stepped out of the bushes that lined the pathway. She was much too old for her chosen trade; only here in the Promise of Heaven could she hope to make a living with what remained of her physical charms. Men didn't come here for porcelain beauty, but for a few quick grunts in the foliage. Still, she did the best with what she had. Goldenwash made her hair too blond, and rouge made her cheeks far too rosy. More rouge colored her breasts, and kohl darkened her lids in a manner that was almost seductive.

Her white dress floated about her as she moved forward. In the pale moonlight it was nearly impossible to discern just how threadbare and worn it really was. There was a certain sad beauty to it and to its wearer.

"Evening, Asphodel," Dayrne said softly. "That perfume. I smelled you before I saw you."

She approached him, grinning, and suddenly she didn't look quite so old. The smile brightened her face, lent it youth. "Sarome's Night," she informed him. "It's in my price range, and it comes by the keg." She ran her fingertips lightly over the jerkin that covered his chest. "If it offends your nostrils, my young friend, then buy me something more expensive."

He caught her wrist, held it for a moment, then lifted her hand to his lips and kissed it. She giggled like a little girl, then pulled away. She touched her own lips to the place where he had kissed, then turned her hand over, opened her palm and exposed the black stone he had pressed upon her.

"You wanted to see me," he reminded her gently.

Whore or not, Dayrne liked the old woman. He'd liked her since the first time he'd caught her placing flowers against the main gate at Land's End. Lots of the townsfolk had left flowers and small gifts there since Cheyne smashed the PFLS. Especially, Dayrne suspected, the prostitutes whose trade that group had nearly ruined by their terrorizing of the streets.

Asphodel, however, had brought more than just flowers to show her gratitude. "Walegrin didn't take that bastard, Zip, to prison at all," she'd revealed in her best conspiratorial whisper. "He let him go." It was the first Dayrne had heard of Walegrin's betrayal, but he'd only just returned to Sanctuary that same day with a hundred men and a missing Chenaya to occupy his time. He'd thanked her for the information, but had taken no other action.

A few nights later, Asphodel had sought him again outside the gate. "There's a plot brewing in the palace," she'd reported. "Nothing is set, yet, and the Prince isn't involved. But some high people want Rashan dead real quick. They don't like his talk about the Lady Chenaya being a goddess. Lots of folks are ready to believe it."

"Why are you telling me this?" Dayrne had asked suspiciously. "How does a Promise Park whore come by such palace gossip?"

That was the first time he'd seen her smile. She'd leaned back against the gate and struck a pose that might have tempted him had she been twenty years younger.

"The ladies who work the park owe much to your Lady," Asphodel had answered. "While Zip and his bloody little boys ran this end of town our customers were afraid to venture out at night. But some of us have children and families to feed. Without the coins we earn in the park we couldn't afford food. Zip starved us as surely as if he stole the bread from our mouths."

She struck another pose. Dayrne realized with a faint grin that she wasn't trying to seduce him at all. Her postures were, instead, matters of long habit, totally unconscious. Long ago, this woman must have been something very special, perhaps madam of her own house. Sadly, times changed for everyone.

"There've been other things she's done, too," Asphodel had continued. "Little things. Many a time your Chenaya has cut through the Promise and scattered a few coins on the path. Oh, she always had a haughty air about her, but those coins sometimes made the difference between a good meal or none at all for someone's baby. We're a close-knit club, we women who work the Promise, and we don't forget favors. Even if people don't know they're doing us favors."

Dayrne wished Chenaya could have heard those words, but she'd left town too soon. "Such information . . ." he'd started to ask.

Asphodel smiled again and rumpled her hair absentmindedly. "How does a common street whore come by such news?" She raised one finely penciled eyebrow. "Sir, it would surprise you the kind of men who seek us out. A fine, soft bed is, of course, a good thing." Her smile turned mischievous. "But a tumble in the bushes, in the open air with the stars overhead and the leaves rustling, a body with no discernible face, and the wind in the crack of your ass. That's more than mere sex, Sir. That's an *adventure*. And men both highborn and low sometimes find their lives turning a bit stodgy. That's when they seek us out."

"And they talk?" Dayrne suggested, gleaning her subtleties.

Her smile faded only a little, replaced by an expression of wisdom and the barest hint of regret. "Ever meet a man who didn't want the woman he topped to know how important he was?"

They'd continued to talk through the night. As the first clouds of morning caught fire in the east they'd parted, her with a full purse in her bodice. She'd tried to refuse it, but Dayrne had insisted. They'd made a pledge to help each other, and it came as no surprise to learn a few nights later that she'd distributed his coins among all the women of the Promise.

The leather purse, though, that she'd kept for herself. She wore it on a thong about her ample waist. As he watched, she opened it and deposited the small black stone that was her means of summoning him. That stone was the only clue Dayrne had as to where Asphodel spent her daylight hours, and he guessed she lived close to the White Foal, perhaps in Downwind.

"Has Lady Chenaya returned home, yet?" Asphodel asked with genuine concern.

Dayrne shook his head. "No word from her, either."

The old whore bit her lip. The gesture touched Dayrne, drew him even closer to his new, unlikely friend.

He glanced up and down the walkway, making sure they

were quite alone. Then, he pulled her gently into the bushes. To his surprise, she didn't make the expected suggestive remark. That told him something was wrong.

"There's trouble?" he whispered, his hand still upon her arm.

She stared at his hand, then away into the dark. "I'm not sure," she said at last. "Maybe I shouldn't bother you with it."

He let go a sigh. If she didn't want to bother him, then it didn't concern Chenaya or Land's End. Still, he owed her. She had done enough for him and those he cared for.

"Bother me," he answered, another suggestive opening that she let pass. So it was big trouble.

Asphodel started to bite her nail, then pulled her finger away from her mouth and folded her hands together. "Some of the ladies have disappeared," she murmured almost too faintly to be heard. Then, her voice grew stronger. "One a night for over a week. And tonight . . ." she hesitated and started to bite the nail again. Again, she caught herself. "A new girl vanished. Sweet child, but a real novice. Her name was Tiana."

"Maybe she went home with a customer," Dayrne suggested.

Asphodel shook her head. "Not likely. We're kind of a family here. We adopt newcomers like Tiana and try to keep an eye on them." Unconsciously, she raised a finger to her lips, inserted it, and bit the nail quite through. She frowned, shook the finger and let go a sigh. "One moment, she was working by the bust of Sabellia. The next, she was gone. Nobody saw her leave. In fact, the park has been nearly deserted all night." She pointed to the sky. "Full moon," she explained. "The brightness keeps the customers away."

Dayrne rubbed his chin. "Are you sure they've disappeared? Maybe they've found . . ." he paused, choosing his words carefully, "better work. Or, maybe they're sick." He tried to think of other reasons a prostitute might take a night off.

"I told you we're close as family," she repeated. "I went to their homes, myself. Two of the ladies had children. Those little ones were all alone. One was a babe, a half-starved suckling. I had to find places for them all."

"Have you taken this matter to the garrison?"

She stared him right in the eye. It was a long, uncomfortable moment. "We're whores," she said at last. "This is the Promise." She didn't have to say more than that.

Raggahs, he thought. Could they be back in the slave trade? He remembered Daphne's experience at their hands, how those desert bandits had kidnapped and sold her into prostitution on Scavenger's Isle. The Promise of Heaven would be easy pickings if those bastards had decided to resume business.

If it was the Raggahs, though, then he had a personal stake in this. Daphne was his pupil. An affront visited upon her was visited upon him as well.

"Have any . . ." he searched for a delicate word, then shrugged helplessly, "bodies turned up?"

"No," she answered. "No traces at all. They simply vanished. Easy enough to do in Sanctuary, and if it was just one or two girls I wouldn't question. But one a night for more than a week?" She gazed around as if she could see through the shrubs and bushes into every corner of the park. Then, she raised the hem of her dress to reveal a small dagger thrust through a garter on her right thigh. "My ladies are scared. I'm scared."

"I'll see what I can learn," he promised, unsure of

what exactly to do. He pursed his lips, then drew a deep breath. "Anything else?"

She also took a breath and let it out slowly. "Just gossip. All those workers who've moved into Shambles' Cross are causing quite a stir. Trouble-making bunch of misfits, all seeking a quick fortune. They like to rough a lady up a bit, you know? They try it up here, and they'll be sorrier than hell." She patted her weapon through the thin dress.

"Doesn't that scare away your customers?" he wondered, amused.

"Easy enough to hide it in this darkness," she answered, grinning weakly. "But it's always within reach."

They stepped out of the foliage and onto the walkway. Once more, Dayrne caught her hand, raised it to his lips, and kissed it. "I'll try to help," he promised again before he turned away. He glanced over his shoulder, but she didn't follow. When he turned a second time she was gone. Asphodel knew the park far better than he did.

Sanctuary, he thought. *The Promise of Heaven.* So many funny names for a town with no sense of humor.

Sunlight shimmered around Daphne as she stepped from her silk palanquin at the Processional Gate. She had prepared for this meeting, dressing in her favorite gown of exquisite blue. It split enticingly to her right hip and draped low, just covering her breasts, leaving both arms bare. She had spent much of the morning piling her hair upon her head, pinning it in place with pins of gold and polished oyster shell. Small silver sandals adorned her feet. A perfume of rare citrus floated about her.

She was not so stunning as Chenaya, but she was beautiful. And before she granted him any divorce, Kadakithis would acknowledge that. So would Shupansea, the woman who wanted her place at his side.

She turned to Leyn and Ouijen who manned the front poles of her transport. "Thank you, brothers," she said formally to the two gladiators. They had helped often with her training, and she bore them great respect. It delighted her heart that they had volunteered to bear her today. The two at the rear poles were new men. She didn't know their names, but if Dayrne had chosen them they also deserved her respect. She made a short bow. "Thank you for this honor you've done me."

"We'll wait here," Leyn said. Then, he put on a grin. "Give 'em a taste of hell."

He was a beautiful man, blessed by Savankala with the same golden hair as Chenaya, tall and strong with the classically sculpted body that only a gladiator's training seemed to give. She looked into his richly blue eyes and smiled half-sadly. Why was it not Leyn she loved?

"I'll try not to leave you long in this sun," she answered. "And a *taste* of hell? I'll serve them a gods-damned banquet." She made an ugly face that instantly transformed to an expression of innocence. "Of course, I'm just a sweet, boring little princess of Ranke." But as she said it, she drew a finger across her throat and turned thumbs down with the other hand.

They laughed together, startling passersby who moved along the Processional on their morning business. Then, Daphne passed alone through the gate, crossed Vashanka's Square, and entered the Hall of Justice.

The hall was empty. Kadakithis had given up any real pretense of governing the city, himself. He rarely held court at all. She paused at the bottom step of a high dais.

At its top rested the throne from which the prince once had delivered his judgments.

For a moment her resolve faltered. She sank down on one knee, staring upward, recalling how she had first arrived in this gods-cursed city with her husband. Kadakithis had been so full of ideals then—almost bloated with plans and schemes to improve this filthy city his halfbrother, the emperor Abakithis, had given into his care. She had loved him at that time, even forgiven him for the harem he had brought along from Ranke. And she, too, had shared his ideals and dreams. Most of all, she had rejoiced at the changes that command had seemed to make in him.

But none of it had lasted. The ideals were shattered and scattered into dust. Kadakithis had so easily relinquished his command, first to Shupansea and her Beysibs, and then to Molin Torchholder and his cronies. She grieved for the Kadakithis that had journeyed—an enthusiastic boy-man—to this city. She despised the Kadakithis he had become.

It was not his fault, of course. It was the city. Sanctuary corrupted from the inside out. First, it shattered your ideals, then it ground your face against the broken edges, held you down with its foot on your neck until you no longer felt the pain. Until you were just numb.

She was proof of that. A once-delicate princess who lived, ate, slept like a gladiator, who cursed like a street whore, who had killed and reveled in the flow of blood. Oh, Sanctuary had worked its brutal magic on her.

Daphne rose from the step, passed through the rearmost door meant only for the prince and his entourage, and into the palace proper. She did not see Lu-Broca, the major domo, anywhere, so she grabbed the arm of the first guard that crossed her path. "There are four good men outside the Processional Gate." She saw by the gleam in his eyes that even a mere palace guard knew who she was, and she smiled inwardly. Intimidation came so easily to her these days. "You, personally, will take them the best goblets and the finest vintage wine you can beg, borrow, or steal from the kitchens. Fail me in this—" She patted his shoulder and winked, "Well, *don't* fail me." She had his dagger from his belt sheath and under his chin before he could draw a breath. "Oops!" she said, passing it back by the point. "You nearly dropped this."

She walked serenely down the corridor, leaving him. Neither Rankan guard nor Beysib dared to bar her way. They knew her, Princess Daphne, who once had dared to call their Beysa a whore to her face and laughed about it before all the city's gathered nobility. They hated her, but they accorded her a measure of awe, perhaps because not even their fish-goddess, Mother Bey, had dared to strike her down.

Or, perhaps that was only her imagination. Sometimes her mind ran away with her. She couldn't really guess what they thought of her, Beysib or Rankan. Nor did she care. It was Chenaya she strove to please, and Dayrne and Lowan Vigeles. And herself. Beyond that, she no longer gave a damn about Ranke or the Beysibs or Kadakithis.

Her loyalty was to Land's End. Chenaya had rescued her from Scavengers' Isle, and Lowan had offered her a home. Dayrne and his gladiators had put strength in her arm, courage in her heart, and a sword in her hand. To them she owed loyalty and love. Anyone else was less than the dirt under her sandaled feet.

She found Kadakithis in his private quarters. It amused her that he thought such intimate surroundings could sway her decision. Well, let him keep his little vanities a while longer. A guard stood by his door, opened it for her, and remained at her side until the Prince stepped through a curtained archway.

Kadakithis smiled his most reasonable smile.

Daphne stifled a sigh. He was still in so many ways the boy she had once loved. He had the same babyish face, the same hair, same thin and spotty beard that probably would never become a man's full mane. He was too scrawny, a mere stick beside Dayrne or Leyn. Yet, she had truly loved him.

No more, though. He had killed that love when the Raggah kidnapped her. Kadakithis hadn't even bothered to look for her or to wonder about her fate. And when she did return— thanks to Chenaya—she had found him with another woman. Hardly a woman at all, but a fish-eyed carp.

She didn't know if she hated him. But he had hurt her. She wanted to hurt him back.

"Daphne!" Kadakithis exclaimed. "You look positively radiant."

She folded her arms and waited for him to come to her. "Flatter me some more, Kitty-Kat," she encouraged him coldly. "Maybe it'll make me more pliant, and I'll give you what we both know you want."

He reached out to her, and she suffered his touch. His fingers brushed over her bicep. "By the Golden Crown of Savankala," he whispered in his best chiding tone, "if your father knew you were working out with a bunch of gladiators!" He squeezed her muscle. "Why it's bigger than mine!"

"Yours was never very big, husband," she answered caustically. "But we both pretended." She changed the subject. "Is Shu-sea hiding behind that curtain?"

The Prince paled briefly and looked back over his shoulder to the archway. "Of course not. We're completely alone."

He never had been much of a liar, not to her, anyway. "Too bad," she said and paced away from him to the far side of the room. "Because I know she'd like to hear my news. I've decided to give you the divorce you've been begging for."

If she hadn't hated him before, that changed instantly. His face brightened; the corners of his mouth turned upward in a smile, and he almost clapped his hands together for joy. Then, he caught himself.

"It's against Rankan Law," she reminded him. "We're both of Royal Families. But let's admit it, my love, we're so far outside Rankan tradition that it doesn't matter spit or blood what we do. The throne belongs to a usurper now, damn Theron's soul. Your loyalty is to your Beysib allies, and mine is to Chenaya and Land's End. You're no more a Rankan prince than I am a princess. I'm a gladiator now, an auctorata. You . . ." she hesitated, then gave him her most withering look. "You're a plaything for Shupansea and a puppet for Molin Torchholder."

Kadakithis came toward her, his arms outstretched. "Daphne, I'm sorry. I never expected—"

She waved him off, and again crossed to the farthest side of the room away from him. "Spare me any more of your whinings, Kitty-Kat." She knew how he hated that name. "You never expected me to be so reasonable? So generous as to give you the divorce? Or such a bitch?" She threw back her head and laughed, pleased by the effect it had on her weakling mate. "Well, I don't intend to disappoint you, darling." She felt the heat rise in her cheeks, though she tried to smother her anger. "I'm not going to be reasonable or generous. I *am* going to show you what a bitch I really can be."

He stared, apparently at a loss for words. She found him funny as he stood there, mouth agape. He persisted in thinking of her as the sweet, demure child he had taken for his bride, the child who'd loved and obeyed him and had never said a word about his philandering or his spineless scraping before his brother, Abakithis.

That Daphne was dead. The Raggah and the filth who lived on Scavengers' Isle had killed her.

"You want your divorce? You want to marry your fish-faced lover?" She laughed again. "You can, my Kitty-Kat." She pointed a trembling finger and released emotions too long held inside her. The bastard! He hadn't even tried to find her! "But there's a price to pay, first." Her lips curled ferally. "There's always a price."

"Anything!" Kadakithis stuttered. "Just tell me—"

She interrupted him. "Oh, you'll regret that word. But not so fast, former love of my life. This is my last grand-stand as your wife, and I want a handpicked audience. Only then will you learn the terms of our divorce."

Kadakithis's face turned stony. He glared at her. "Is this another game you're playing?"

If she'd had something close at hand she'd have thrown it at him. In fact, she wondered now if he'd had the room cleared just to avoid such an incident. It was remarkably bare of small objects. "Of course, it's a game," she answered, recovering a measure of calm. "You poor boy. Will you ever grow up and open your eyes? It's all a gods-damned game. You'd better learn to play, instead of hiding here behind your nice safe walls. As it is, you're nothing but a pawn for Shupansea and Molin. Be a player, damn you! For once in your innocent, naive life open your eyes and be a man! Until you manage that nothing here will ever truly be yours. Not this city, not Shu-sea, nothing."

He trembled visibly. She saw that from across the room, but strangely she found little joy in her triumph. She knew

few people had ever dared to talk to him that way, or
dared to tell him such a truth.

"Your audience," he reminded her. He could barely get
out the words; his lips made a thin, taut line, and his eyes
were narrowed slits.

Daphne drew a slow breath, her anger finally spent. She
had not realized the depth of the bitterness she'd harbored
against her husband. But that was suddenly gone, at least
for the moment. There was still the purpose though—the
reason she'd decided to grant the divorce.

"You," she said softly, "and Shupansea, and Molin."
She raised a finger for each name. Lastly she lifted the
little finger of her right hand. "But most importantly, our
dear garrison commander."

The Prince raised an eyebrow suspiciously. "Walegrin?"

She allowed a small, cruel smile. "His fame precedes
him, does it not? My terms will be of special interest to
sweet Walegrin."

There was no love in the look he gave her, no regret. A
shared past, shared dreams and ideals, they meant nothing
to him anymore. He wanted only his divorce, and as
quickly as possible, she saw that in his gaze. The chill in
his voice made even Savankala turn his head away, and
the room grew darker as, beyond the window, a cloud
passed over the sun. "When and where do we play your
game?" he said.

There was only one place. "The Hall of Justice," she
answered. "Tomorrow. You can sweat for awhile wondering what I'm planning."

Kadakithis folded his arms over his chest. "Then the
gods be with us all."

She spat on his lovely, marbled floor. "Don't blas-
pheme," she advised acidly. "The gods have nothing to
do with this business."

She left him then, passing within a hand's breadth of him on her way to the door. She smelled his essence and the clean crispness of his garments. She felt the warmth of him they passed so closely. But she gave him not another glance. She was numb, she told herself, numb.

In a strange kind of serenity she walked through the palace, through the Hall of Justice, and across Vashanka's Square. Her palanquin and her friends waited at the Processional Gate. They hailed her as she joined them. Each man held a fine silver goblet.

"We sent the wine back," Leyn informed her, "and requested water, instead. There's still a day's training ahead of us when we get back to Land's End."

She didn't have it in her to smile. She parted the curtains of her transport and climbed inside. "Take me home, Leyn," she whispered. "Please take me home." She let the drape fall between her and the rest of the world and did her best to smother the sounds of her tears.

Dayrne fed scraps of freshly killed meat to Chenaya's falcon. Reyk was reluctant to feed, however. The bird took the bits, chewed them briefly, and dropped them to the bottom of his cage. He emitted a long, shrill call, spread his wings to their fullest, then folded them again. He crawled into one corner, finally, and turned away from his feeder.

Dayrne gave up. He set the bowl inside the cage where Reyk could reach it if he changed his mind.

"He misses Chenaya."

Dayrne looked around. He hadn't even heard Daphne approach. A frown creased his lips. Didn't she ever wear anything but her training garb anymore?

"You're armed," she noticed. "Going out?"

He glanced at the sky. Twilight crept slowly over the
heavens. It would be dark soon. Asphodel would be in the
Promise like a mother hen protecting her clutch. He remembered the small dagger she wore in her garter and
smiled grimly. If the Raggah were involved, she'd need a
hell of a lot more than that.

"Personal business," he told Daphne. He turned and
walked through the aviary, paying no attention to the other
falcons in their cages. Birds were Lowan's hobby, not his.

Daphne kept pace beside him as he headed for the
estate. "Let me help," she offered.

Dayrne paused. If there were Raggah to hunt, didn't
Daphne have the right to join him? He shook his head.
Despite all her training and skill, she was a princess of
Ranke. He had no right to risk her safety. Besides, he had
no proof that the Raggah were his prey. Only a suspicion.

"Personal," he repeated. He increased the length of his
stride, leaving her behind. She didn't try to keep up, but
stopped instead and glared. He could feel the power of her
anger at his back.

The twelve original gladiators who had accompanied
Lowan Vigeles to Sanctuary had all been quartered within
the estate. Two were dead; they were only ten now, but his
grief was eased by the knowledge that his brothers had
died bringing an end to Zip's tyranny. There was honor in
that, so their deaths were good.

He sought Dismas and Gestus in the rooms they shared.
Dismas was curled on the edge of the bed with a book of
poems. His lover, Gestus, busied himself with a whetstone
and a favored dagger. They looked up when Dayrne entered.

"I'll be gone most of the night," he said softly. "Perhaps for the next few nights as well. I'd like it if the two

of you took charge of the watch tonight. Double the guards on all the other gates, too."

Dismas closed his book. "Expecting trouble?"

"In this town?" He didn't need to say more. His comrades set aside their diversions and rose to follow him out.

"I won't ask your business," Dismas said as they closed the door behind them. "But do you need any help?"

"Personal," Dayrne answered as he had to Daphne. Among the ten no other explanation was ever necessary. They were all auctorati, free fighters, at liberty to come and go as they pleased.

He left them, strode through the estate and out to the main gates. Leyn and a dark-haired giant named Dendur, one of the new recruits, stood duty. He exchanged a few words, then passed into the street.

The entrance to the Promise was as dark as ever. There was no stone waiting on the pillar for him, though. It didn't matter; he didn't plan to let Asphodel know he was here. He stole into the bushes and glanced at the sky again. One night past full moon, Sabellia still filled the world with her pleasure.

Light enough to see by—enough light to be seen.

He crouched lower and began to move.

The Promise of Heaven was a large park, triangular in shape. Three entrances and three main walkways welcomed visitors, but dozens of smaller trails snaked among the trees and foliage. All along these trails in small, secluded niches stood pillared busts and statues, little shrines to all the various gods and goddesses that had ever been worshipped in Sanctuary, each cared for by their various priests.

By daytime, the park was the shaded haunt of those priests and their acolytes, of philosophers and their students. It was a school where learned men met to share discourse, where supplicants sometimes came to pray.

By night, however, the niches belonged to the prostitutes—and to their supplicants who came to play.

Or prey, Dayrne reminded himself as he crept from place to place. Here and there, a giggle rose on the breeze. Here and there, the sounds of quick and furtive lovemaking. Dayrne was above embarrassment. He went about his search with a singleness of mind.

Sabellia sailed serenely through the night, marking the time.

He wasn't sure when he first felt eyes upon his back. He realized only that someone watched him, someone as quiet and subtle as he. He moved to his right, and they moved with him. He circled left, and they followed. Oh, they were good, indeed! Whoever his companion was, he couldn't spot him. But he knew someone was there.

He headed for the idol of the Ilsigi goddess, Shipri. A large niche, he remembered. There would be plenty of moonlight. If he was clever, he might lure his tag-a-long into that brightness. He fingered the pommel of his sword and pressed on.

Then, he cursed. There were voices in the niche. Of course, there would be! Shipri was a goddess of love and motherhood. What better place for a prostitute to set up shop? He parted the bushes for a look.

The voices stopped suddenly. At first, he feared he had been seen. But neither the man nor the woman there turned his way. Indeed, their eyes never seemed to move at all. After a moment, the man resumed the conversation, but the woman gave no answer. She didn't speak a word. Neither did her gaze leave her partner's face.

An alarm jangled in Dayrne's head. He peered closer at the black-cloaked man, unable to tell much about him save his height. A hood concealed his features, also any weapons he bore. But he was tall, much too tall for a Raggah. And he spoke Rankene.

"Come with me," the man said, crooking his finger. The prostitute smiled and fell into step beside her suitor. They left the niche and walked down the pebbled path.

Their tread made no sound!

Almost, Dayrne leaped from his hiding place, drawing his sword. Sorcery! If he struck swiftly, the fiend might not have time to react. A clean stroke through the neck—separate the head from the body—that was the best way to kill a wizard.

But he stopped himself. That might save this lady, but what of the other missing whores? He owed it to Asphodel to try and find them. He didn't relish the task, and he cursed his own sense of loyalty. Still, he *owed*. There was no more to be said about it. Of one thing he was sure, though. This villain was no Raggah.

Dayrne followed the pair. Apparently, the wizard knew the park well. Shipri's grove was isolated in a little-traveled area of the Promise. The walkways were empty. They wove a careful course toward the high wall at the southeast corner. Dayrne rubbed his chin. He'd expected them to make for one of the entrances. Where could they be going?

In the very corner where the two walls joined stood one of the tallest of the park's god-sculptures. Dayrne ducked behind a shrub while the wizard and his catch approached the Father of the Ilsigi pantheon, mighty Ils.

The wizard left the prostitute in the god's shadow while he went to the jointure of the walls. He put his left hand on a certain brick about shoulder high in the east face. His right found another brick in the south face at belly level.

The two bricks were barely within his reach, and he strained to press them inward.

Dayrne heard a grinding of stone against stone as the statue of Ils moved on its base.

The wizard crooked a finger, and the prostitute went to his side. He led her down into a black crack at the idol's feet and the darkness swallowed them. Dayrne bit his lip. She'd gone like a sheep to slaughter, without protest, smiling as if she'd smoked a whole bag of krrff.

Again came that grating sound, and the pit suddenly sealed. Dayrne leaped out of his concealment and raced to the wall. Which were the right stones? He strove to remember. He was taller than the wizard, and his arms were longer. He chose a pair and pressed. Nothing happened. He tried again. Still nothing. He was sure he had the correct left-hand brick. But which was the right?

Suddenly, Ils moved. Dayrne thanked his own gods, stepped to the edge of the opening and looked down. A set of stone steps descended into utter blackness. He spent only an instant wishing for a lamp or a torch, then took the first step.

The air was oppressive and stale. He glanced back upward at the square of moonlight and drew a final fresh breath. He didn't take time to search for the closing mechanism, but drew his sword and began to feel his way forward, brushing one hand along the slime-slicked wall.

The tunnel led in only one direction. He'd heard rumors of such tunnels, but all reports had confined them to the Maze. Apparently the reports were wrong.

The darkness made him pause. It was worse than being blind because he *knew* that he could see. His eyes were wide open, shifting from side to side, straining for some object or bit of light to fasten onto. His heart thundered in his ribs. Still, he pushed on, mindful of the promise he'd made to Asphodel.

A web draped over his head. He opened his mouth, a shout rising in his throat. Barely, he choked it back, and he rubbed his sleeve over his face in a frantic haste to free himself from the sticky strands.

Now, how in hell had that damn wizard dodged that?

He crept on, all too aware of the closeness of the walls, of the weight of the earth over his head.

Then—was that a light?

He moved a little faster, careful still to make no sound. The tiny spot of light became a flame in the distance, then a sconced lamp with another just beyond it. Dayrne hovered at the edge of the darkness and listened.

A low voice rode on the stagnant air. Impossible to distinguish the words, but by the rhythms and stresses, Dayrne thought it some kind of chant. He saw nothing ahead, though, so pressing against the wall, he ventured on into the light.

He stopped again. A too-familiar scent wafted through the tunnel. Dayrne sniffed. His brows knitted together for an instant, and he clenched the hilt of his sword.

A death smell hung in the air, the unmistakable odor of rotting flesh. Too many years in the Rankan arenas as a slave and as an auctoratus had made him familiar with that stench. Gritting his teeth, trying not to breathe too often or too deeply, he followed the scent and the voice.

A shriek ripped through the tunnel. The fine hairs on Dayrne's neck rose straight up. A woman's voice! Another cry echoed after the first, then a pause, and a long series of screams and broken sobbings.

Dayrne abandoned stealth and ran forward. The chant had risen to match the intensity of the screams. A mad cacophony of sound swirled around him. He ran wide-eyed and fearful, yet the fear did not stop him. It drew him, instead, until he found the entrance to a side room off the tunnel.

He realized at once the tunnel's original purpose. He was surely close to the palace by now, and this was an old escape route used in times of emergency, built by the Ilsigs, perhaps still unknown to the current Rankan occupants. The side room was full of empty weapon racks where fleeing men might once have grabbed swords before emerging aboveground in the Promise.

But not all his arena experience had prepared him for the rest of the sight.

In the light of a dozen oil lamps Dayrne saw the bodies of Asphodel's missing prostitutes. They hung by their necks from metal spikes driven deep into the walls, twisted ropes biting through the bloated flesh of their throats. Plainly, though, they had been killed before they were hanged.

The first few women had merely been stabbed through the hearts. The purpled, crusted wounds showed visibly on their bare breasts. The next one had been disemboweled; the flesh of her belly had been peeled back to reveal emptiness; she looked like nothing more than a gutted fish. The mutilations grew progressively more cruel. The skin and muscle had been sliced from one, leaving the organs in full view. Another had been left relatively intact with only dark holes showing where the organs had been removed. On yet another body the visible veins and arteries had been precisely, surgically opened, making a strange and gruesome mapwork.

Blood had stained the wall a nauseating color where the corpses hung. Old puddles and rivulets of blood had dried and crusted on the floor beneath them.

Dayrne reeled at the insanity of it.

He fixed his eyes on the center of the room. Bound upon a cross-shaped altar a woman screamed again, her terror filling the chamber and the tunnel beyond. It was the whore he'd followed from Shipri's niche. Whatever entrancement her captor had placed upon her had faded. Her feet and wrists bled as she struggled in her ropes.

At her head stood her captor. The wizard's eyes snapped open and fixed suddenly on Dayrne. The chant died in his throat. The gleaming knife he'd brandished over the prostitute turned point first toward the gladiator, and he snatched a second dagger from a table of instruments close at hand.

Outrage smothered any thought of fear. Dayrne started across the room, raising his sword. The wizard stepped swiftly to the altar's far side, putting his victim between himself and his unexpected attacker. As he moved he brought the points of his two blades together and barked a short command in a language Dayrne didn't know.

A pain stabbed the gladiator's heart. The breath rushed from him, and he clenched his teeth. Still he forced another step forward, fighting the sudden agony. The pain struck him again, and as he took another step, yet again stronger than ever. His knees buckled; the arcane fire in his chest consumed his strength. A red tide flooded his vision. His fingers trembled with seizure on the hilt of his sword.

He forced his head up, expecting a death stroke from one of the daggers. The wizard had felled him easily; Dayrne was helpless at that moment. Yet, his foe kept his place behind the altar and his victim.

Then, Dayrne saw fear, not triumph, on his foe's face.

Fighting the pain, he crawled back toward the entrance. With each retreating step the pressure on his heart lessened. He leaned on the jamb and slowly pulled himself to his feet, gasping for one good breath.

The wizard lowered his blades. A fine sweat sheened on his brow, and the glow of the oil lamps lent him a strange countenance.

Still, the fear was unmistakable; Dayrne saw it in those dark, deep-set eyes.

The prostitute cried piteously. "Help me!" she begged Dayrne. "Don't let him kill me, I'm with child!"

Dayrne stayed by the door. He needed a moment to recover his strength and to think. For all the wizard's apparent power, he feared Dayrne. Why?

"Don't just stand there like a worthless eunuch!" the whore shouted when her rescuer didn't move. "He's going to—"

The wizard frowned and touched her temple with one finger. Her head sagged back before she could say another word. Her eyes fluttered shut. She sighed, then went limp.

But almost instantly, her lids snapped open again. She screamed and cowered away from the wizard's hand as far as her bonds allowed.

The wizard roared in frustration, grasped both his blades in his right hand, and seized the woman's hair in his left. He jerked her head up then sharply down on the altar. She let go a short gasp as her eyes rolled and closed. A fine trickle of blood oozed down the cross under her head and dripped to the floor.

"I get so tired of the noise," the wizard said in exasperation.

Dayrne leaped across the threshold, but his foe was just as fast. Again the points of the blades touched, and again he shouted in that strange tongue.

Dayrne screamed as fire exploded in his chest and a rush of tears half-blinded him. But he kept his feet and flung himself at the altar. Wide-eyed, the wizard sprang back against the wall, clutching the daggers in shivering hands.

"Whatever god has siphoned my power, I've still more than enough for you," the wizard hissed. But his voice quavered.

Dayrne sprawled over the altar and over the woman's limp form, his fingers clutching her thighs for support. He sucked for air to relieve his tortured lungs and tried to fight the weakness that numbed his limbs. He lunged with the point of his sword, but his strength faded too swiftly, and his foe retreated beyond his reach.

The wizard flattened against the wall, and his fear was a tangible force. Then, fear turned to anger as he realized Dayrne's impotence. "All the way from Carronne I came to this miserable dung-hole!" He was still careful to keep his blades touching and pointed at the gladiator. "The tales had reached even that far of the strange affairs transpiring here, stories of gods and demons and dead souls that walked the streets. Clearly, there was power here for the taking, and who deserved it more than I? So I came disguised as one of the laborers who build your walls."

Dayrne hissed through his teeth, barely able to form words. "Human sacrifice? Never in our empire—not even in this rotten town!" He tried to glance over his shoulder, wondering if he could make it back to the safety of the entrance where the wizard's spell didn't reach. But he knew that was useless. It was a struggle even to raise up on one elbow and look his foe in the eye.

"The sacrifices are to placate whatever god has stolen my magic!" The wizard dared to come closer. "In Carronne I was a hazard-class magician—curse the fate that brought me here! My simplest spells go completely awry. All those stories of power—there must be some secret!"

"No secret," Dayrne managed. "Go back to Carronne." He dragged one foot, then the other, under himself and tried to stand. It was useless. His heart hammered against his ribs; the room spun crazily. The wizard's face swam out of focus. "Tasfalen's,"—he fought to get the words out—"magic burned out!"

But the wizard didn't hear or didn't understand. "I'll find the god who has cursed me and broken my skill and offer blood to appease him, until I'm strong again—strong enough to break your secret and seize the magic that pervades this city!"

Another voice called suddenly from the entrance. "It's always good to have dreams." Dayrne recognized it immediately and turned to shout a warning. All he managed to do was fall. Daphne didn't spare him a glance. "Have a long one in your death sleep." Her dagger flashed across the space.

The wizard cried out and bounced against the wall, clutching his shoulder. When he straightened, Daphne's blade protruded near his collar bone. A wet stain blossomed rapidly on his dark garment. Still, he managed to lift his own daggers and slam the points together and breathe his Word of Power.

Dayrne thought his heart would burst. From the corner of his eye he saw Daphne double over as she stepped across the threshold with drawn sword. The weapon tumbled from her grip.

But then, impossibly, she began to laugh. She straightened, threw back her head and let the mirth flow from her lips. She looked around for her sword, but as she bent to retrieve it she tripped on her own foot and fell, only to clamber up again laughing.

Dayrne felt it, too. The hand that squeezed his heart began, instead, to tickle it. His pain turned slowly into renewed energy. Strength flooded his limbs. He chuckled. Then, uncontrollably, he laughed. He looked at the bodies suspended on the walls, at the prostitute bound to the cross, at the astonished expression on the wizard's face.

It was all so funny!

The wizard smashed his daggers together, cursing, and stamped his foot. With a bellow he struck them once more. The blades shattered under the impact, and the pieces fell at his feet. His face paled, and his mouth gaped. Then, gathering his robes about him, he raced from the room and into the tunnel.

Daphne shot out a foot as if to trip him, but he was already gone. She rolled kittenlike onto her back, clutched her stomach and howled.

Moments passed before the twisted spell dissolved. Dayrne got to his feet, wiping spittle from his chin. He sheathed his sword and turned to help the princess.

But Daphne rose on her own. "If you breathe a word of this," she threatened, red-faced, "I'll wear your mouth for a garter."

"Just see to that one," he snapped, pointing to the prostitute on the altar. "Later we'll talk about your following me. I told you this was personal business."

She put a hand on his chest before he could pass her. "You're my business," she answered stubbornly, her gaze hard and glittering. "Good trainers are rare."

He regarded her for an instant, then remembered the wizard. "We'll talk," he said, and he ran into the tunnel.

The echo of fleeing footsteps sounded from the direction of the Promise. Dayrne sped after, drawing his blade once again. He quickly passed the final lamp and plunged ahead. The darkness, though, forced him to slow. He put a hand to the wall and hurried as rapidly as he dared, cursing under his breath.

The wizard's footsteps faded. Had he reached the tunnel's end at the shrine of Ils? If he had emerged, Dayrne knew he might never find him.

His answer came as he spied the shaft of moonlight that lanced the blackness. But strange sounds wafted through the opening, swelling as he approached—shouts and curses, high, frantic voices.

Dayrne raced toward the moonlight. It had to be the prostitutes! He took the steps two at a time and ascended into open air.

The women of the Promise surrounded the wizard in a wide ring. He spun in confusion, weakly brandishing Daphne's dagger. It gleamed wetly with his blood. The whores, too, waved daggers, the small weapons they wore in their garters. Still, they didn't know their foe's power!

Dayrne tried to warn them. "Asphodel!"

At his shout, the wizard whirled. Their eyes met for an instant. Hatred and anger burned in that furious gaze, and Dayrne felt a force reach out for him.

The prostitutes saw their chance. They fell on the wizard, hacking and stabbing with their tiny blades. Arms rose and plunged with frantic outrage and swiftly blackened with the blood of their stalker.

Dayrne could only stare as the wizard sank under the onslaught. The women did not stop. They stabbed and stabbed, giving release to all the rage and terror they had lived with the past nights. Then, Asphodel stepped back gasping and wide-eyed, her white dress a stained ruin. Dayrne went slowly to her side.

"Who was he?" she asked, barely able to speak as she trembled.

She might have been a spectre that haunted the park the way she looked. Dayrne wiped a smear of blood from her cheek and patted back the hair that had fallen around her face. "He came from Carronne," he finally answered. "I never learned his name."

Asphodel sighed and looked over her shoulder. The whores stood away from their grisly work. Pieces of the corpse lay hacked and scattered around their feet. The women stared from one to the other with expressions that betrayed confusion in some, fury and vindication in others. One by one they drifted back into the bushes. From somewhere in the foliage came the sound of weeping.

"I guess it doesn't matter," Asphodel said. "One of my ladies found this opening, and we waited to see who came out. I knew it had something to do with my missing ones." She sighed again and peered into the tunnel's gloom. "They're dead, aren't they, Tiana and all the rest?"

He nodded quietly. "All but the one he took tonight. She's still alive, though somewhat battered."

Daphne chose that moment to emerge from the opening with the prostitute slung over her shoulder. She dumped her burden unceremoniously in the grass.

Dayrne frowned and knelt beside the woman. "He didn't hit her that hard. She should have come around by now."

Daphne spat. "She did. Then, she took a good look at—" the one-time princess, hesitated, looked at Asphodel, and spoke more softly. "She saw her friends and realized how close she'd come to joining them." Daphne shrugged and cocked her head to one side. "She fainted."

Asphodel glanced from Dayrne to Daphne and back again. She realized who the princess had meant, and that the younger woman had tried to spare her some horror. Her old eyes misted over, but she blinked back any tears.

"Some of my brothers will bring them up in the morning," Dayrne said gently. "There's no need for you to see them the way they are."

"They're family," Asphodel answered. She held up her dagger. With a look of disgust she flung it aside and wiped her hand on her dress. "I'll be here to help."

Dayrne started to protest, but Daphne touched his sleeve. "It's her decision," she told him. "You know, *personal business*." Then, with her usual tact, she pointed to the wizard's remains. "Besides, they don't look any worse than that."

Asphodel walked to the corpse and stared at it for a long moment. Daphne went with her, bent down and retrieved her dagger from the ground near the wizard's hand. "It's Chenaya's," she informed Dayrne. "She'd be pissed if I lost it." Then, she turned away and vanished into the park.

Alone, the old whore turned to Dayrne and touched his arm. "Thank you," she said.

"For what?" he answered with a shake of his head. "I didn't do anything."

It was almost true. With all the blood spilled this night, his was the only clean blade in the park.

Daphne scandalized the palace by arriving, not in a gown, but in an outfit borrowed from Chenaya's closets. She looked as beautiful and deadly, all in soft black leather, gleaming with buckles and ringlets and weapons. Her night-black hair flowed over her shoulders. Pride stiffened her spine; she lifted her chin high as she strode into the Hall of Justice.

Two seats had been placed upon the dais. Kadakithis and Shupansea sat there side by side, looking down upon her. Molin Torchholder stood beside the Beysa, Walegrin by his prince. It was the audience she'd requested and no one else. Her husband simply had no sense of theatrics. But then, he had no sense, period.

She looked up and met his stare as she stopped at the lowest step. His jaw gaped in astonishment. It was the acknowledgment she had sworn to get from him—and it tasted sweet indeed.

"Second thoughts, my husband?" She rested one hand on her hip, taunting him.

His hands fluttered. "You look—" he bit his lip and cast a sidewise glance at Shu-sea. The sentence hung unfinished. The Beysa at that instant looked less like a carp, more like a shark protecting her catch.

Daphne had expected to gloat, to draw out the moment of her triumph, but she found now she had little stomach for that. Better, she decided, to end this quickly, break her ties with this pathetic little man, and get on with her new life.

"You want a divorce, Kitty-Kat?" She looked at each of the four on the dais and grinned. *It's all a game*, Chenaya had once told her, *everything is a game*. Daphne realized the truth of that. These were the master gamers of Sanctuary she faced. "These are my terms."

"List them, Princess, and we'll consider."

Daphne shot Molin a withering look. "Shut up, Torch. This is between Kadakithis and me. You're merely here to witness, and I extend you that courtesy only because I know you're even more eager for these two to wed than they are. I half expect you'll share the marriage bed."

Molin maintained an outward calm, but Daphne knew him better than that. She turned back to her husband.

"First, I want the estate immediately south and adjacent to Land's End. It's abandoned right now, but the way people are flocking to this pisshole these days it's not likely to be so for long." She paused, and her brows narrowed. "I require agreement. None of this is negotiable."

Kadakithis rubbed his thinly bearded chin and glanced at Molin. The Torch gave a not-very-subtle nod, and Daphne smiled to herself. Puppet and puppet-master.

"We'll draw up a deed," the prince answered.

"Second term," she continued. "One half of your personal fortune."

Kadakithis rose from his seat. His eyebrows shot upward, and he gripped the arms of his chair to steady himself. "What!"

Daphne clucked her tongue. "Won't it be worth it to get rid of me? Besides, think of all that gold on the Beysib ships. I'm sure your bride will offer a dowry worthy of a man like you."

The prince sank back into his seat. At last, he waved a hand. "All right, damn you! Yes, I'll even agree to that. As you say," he added caustically, "it'll be worth it to be free of you." He glowered down from his high position. "You're not at all the sweet wife you used to be."

The accusation caught her completely off guard, and she barked a short laugh. To her utter surprise she found within herself a sudden sympathy for Shupansea.

"Third term," she said, regaining control of herself. "I retain all my titles and any property in Ranke that Theron hasn't seized along with the throne."

"Done," Kitty-Kat agreed disinterestedly. "What else?"

She rested a hand on the pommel of her sword and let go a small, inaudible sigh. "There was one more term, originally," she said. She faced Walegrin and waited until he shifted uncomfortably. "I wanted the first knuckle of the little finger of your right hand to wear on a chain about my neck," she told the garrison commander. She watched all their faces as she said it, and she wasn't disappointed by their reactions. "Look at them," she said, addressing him directly. "They'd have given it to me, too."

Molin stepped to the very edge of the platform, but Kadakithis caught his sleeve and pulled him back. "You're insane!" her husband shouted.

"That's right!" she shot back. "You made me insane when you abandoned me to the gentle mercies of Scavengers' Isle!"

Only Shupansea kept a measure of her composure. She leaned forward, regarding Daphne with sudden interest. "Why our commander?"

Daphne faced Walegrin again. "You betrayed the Lady Chenaya," she charged, "and let Zip go free after she handed the little bastard over to you. Now, the common people of the city shower her name with praise and beflower her gate while Molin and the powerbrokers of Sanctuary rant and rave about her so-called treachery. Yet, no one speaks of your treachery, Walegrin. You made love to her, then you betrayed her. You helped shape her plan, and you killed piffles right beside the rest of us." She stabbed a finger at the Torch and Kitty-Kat. "Then, on their orders, you freed the man who murdered your little niece and gutted your own sister with an ax." She gave him a cold look, finding small reward when he turned away from her gaze. "You've thrown away your honor, Commander. Molin and his cronies may praise you for your obedience and sense of duty. But the common men and women of this town know you now. Look in their eyes the next time you walk the streets. You'll find reflected there nothing but scorn."

She turned to Molin who seemed ready to swoop down on her like the carrion bird he so resembled. "Keep your toy soldier, Torchie. But keep him away from me. He pollutes the air."

"I am curious," Shupansea spoke, leaning forward. "If you wanted our commander's finger, why did you change your mind?"

Daphne allowed a wan smile. "It's nothing any of you will ever grasp," she answered. "But I found true honor in this city last night among some whores in a dirty park, where a group of women struggle every moment of their lives to eke out an existence you and I would die to avoid. For all their misery they take care of each other like a kind of family." She hesitated. "I've found a similar kind of honor at Land's End, but you wouldn't understand that, either. Walegrin can keep his finger." She cocked her head to one side, recalling her night in the tunnel and an odor that still lingered unpleasantly in her memory. "It would have made a smelly bauble, anyway."

She gave her back to the masterplayers, then, winning her best victory by walking away from the game.

Just beyond the Processional Gate she found Dayrne waiting. He'd washed and changed since the morning's training session, and his essence was sweeter than the day, itself. "I thought I'd walk you back," he said.

She grinned up at him. He really was the hugest man she'd ever seen, yet she found in him the most unexpected gentleness. Chenaya was a fool not to love him. Daphne shielded her eyes from the sun as she gazed at his face. The brightness lent a halo to his features.

"How about I buy you a mug, instead," she offered. "You pick the tavern. Make it someplace raunchy."

He frowned. But then, he clapped an arm around her shoulders, and his lips curled upward into the barest smile. "I think I can find a place to make you blush," he said.

"A gold sheboozh," she answered, "that you can't."

THE VISION OF LALO

Diana L. Paxson

Lalo twitched the mask back into position over his nose and mouth and dipped his brush into the gray paint once more. Another three feet of this wretched wall and he could stop for a bit. The brush rasped the coarse canvas, deftly suggesting texture; a touch of black gave it depth, and another stone was finished. From somewhere out front he heard hammering. The opening of the second production of Sanctuary's first and only resident theatre troupe was two days away. The painter wondered if either their rehearsals or his sets would be finished in time.

Lalo stepped back to consider his work and grimaced beneath the mask. Even with shading the canvas looked like a collection of blobs. He supposed that from the audience the flat would create the illusion of reality. It occurred to him then that if he took off his mask and breathed on those rocks that they would *be* reality. . . . Was he resisting the temptation because he was not sure the stage would take the weight of the stones, or because he feared that he had lost the power to make them real?

Lalo told himself it was a small price to pay for the

return to (relative) normalcy in Sanctuary. Perhaps his son
Wedemir and that girl he was courting up at the Palace
would be able to raise all of *their* children in peace. Except
when some spell-supported building collapsed as its magic
decayed, the debris of the explosion of sorcery that had
nearly destroyed Sanctuary had been cleared away. The
town was rebuilding. Lalo supposed he should be glad.
But the period of escalation in magic had also seen the
flowering of his own creativity. He was not sure now
which of his talents were magic, and which had been
simple craftsmanship. He felt half-blinded—"head-blind"
the mages called it. But he dared not try to see.

And so he was painting scenery for a production of something called *The Accursed King*, which seemed more de-
pressing the more of it he heard.

"We'll take it again from the beginning, then," said
Feltheryn over his shoulder as he strode onto the stage.
"Two days to opening, dear gods! But at least *this* piece
can offend no one . . ." The repercussions of the troupe's
first production were only now beginning to fade in public
memory.

Feltheryn the Thespian, the troupe's founder, director and
star, took his place before a post that was going to become a tree as soon as the carpenters got around to it, and
thumped his staff against the floor. Simpering girlishly,
Glisselrand scurried across the stage after him and took his
elbow.

> *"Tell me, my daughter, where have you come to now*
> *With your blind old father? What is this place, my*
>   *child?"*

Feltheryn's stentorian tones rang out with remarkable
resonance for a monarch as enfeebled as he was supposed
to be.

"It's little I ask, and am well content with less.
Three masters—pain, time, and the royalty in the blood—
Have taught me patience—"

The stage shuddered as something large and heavy hit the floor. Feltheryn broke off and turned. "Patience!" he roared. "Gods give *me* patience—I have to work with fools!"

"It was the hoist," came a plaintive voice from backstage. "It wasn't my fault, master—the rope slipped—"

"Lempchin! You misbegotten son of a sheep-swiving Rankan!" He gathered breath, and ominous tones rolled across the stage. "What fell?"

There was a silence, and Lalo bent to gather up the brushes that had been knocked from their stand.

"It was . . . the thunder machine."

"Vashanka's rod! Do you know how much that thing cost? A gift from the Prince himself it was, and after everything—" he took a deep breath, then launched into a monologue of sorrows as eloquent as anything in the play.

Lalo found that he had put the brushes back into their case instead of on the stand, and grimaced. How could anyone be expected to paint—even to paint scenery—with this sort of thing going on? Darkness had fallen an hour ago. Gilla would already be angry with him for being late, but perhaps dinner would not be completely cold. He was hungry and tired. As Feltheryn stormed backstage to survey the damage. Lalo finished capping his paints and putting them away, strapped the brush case to his belt, and headed for the door.

"Oh Lalo, are you going already?" Glisselrand called after him. He mumbled something about Gilla and continued up the aisle. "Yes, do give my love to dear Gilla—I'm working on a shawl for her—rose-colored yarn with lemon

yellow and a lovely purple from Carronne. . . ." As the
door closed behind him Lalo could still hear her describing
the color scheme.

He shook his head. The tea cozy had been bad enough.
The thought of a shawl large enough to cover Gilla. . . .
He shuddered. And Gilla would insist on keeping it! He
wondered if he could persuade her to keep it somewhere
out of sight. . . . Still contemplating the horror of Glisselrand's sense of color unleashed on something the size of a
shawl, he hurried on through the darkness.

Lalo had rounded the corner of the Serpentine and was
starting down when he became aware of the footsteps
behind him. Close—too close—they must have been waiting in an alley, or perhaps his own abstraction had kept
him from hearing them before. Reaching for his knife, he
started to turn.

Shadows rushed toward him. Beyond them he glimpsed
the mocking grimace of the Vulgar Unicorn on its sign as
the door of the tavern opened and light streamed into the
road.

"Help! Thieves! Help me!" Lalo knew the futility of
his shout even as it left his throat. His knife glinted as he
brought it up. He struck something soft, heard a grunt and
leaned into the blade. Then a blow numbed his hand and
the knife went skittering across the stones. He lifted his
useless arm to guard his head. Someone laughed—his
attackers, or the men who were coming out of the Unicorn?

This can't be happening now, Lalo thought in confusion
as he was knocked against a wall. *Not after so many years!
Not so close to home*—a blade flashed toward his shoulder;
he dodged and felt the sting as its tip scored his arm—*as if
I were a foreigner or a fool!*

How could he have been caught this way? Someone

grabbed for the case that held his brushes and Lalo struck out, tried to duck as he sensed something falling towards him, but not fast enough, not quite fast—

The shock of the blow stopped the world.

Light and shadow, the hoarse gasps of his assailants and the shouting beyond them all faded as his senses whirled away.

Gilla, I'm sorry—

And then both regret and pain were extinguished as Lalo fell endlessly downward into the dark.

Darkness . . . a musty smell that makes the nose wrinkle. Limbs stiff from spelled sleep, stretch, lungs draw in stale air. Dust tickles dry nostrils, and Darios wakes fully with a sneeze. Ears strain, but there is only the sound of his own ragged breathing. He sneezes again.

I'm alive! I survived! *Even in the darkness, Darios can feel his skin flush with pride. He remembers the panic as the defenses of the Mageguild began to unravel, remembers collapsing walls, and the roar of rioting crowds. They were all running—apprentices and masters as well. Did none of the others remember this vault beneath the stables sealed by potent magics before ever the Nisibisi rose in the North or the Beysib sailed into Sanctuary's bay? Those magics would last as long as the Mageguild, preserve him in a timeless trance as long as—*

—As long as its wards remained intact, until a ranking Hazard came to set him free. . . .

But Darios is alone in the vault, and the doors are still sealed.

He swallows, reaches out and touches cold stone. Exploring fingers find wetness. Water is sliding down the wall from somewhere above. Darios brings his fingers to his mouth, and the moisture enables him to swallow. He takes a deep breath and pronounces a Word . . .

But the darkness remains unbroken. For the first time, Darios feels the chill touch of fear.

From the sounds around him it must be morning. Lalo took a deep breath, winced as pain split his skull, and thought better of trying to open his eyes. But it was not the throbbing ache that came from drinking—it had been years since he had felt that particular pain—and already he was remembering swift footsteps and the scuffle in the dark.

I'm still alive! he realized in wonder.

"Are you back with us, then, you foolish man?" asked Gilla. "What were you thinking of, to take that route home at night, alone?"

Anxiety had sharpened her voice, but Lalo smiled. Even her scolding was welcome when he had not expected ever to hear it again.

"You've been luckier than you deserve!" she went on. "Dubro was sure you were dead when he found you with that great gash in your skull." That was probably true, thought Lalo, remembering the blow, as if Feltheryn's thunder machine had fallen on *him*. "Sit up now, and I'll give you something to help with the pain."

Biting his lip, Lalo got his elbows under him, and then, very carefully, opened his eyes. But he must have been wrong about the time, for it was quite dark still.

"Open your mouth—"

"Light a lamp first," he answered. "So that I can see the spoon."

"A lamp? I'll open the shutters wider if you want more light, but why—" Gilla did not finish. There was a moment's silence, then a breath of air brushed his forehead.

"Lalo—" she said tightly. "Why didn't you blink? Didn't you see my hand?"

"No . . ." He turned towards the sound of her voice, straining to see despite the pain that pulsed frantically against the confines of his skull. He reached out, and felt the strong grip of her work-roughened fingers clasp his.

"No. Gilla, I can't see anything at all!"

After that, Lalo supposed he must have become hysterical, tearing at the dressings on his head until agony slammed shut the doors of consciousness again. When he woke once more, his eyes were bandaged. *Blind . . .* he thought, as memory replayed what had happened. *Will it go away? What am I going to do?*

For a week they waited for his head to heal, hoping that the blindness would go away. The Prince sent his own physician, who examined the wound and clucked solicitously, prattling of evil humours and the aspects of the stars until Gilla booted him out the door. Wedemir came, and came again with the chirurgeon from the garrison, a man who seemed more knowledgeable, but hardly more encouraging. He could only tell them that he had seen a blow on the head cause blindness on the battlefield. Usually sight returned in a few days.

"But not always?" asked Wedemir. Lalo could hear them whispering in the corner. They did not realize how the loss of one sense focused concentration on those that remained.

"Not always—" the soldier agreed. He did not know why Lalo's sight had been affected, and the only treatment that he could recommend was time. "Are you coming, Wedemir?" The chirurgeon's voice faded and then grew louder, as if he had reached the doorway and then turned.

"Yes—just a moment—"

Lalo felt the rough grasp of his oldest son's hand.

"Papa, I've got to go back on duty now. I'll be back soon, though, to see you!" The tone was bracing, but Lalo could hear the waver that Wedemir tried to hide.

"Duty, hah! You just want to see Rhian again, I know!" piped up Latilla. "Did you know he's got a girl at the Palace, Papa? A Rankan lady, she is, and very pretty. I saw her when I was visiting Vanda last time."

"She's not my girl—not yet, anyway," Wedemir interrupted. "She was pledged to an apprentice in the Mageguild, and she says she is still bound . . ."

"The Mageguild?" said Gilla. "But the ones who survived are scattered throughout the city now, or fled—"

"Don't you think I've tried to tell her?" asked Wedemir. "If her lad were still alive, surely he would have sent her word by now! It has been almost a year since they broke the Globes of Power. If he is still living, he doesn't deserve her!"

"Wedi's got a girrill—Wedi's got a girrill!" Latilla sang, until a squeal and a torrent of giggles told Lalo that her brother was tickling her as he used to when they were younger. Lalo tried to imagine what was going on, but he could only remember how they had looked as children, long ago . . . when he could still see . . .

Lalo felt his cheeks grow wet with easy tears.

Wedemir accompanied the chirurgeon back to the barracks, and Vanda went back to her Beysib mistress in the Palace. Glisselrand sent over a crochetted bed-shawl which Lalo was glad he could not see. The household began to settle into a routine.

Lalo dreamed of the paintings that he had never found the time to do and hardly noticed what they fed him, but he heard Alfi and Latilla complaining and realized that Gilla had stopped buying the delicacies the family had become used to. She was shifting back to a style of cooking he remembered only too well—beans and whatever protein was cheapest—poverty cooking. Once more he felt the treacherous tears slide from beneath shut lids.

She does not think I am going to get well. . . .

Did he?

During the first week Gilla had been always with him, her sharpness sheathed in uncomplaining, patient care. But that was changing. His wife still made sure he was fed and tended, but now it was Latilla who sat with him, Latilla who cut his meat and set the spoon into his hand.

"What is your mother doing?" Lalo asked one morning —he could tell it was morning because of the freshness in air that would be weighted with all the smells of the city by the advancing day.

"She's gone up to the Palace to visit Vanda," answered his daughter brightly. "Vanda says the Beysib ladies need a lot of sewing done, because of the wedding, you know, and Mother does lovely work—"

Lalo groaned.

"Papa—are you all right? It doesn't matter if Mama's not here—*I'm* here, Papa, and I'll take care of you! Please, Papa, don't cry!"

He felt the soft touch of her hands smoothing his hair, the coolness as she sponged his tears away.

"*I* won't leave you!"

Lalo reached out and found her shoulder and Latilla hugged him fiercely. Her arms were still thin—a child's arms, but her body was beginning to ripen. She was twelve now. Would he ever see her promise of beauty fulfilled?

Gilla is looking for sewing to do because she does not think I will ever work again—the cold fact of it shook him. Was that why she had drawn away? Lalo wondered if he was seeing what Gilla herself did not yet consciously know. He thought he understood. He had failed her for the last time. Gilla's first responsibility was to her children now. Though Lalo's body still lived, his life, and their marriage, were at an end.

Without meaning to, his grip on Latilla had tightened; she squirmed, and abruptly he let go. The girl straightened with a sigh and began to prattle about the bird that was perching on the windowsill. Lalo lay back against his pillows, hardly hearing her. Was this the way it was always going to be?

He supposed that Gilla would bear her fate in uncharacteristic silence. But Lalo was consuming resources that should have been used for the children. And Latilla—all she knew now was that she had her father to herself at last. But Lalo could see clearly how her care for him would steal her youth away.

Perhaps he could sit at the corner and ask charity of passersby. . . .

In Sanctuary? As well seek warmth from a beynit, pity from a Stepson, motherly love from Roxane! A bark of bitter laughter brought Latilla back to his side.

"Help me get dressed!" he said with sudden energy. "Without exercise, my legs will be as useless as my eyes! Come, Latilla—I want you to guide me through the town."

Once, long ago, Lalo had observed that the blind might be blessed, because they could not see the squalor of the town. Gods help him, he had thought it funny at the time. Now, holding to Latilla's shoulder, he realized that he should have known it was not true. As they moved through the town, memory and imagination supplied images to go with the sounds and stenches around him, picturing a thousand evils and never knowing which of them he imagined and which were true.

The Maze at night was like that, when danger coiled in every dark alley, and only the glare of a torch could burn the fear away. But all of Lalo's roads led through darkness now.

Slowly they made their way through the conflicting enticements of perfumes and cooked food in the Bazaar, the cacophony of hawkers crying their wares and the babble of not always good-natured chaffering. Lalo's nerves were still twitching as they passed the mournful lowing and the sick stench of cow shit that came from the pens of the Shambles, and went on towards the harbor, where a brisk sea breeze did battle with the myriad odors of the town.

Gulls screamed around him as they neared the wharves. Lalo could hear the flap and the flutter as they swept past, squabbling over spilled fish guts. As Latilla led him out along the echoing wooden planks of the pier, he tried not to remember the dazzle of sunlight on waves, the pure beauty of the birds when their wings drew a silent arc across the bright sky.

In the play, thought Lalo, the king had lost his sight because he insisted on seeing too much—on bringing things better left hidden into the light. *Am I being punished for my vision? Have I been blinded because I dared to look upon the faces of the gods?* he wondered then. But Ils himself had given that gift to Lalo, and if the gods had wished to chastise him, the past few years had offered them some spectacular opportunities to strike him down.

Or was it because I wept for lost magic and never

*thanked the gods for the blessings that I had? I have
nothing now. All my visions must remain imprisoned behind my eyes, and I in this useless body, a burden to those
I love!*

" 'Tilla—Latilla! It is you! Where have you been?" a
girl's voice cried.

"Hello, Karis—" there was a pause, and Lalo knew
that Latilla must have made some sign that indicated his
disability, for the other girl's voice was decidedly subdued when she replied.

Lalo's hand touched the splintery, weathered wood of a
piling and he guided himself down.

"Are you all right, Papa?"

"Yes—yes—" he forced an answer. "Just a little tired.
Let me sit here with my back against the piling for awhile.
You go on—talk to your friends. I will do well enough
here."

For a few moments he could feel her near him. Then her
light footsteps grew fainter as she moved across the planks.
Soon he heard the ripple of conversation, and a girl's light
laughter.

Waves lapped against the base of the piling as a fishing
boat came in, timbers creaking, sails flapping as the curve
of the land cut off the wind. A man hailed the shore. Lalo
felt the pier shake as someone ran forward to catch the line
and make it fast. Familiar sounds, all of them—he tried to
visualize exactly what the boat would be doing now, how
they would take down the sails and warp the craft in to lie
snug against the pier. But he could not remember.

He rested his face in his hands. How many times had he
come here to think, sometimes in joy, sometimes in despair? Why had he never set his mind to really *seeing* what
was going on around him, instead of chasing his own

thoughts until he grew tired, or Gilla came to drag him home?

Memory moved back to the time of his greatest agony (until now) when Enas Yorl's gift had turned to a curse from which he saw no escaping. Lalo remembered how he had gazed into the polluted waters of Sanctuary's harbor. He would have thrown himself into them that day if it had not been for the horrors he saw floating there.

But you cannot see what is in those waters now. . . . .

Were the words that came to Lalo's mind his own? Softly, how softly, the wavelets were lapping—they made a hushed, soothing sound, like a lullaby. He turned a little, head tipped toward the water, listening.

Gently rocking, peacefully floating . . . soon the tide would be turning, and all broken and useless things that had been cast into the bay would be carried out to sea. The weight of his head drew him downward . . . moist air cooled the tight skin of his brow. How easy it would be to let himself fall . . . When the dark waters had closed over him it would not matter if he could see.

He let out his breath on a long sigh, not allowing himself to think, wanting only coolness, darkness, rest. . . .

"Papa, Papa! Watch out!" Sharp fingers pulled him upright. For a moment Lalo tensed in resistance. "Papa, were you asleep? You almost fell in!"

Lalo shook his head despairingly. He had been so close! He struggled to his feet and took a step forward, then stopped, confused. Which way was the water?

Latilla's thin arms closed around him. "It's all right, Papa. You're going the right direction—I won't let you fall!"

The water was behind him, then. All he would have to do was turn, and leap—he felt wetness on his hand. Latilla's tears. . . . One leap and it would be over for him, but not for her. The child would have felt guilty even if his death had appeared to be an accident. Latilla thought she had saved him. Lalo could not kill himself before her eyes.

Oh, my little one—he thought, holding her, *if only you could set me free. . . .*

He let Latilla lead him homeward without even trying to keep track of the way, let her bright chatter flow over him without answering. The house was full of the rich odor of roasting fowl as they came in the door, but even the relief in Gilla's voice as she announced that the Prince had awarded Lalo a pension could not cheer him. He told them that the walk had tired him, and lay down with his face to the wall.

Darios breathes slowly, deeply, trying to control panic with the knowledge that he is not going to exhaust the air in the room. The water that drips down the wall proves the vault is hermetically sealed no longer. That must be why he has awakened—even the magic that made this place is finally beginning to decay.

But not entirely. The spells that hold—and hide—the door are still intact. Darios has worn his fingertips raw, feeling every inch of stone. He has even spent some of his dwindling strength to conjure up a magelight, but the blue flicker shows him the same blank surface his fingers have found. Without some way to replenish his energy he dares not try that again. He will not die of thirst or suffocation, but without food, how long can he survive? If he uses no energy, and stills his bodily processes in trance, Darios can extend his existence. But why? Why, if he is bound to starve to death in the end?

If only he could remember the Sigil on the outside of the door!

That night, he had thought only of getting into the vault—he had been sure that his master was just behind him. . . .

Darios takes a deep, shuddering breath and forces himself to stillness again. Are all the wizards in Sanctuary dead? He tries to use his inner vision, but he has not received the proper initiations to walk the Wizards' road. All that comes to him is the face of Rhian, gray eyes clear as rainwater, auburn hair taking fire from the setting sun. . . .

Am I being punished for deceiving her? *Darios wonders.* It was only a little magic, a small glamor to make her look at me! *He was a student, and he looked like one—a little round in the shoulders from hunching over a desk, and in the belly, too, though he supposed his gut was growing concave by now. Pale from long hours indoors, how could he compete with the hard-muscled, bronzed men of the Palace guard? But he had skills a soldier never dreamed of, and it had only been a small spell to make him look taller, to broaden his shoulders, to give his dark eyes a mystic gleam.*

And it had worked! Rhian had given him her love!

Oh my sweet girl! *His heart cries.* Where are you now? Did you survive, do you remember me? *The brightness of her eyes holds his fear at bay. Still clinging to that image, Darios forces himself back into the half-sleep that will preserve him another day.*

''Papa—I've brought Rhian to see you—''

Wedemir's voice, brittle with that conscious cheerfulness with which everyone spoke to Lalo these days. Did

they think he could not hear? He heard the rustle of silken
skirts and turned his head toward the sound. What did she
look like, this girl with whom his eldest had fallen in love?

"I'm glad to meet you."

Her voice was subdued. Lalo wondered if she were
embarrassed because of his blindness, or whether she had
her own sorrows? Even the privileged ones at the Palace
had reasons to grieve, these past years.

"You are in service with the Beysa?" he asked. He
wanted to hear her speak again. Silk whispered as if she
had shrugged.

"The Prince wants to build understanding between our
people and hers. I was glad to be offered the position. My
father brought his family here when the Prince was made
Governor, but my parents had gone back to Ranke on a
visit when the Emperor . . . fell."

Lalo thought she sounded more wistful than bitter. Her
voice had a spicy warmth to it. What kind of face would go
with those tones? Drifting, he visualized cleanly modeled
features, bright eyes, and hair of some warm color—
something like cinnamon, perhaps.

He could hear Wedemir talking to his mother in the
other room.

"They tell me that my son is courting you," Lalo said
then. There was a pause, as if Rhian had looked around to
see who else was there.

"Wedemir is a good man," she said slowly, "but—"
Suddenly it seemed to him that her Rankan accent was
very clear.

'But he is Ilsigi, and a commoner!" Lalo fought to
subdue a bitterness he thought he had forgotten.

"Oh, it is not that!" Rhian said quickly. "What does all

that matter, now? But before I met Wedemir, I had given my word—".

"To a mageling—" Lalo remembered now. "Wedemir was telling me. Did you love him so much, then?" He stopped, wondering why he dared question her so sharply. Was it perhaps just because he could not see her? And was she answering so freely because she did not fear to read condemnation in his eyes?

Rhian sighed. "Wedemir is very warm and alive. When I am with him, I feel safe. I know that I am loved. But I gave Darios my word."

"Death cancels such pledges," said Lalo.

"Darios is not dead."

"She keeps on saying that!"

Lalo started, realizing that Wedemir had come in from the other room.

"Rhian, if he is not dead, he has deserted you! You owe him nothing either way!"

"I can feel his presence! If he is dead, then his spirit is haunting me!"

Her tone had sharpened, and Lalo's sense of her presence grew clearer. She was turning from him to Wedemir, her gaze more luminous, as if her eyes had filled with tears. Or was it only the pain in her voice that made him think so?

"In my dreams I see him, Wedemir . . . Darios is trapped in darkness, and he cannot get free!"

Trapped in darkness! thought Lalo. *Like me! Like me!* For a moment a terror that was not his own washed through him. But he could hear voices, feel the sun on his face and breathe in the wind. It occurred to him for the first time since he had been blinded that there were worse fates than his own.

"He is not dead yet," Rhian continued. "But he is dying. He has been buried alive, and if I can't find him, he will starve to death in the dark. He has lost hope, but still he thinks of me. . . ."

Again, the sense of panic washed through Lalo's awareness, as if what the girl was feeling had somehow been transmitted directly from her to him.

"But where?" exclaimed Wedemir, humoring her. "Most of the wreckage from the riots has been cleared away."

"Not all of it—" said Rhian slowly. "No one has dared to touch the parts of the Mageguild that fell down. That's where Darios was living. What if he sought shelter in the cellars and was trapped there? The possibility comes between me and sleep!"

"Well that's easily checked out!" Wedemir laughed. "I'll get a permit from the Palace to excavate, go down there with a few of the lads and some picks and shovels and dig the rubble out. We'll lay your ghost for you, Rhian."

Lalo could feel the sudden hostility between them. He understood Wedemir's reaction—he was fighting for his love. But beneath her Rankan elegance this woman was the true steel. The boy would ruin his chances with her if he went on this way, no matter what the diggers found. Why couldn't Wedemir see that? Lalo felt himself straining, as if a look could silence his son. But he knew that he was seeing through both of them, seeking, like Darios, to pierce the dark.

Darios knows when he is dreaming, because in his dreams, he can see. But when he opens his eyes into darkness, he is afraid. He is going to die. . . . Why does he keep trying to keep his body going when there can only be one end? He will go through the only door that will open for him now, and hope the gods will forgive him all the petty deceptions and angers of a student mage.

I have done nothing really bad, *he tells himself.* Nor anything particularly good, either, *his thought goes on. But he has done one thing for which the Judge might indeed condemn him, though he supposes that hardly a man in the Mageguild or out of it would care. He has deceived a woman in order to compel her love.*

Was that evil? *He asks himself.* What would that deception do to me—to us—if I were to live? *He thinks of Rhian's bright beauty, and knows that his own falsehood would stain it for him, in time. As outer vision is denied, his inner awareness becomes clearer, showing him a future in which one deception leads to another, until he hates Rhian's truth for showing him his own deficiency— until he hates, and at last destroys, the clear gaze that would prevent him from seeing himself as he has made her see him.*

Is this knowledge why he is suffering? But now Darios knows his sin. Surely he has been punished enough. Once more, he tries to remember the Sigil on the door, the pattern which he must trace in order to be free. . . . But he cannot see it!

And there is no use in praying for rescue. Darios remembers only too well how the Spell that seals the vault is set to respond if anyone tries to open it by physical means. . . .

Lalo knew that he must be dreaming, because he could see. He dreamed with a clarity of vision that had never been his in waking life, or even in sleep, before his sight was taken away. In his dreams, he ranged through Sanctuary at will, invisible, invulnerable, as if all the energy that had no outlet by day was fueling his nocturnal wanderings— nocturnal in their beginnings, though once he had begun his dreaming, Lalo might find himself moving through night or day, through scenes from the past, or sometimes among people and events whom his waking mind would not have recognized. But he had never tried to bring these visions into waking memory. The contrast would have been too cruel.

It was morning now. The clear light glowed in the faces of the young, who woke wondering what the new day would bring, and revealed without pity every line and shadow in those of their elders, who knew only too well. Still, there was a welcome freshness in the air, and the sunlight gleamed cheerfully from the temple domes. For a moment Lalo thought that he had gone back to his own youth, when the great caravans used to bring the town a rough prosperity. But as he looked more closely he saw the mended cracks the new gilding tried to hide, and turning a corner, recognized the jagged outlines of the Mageguild. This was the present then, or perhaps the future, for the City walls beyond it were perceptibly higher than he remembered them.

For such an early hour, the place seemed very active. . . . Lalo moved closer, and saw a familiar curly head—his own son Wedemir, with a crowd of his friends from the garrison, big, bronzed men, who laughed and traded good-natured obscenities. But they were carrying picks, not pikes, and instead of swords they swung shovels. Wedemir was trying, with indifferent success, to get them organized. A short distance away Lalo saw his daughter Vanda, and with her another girl whose auburn hair glinted beneath her veil. *Rhian*—suddenly Lalo was certain who this must be. But how had he known?

He moved toward them, calling a greeting, but they looked through him, no more able to see his spirit than he had seen their bodies when they visited him.

Sight and vision are not necessarily the same . . . The awareness came to Lalo like the answer to some long-debated question . . . He was on the edge of understanding when a shout distracted him. The soldiers were attacking the rubble at the edge of the Mageguild's great hall. Dust puffed up as the first of the great stones was moved. Wind lent the moving particles form and substance. Figures for which ordinary humans have no names seemed to hover for a moment above the workers, then the wind swirled them away. Was that a trick of the light, or was Lalo perceiving the elementals that had been bound to those stones?

Sight . . . or vision?

That first success had encouraged the diggers. Picks shattered stones into fragments small enough to be carried away. Now they had bared the ground level. Someone shouted, and the men crowded around a rubble-choked depression next to the wall.

"What have they found?" Vanda asked her friend.

"It should be the stairs to the vaults beneath the Mage hall," answered Rhian. "Darios boasted that he knew the way—he should not have told me, I suppose, but he would never believe he did not need to impress me. . . ."

"His indiscretion may save his life," said Vanda. "If they do find him alive, what will you do about Wedemir?"

Rhian shrugged a little and colored. "I don't know. I love them both—can you understand that? I love them in different ways."

Vanda shook her head. "I have never been in love with one man, much less with two. Perhaps I am the lucky one . . . Oh, look—" she added suddenly, "the men have found a door!"

The digging had continued while the girls were talking. As the last stones were removed, Lalo saw what seemed to be an unbroken slab of stone. A symbol was cut deeply into the smooth surface; Lalo drifted closer to see. It was nothing he knew, but its loops and angles teased at the memory. Had he seen something like it at Enas Yorl's?

But he had no time to study it. Wedemir heaved up his pick and brought it down with all his strength upon the stone.

Violet light blazed from the sigil, then burst outward in a flare that burned sight away. But Lalo heard the sharp crack, the clatter of falling rock and then screaming and the ominous, agonized rumbling of settling stone. His cry mingled with the others', but the rush of displaced air was whirling him away. Vision was still darkened, but upon his inner eyelids he saw the Sigil imprinted in lines of fire.

"Wedemir! *Wedemir!*"

Anguish tore Lalo's throat. He fought the darkness; his flailing hands found something soft and solid, he was held, and presently his breathing steadied. An awareness deeper than sight told him who held him. With a shuddering sigh Lalo rested his head on Gilla's ample breast and breathed in the sweet scent of her hair.

"It's all right—I'm here . . . hush, my love—it was only a dream. . . ." Gilla was patting his back as if he had been her child. A coolness in the air told him that it was still nighttime. He could hear the distant barking of a guard

dog, and a scream, cut short abruptly, from the direction
of the Maze.

"A dream—" he muttered. "Dear gods, I hope so!"
He waited for his heartbeat to steady. Images replayed
themselves in his awareness—the Sigil, Wedemir's face as
the stones crashed down. . . .

"Wedemir said he would excavate the rubble of the
Mageguild," he said finally. "When, Gilla—did he say
when?"

"I don't really know," she began, and winced as his
fingers tightened on her arm. "Tomorrow, perhaps. Does
it matter?"

"We've got to stop him, Gilla. If Wedemir tries to
break those wardings, he'll be destroyed!"

"What wardings?" He felt her pull away a little to look
at him. "The Guildhall is a ruin, Lalo. I've seen it!"

"So have I!"

"Lalo, what are you talking about?" Gilla said sharply.

"In my dream I saw Wedemir digging among those
ruins, and I saw him crushed beneath falling stones."

"You are worried about him—well, so am I—" she
said carefully. "It's part of parenthood. I've had any
number of nightmares in which the children were endan-
gered. It was a nightmare, nothing more." Her voice was
so reasonable, so soothing. . . .

Lalo shook his head. "Gilla, don't talk to me as if I
were one of the children! You're acting as if I'd lost my
mind along with my sight! Listen to me, Gilla!"

"What do you mean? I've been treating you the way I
always do. I've had to take care of you, of course, but—"

"Have you always secretly despised me, then?" he
shouted. "Even in our worst times, you never slept in the
other room."

"You were hurt," she began. "You needed to sleep alone—"

"Gilla, my head healed weeks ago! I'm still your husband—I'm still a man, even if I can't see!"

There was a silence. He heard her shaken breathing and fought to control his own. Her flesh was so familiar . . . Lalo knew the luxuriant hills and valleys of her body better than he did his own. But now he felt as if a stranger were lying there.

"Is that the way it seemed to you?" she whispered finally. "I didn't intend it. But you may be right. I was afraid—all I could think about was protecting the children. Oh Lalo, what can I do?"

Lalo was glad that the darkness hid his involuntary grin. Her question had sounded too much like a verse from a bawdy song that he doubted Gilla knew.

"Let me inside your defenses, love," he whispered, touching her cheek with fingers that had grown more sensitive, moving his hand gently downward until it curved around her breast, teasing her nipple until he felt it harden, and she gasped. For this, he did not need to see.

"Please, Gilla, let me come in. . . ."

The air had freshened and the hush of early dawn lay on the town by the time they were quiet again.

"After so long, you would think there could be no surprises," Gilla murmured drowsily, rolling away from him. "But each time we make the world anew. . . ."

Lalo emerged from the deep well of pure sensation reluctantly. He could view the images of his nightmare with some detachment now, but they retained their clarity.

"Gilla . . . there's been so much strangeness in my life. Do we dare assume there was no truth in what I saw in my dream? Listen—" he went on as she mumbled sleepily.

"We never met that girl, Rhian, until after I was blinded, but I can describe her—someone might have told me the color of her hair and eyes, but would they have said that Rhian wears a blue gauze veil with golden scallop shells embroidered on the hem, or that she has a dark brown mole on the back of her right hand?"

"That's true." said Gilla, fully awake at last. "You have described the girl." Her voice sharpened. "But if what you saw was a true vision, then Wedemir is going to die!"

"It may be a possibility only!" Lalo answered more confidently than he felt, holding her until he felt her tension begin to ease. "You must take me to the Mageguild, Gilla, as soon as it's light. We can save our son if I stop Wedemir from breaking down that door!"

Once, when he was first apprenticed, Darios had broken a flagon in his master's workshop, and screamed and ran as its contents exploded in fire. A prompt spell from the senior mage had sent the flames running back upon themselves until all the stuff was consumed, but the master had afflicted Darios for several days with a demon who tormented him with little pricking flames. Now he dreams that the fire is spreading, licking up the heavy draperies, even consuming the stone. The Mageguild is an inferno; the heat blisters his skin, the light blinds him. He writhes and shrieks and wakes to the cold silence of his tomb.

Shuddering, Darios composes himself to trance again. And again the dreams torment him. This time it is a book which he has been forbidden to read. But if he once opens it, he can escape the tyranny of his masters, for their knowledge will be his own. He makes his way into the chamber and sets his hand to the cover. Light spills from

*within as he lifts it, brilliance explodes as it flies open.
Darios strives to force the cover down again, but he does
not know the spell. He screams as the world whirls away.*

*To wake twice from such a nightmare is an evil portent.
Darios would try to stay awake, but awake he is aware
that he is cold, and hungry, and alone. Guarding himself
with all the spells he knows, he seeks stillness once more.
But yet again he dreams, though he struggles against it.
This time he is with companions, fellow-students, perhaps,
who are on the track of some treasure. They begin to pull
down a pile of rocks, laughing and tossing away the
stones. He tries to stop them, but soon they come to a slab
set into the ground. Something is written there—Darios
tries to see it, but the others are in the way. He sees them
pulling at it, and then light explodes from the earth,
flinging him away. In despair he cries out Rhian's name
and wakens, hearing the regular clank of metal striking
stone. . . .*

Lalo and Gilla reached the Mageguild as the sun was
topping the newly gilded dome of the Temple of Ils.
Wedemir and his friends were already working. Over protest Latilla had been left behind to watch Alfi, but Vanda
and Rhian were here, as Lalo had known they would be.
From his tone, Wedemir seemed mildly annoyed to see his
parents, and more than annoyed when Lalo asked him to
stop. Lalo sighed. It had been hard enough to get Gilla to
believe him, why should his son listen to a blind old man?

"For Shipri's sweet sake, hear me out!" he exploded
finally. "Wedemir, do you remember the Black Unicorn?"
There was an uncomfortable silence. Behind him, Lalo
could hear two of the soldiers whispering. He supposed
that by now even new recruits must have heard the tale of

the creature that Lalo had unwittingly created and unleashed upon the town.

"What does that have—" Wedemir began, but Gilla interrupted him.

"You're a grown man now, and so you think you have nothing left to learn?" she said scornfully. "Especially from your parents? You were not so proud when your father destroyed that black beast—don't you yet understand that he is not like other men?"

"Father—" Wedemir sounded subdued when he finally replied. "You know why I am doing this. I must have some reason beyond a dream to give up now . . ."

"Rhian is here, isn't she—" said Lalo.

"You might have heard her voice; you might have guessed she would be here."

"You don't believe me? Keep on digging then. When you have cleared away the rubble, you will find a staircase leading down to a stone slab. There is a symbol carved on it, Wedemir. You must believe me then, for if you touch that doorway, you will die!"

"I'll admit there's no normal way you can know what's under there," said his son. "If we find the door we'll stop. Does that content you, Papa? We will stop, but you will have to choose what we do then!" Emotion trembled in his voice.

That girl, thought Lalo. *He won't give her up any more than I would have given up Gilla at his age.*

They sat with Rhian and Vanda as they waited. Lalo could hear the sound of the digging, and memory supplied a picture of the scene. He knew it when they reached ground level and uncovered the beginning of the staircase. He knew when they finished digging it out, and found the stone slab.

The men were very quiet as Rhian led him to the doorway. Delicate fingering confirmed that the sigil was the one that he had seen. Lalo's fingertips tingled as he touched it, and he knew that the magic that warded it was still alive.

And in the silence after he took his hand away there was a sound—too faint to be heard above the noise of pick and shovel, or even over normal conversational tone—a distant voice that called, "Stop! For your life's sake, you must not touch the stone!"

"He's alive!" whispered Rhian. From Wedemir came something like a muffled groan. Lalo winced, recognizing that at this moment his son might well have preferred to have been crushed by falling stone. But he had no choice. He bent until his lips were nearly touching the rock and took a deep breath.

"What must we do to free you?"

"You cannot," came the faint reply. "The vault can only be opened by drawing the sigil, with the proper words, from inside . . ."

"Do you know the words?" Gilla's voice sounded very loud in Lalo's ear.

"I know the spell, but not the Sign," came the answer. "Pray for the spirit of Darios, son of Wint, and may the gods bless you for attempting to help me."

Rhian had begun to sob. Lalo bit his lip, thinking. The contours of the sigil were still vivid in his memory. He could have drawn it, but he could not describe it. The peculiar curves and angles of which it was composed followed no normal human logic, could not be explained in human words. Could the puzzle have been unlocked by the Rankan wizard, Randal, or even by Enas Yorl? Lalo wondered. The foundations of the Mageguild had been

here before either. They felt old—Ilsigi magic, or perhaps
something that had been here even before. . . .

"He knows the words, and you know the Symbol,"
muttered Gilla. "Surely there must be some way—" Lalo
sighed. He was glad to know that Gilla really believed
him. But even if he had been able to see, he and young
Darios were still on opposite sides of the door.

"A doorway—it is only a doorway—" she murmured.
"But you can go through such things, Lalo. Remember
how you took me with you through the image on the card?
Can't you do the same thing for the boy with words?"

Frowning, Lalo reached out and felt her clasp his hand.
"I suppose . . ." he said slowly. "Wedemir, my son—do
you understand why I must try?"

"Yes, Papa," Wedemir said harshly. Better to have it
over with now, whatever the outcome might be. If he had
not won the girl when Darios's fate was still in doubt, he
would never get her while her first love was slowly starv-
ing to death beyond this stone!

"Darios, can you hear me?" he said more loudly.
"Listen—I know you've been trained to this—listen, and
see what I say—"

"I don't understand . . ."

"Just listen!" From habit, Lalo closed his eyes. He had
had the S'danzo card in front of him before, but he remembered each brushstroke vividly. "Calm down, steady
your breathing—you know how. . . . Imagine you are
looking at an archway—the arch of a gate big enough to
drive a chariot through. Look at the stones. They are pale
granite with dark flecks that glint in the sun . . . six great
stones on each side, and a larger cap, three on each side of
the arch, and a trapezoidal keystone. Do you see it, boy?"
Lalo saw it clearly in his mind's eye, not a thing of paint

and pasteboard now, but a real gateway, solid stone. There
was a faint murmur of assent from within.

"Look through the archway now—you see a garden. . . ." Lalo began to describe the sweep of green
grass, the roses, the trees. And as he spoke, he himself
saw them. He moved forward. "Go through the gateway,
Darios—go into the garden . . . into the garden. . . ."

Lalo hardly felt Gilla's arms go around him as he left
his body behind him and his own words carried him
through. It was no shock to find that he could see, for this
was only a continuation of his inner vision. He turned, and
saw someone coming toward him. It was a tall young man,
well formed, though his skin had the pallor of one who
spends his days indoors. His curling black hair and beard
were as glossy as the coat of one of the Prince's pampered
horses, and his dark eyes glowed.

A handsome man, thought Lalo. *No wonder Rhian loved
him.* A mental adjustment to his own dress clothed him in
a clean shirt and one of his better coats. He lifted his hand
in greeting.

The young man's eyes widened. "Who are you?"

"Lalo the Limner." It seemed such an inadequate answer to offer this young man who stood in the rich robes
of his Order, watching him in wonder.

"I've heard of you. But you're not a mage!"

"I'm not sure what I am anymore . . ." Lalo looked
around him. If only he could stay here, where it was so
beautiful—where he could see. But at least he knew the
way here now.

"But unless we do something, you, my son, are going
to be dead very soon!"

A moment's concentration brought a tablet and stick of
charcoal into his hands. The Sigil still blazed in Lalo's

memory. He could not have described it, but his arm
moved easily in the contorted swirls of the figure, and he
felt a swift rush of delight in the sureness with which he
drew, recognizing only now how the frustration of being
unable to do so had galled him. Here, he could paint
again, even if there was no one to see.

"Can you remember it?" He held the tablet out to the other
man. Darios gazed at it, his eyes going glassy as ingrained
disciplines committed the curves and angles to memory.

"I will remember," said Darios grimly. "I never saw it
properly. The Sigil was not in the book I found—only the
spell. And if I fail," his lips twisted a little. "At
least you have shown me the way to an easy passage. My
thanks to you, Master Limner, for that." For a moment
the two men clasped hands.

They both looked toward the archway that led back to the
world's darkness. Lalo straightened, realizing that he was
almost as unwilling to return to the prison of his body as
Darios was to go back to his tomb. But he could feel the need
of those he had left behind him tugging at his awareness.

Together they moved forward.

Then Lalo was shaken in a tumult of darkness through
which he heard a great voice crying "Be opened!", and
the Sigil blossomed upon his vision in lines of white fire.
There was a moment of disorientation. Lalo felt strong
arms supporting him. He gazed as the Sigil coruscated
through all the colors of the spectrum in a blaze of opales-
cence, and then both Sigil and stone misted away, and a
gaunt figure staggered forward and collapsed into his arms.

"Darios!" shrieked Rhian.

But Lalo had not needed that to identify him. Something
in his spirit had recognized the essence of the man he held,
that wavered like a guttering candle flame. He stared down
at matted tangles of black hair, a patch of blue robe whose

cloth was of rather poorer quality than the fabric Darios had worn in the Otherworld, and beyond, to a patch of dusty stone. The bent back heaved; bony fingers clutched at Lalo's arms.

"My son, my son, don't weep!" He stroked the dusty locks as if Darios had been his own child indeed. "It worked, lad—you are free—you are free!"

And then Lalo's hand stilled. When he closed his eyes, he saw the glossy hair and tall strength of the man he had met in the Otherworld. But when he opened them, he knew he held a youth who would be no more than his own height even when full-fed. Instead of a verdant garden, he saw the sordid, soiled reality to which he had been born . . . he saw every stinking turd and blessed battered stone . . . he *saw*!

Vanda and Rhian were on either side of Darios now.

"Darios—my poor darling! You look like one of your own spirits!" Rhian drew his arm across her shoulder.

"Starved—" whispered the mageling, "but even before that . . . wasn't handsome. A spell, Rhian . . . to make you think so. Forgive me!"

"You silly boy!" Rhian shook her head. "Do you think it mattered?"

"We'll take you home and let my mother's cooking put some flesh on your bones!" said Vanda, taking his other arm.

Lalo let go, and the two girls supported him as he stumbled toward the stairs. Gilla set Lalo's hand on her shoulder.

"No—" his voice cracked, and he laid his own hand over hers. "I can see my own way now." She started, and her gaze came back from Darios to meet his own.

"Oh! Oh Lalo!" Her arms closed around him, and he felt her tears wet on his neck. He blinked, and looked past her bent head to the stairs.

Darios and the girls had nearly reached the top now. Wedemir was waiting for them, stiff as a statue, with all his agony blazing in his eyes.

"And what of me?" he asked as they passed him, as tragically as any character in one of Feltheryn's plays. "Rhian, what about me?"

Rhian turned to face him. "I am taking this man to shelter, Wedemir, not marrying him," she said tartly. "At this moment, I don't know if I want to marry anyone—not him, or you!" She and Vanda helped Darios on, leaving Wedemir staring.

Lalo began to laugh, because of the swift toss of Rhian's bright head, and the look on Wedemir's face—and for sheer simple joy because he had been healed.

"I still love you, lambkin—" Lalo put his arm around Latilla, who sniffed and turned her face away.

"You love Mama better . . ." she mumbled.

Lalo sighed, aware that there was a part of his daughter that wished he were still blind. But it would do no good to tell her so.

"I love Mama differently—but not more than I love you. That's the way it's supposed to be. Someday you'll find a young man who loves you that way, and you'll have a daughter of your own. You'll see. . . ." He sighed, remembering how he had rejected this kind of reasoning when he was her age.

"Nobody will marry me—I'm ugly!" she whispered then.

"Did the other girls tell you so?" He squeezed her hand. "Listen to me, Latilla—you will be beautiful! This isn't just your father's love talking, sweetling—I *see* what you will be!" Gently he turned her to face him, and let outer and inner vision merge, seeing the color of Latilla's mouse-fair hair deepen to old gold, the fine bones define the face beneath the translucent skin.

It was becoming easier. When his sight first returned, Lalo had sometimes had to shut his eyes because the confusion of shape and color was too painful. While Darios lay in the next room, eating Gilla's good food and growing back into his body, Lalo had learned to see once more.

But it was different now. He saw the shabby streets of Sanctuary as a man long away looks upon his childhood home. Recovering one kind of vision had given him all of them, for to Lalo, the ordinary light of day was now as wonderful as the clear light of the Otherworld. He had begun to use inner and outer vision equally as he had never done before.

"I could paint what I see in you so that you can see it too—would you like me to?"

Latilla looked shyly up at him, then away again.

That's the first time I've ever boasted of it, Lalo realized. No, not boasted, but accepted as one of the things that he could do. *I am no longer simply Lalo the Limner.* he thought. *But what am I?*

"I . . . don't think so. I believe you—" she added swiftly, "but I don't think I should know."

Lalo nodded, wondering how many girls twice her age would have been so wise.

"You tell me when I get there, will you, Papa? And then, maybe if Darios doesn't marry Rhian he will marry me. Do you think he might?" She broke off suddenly, blushing, and Lalo saw the student mage standing in the door.

"He might—who knows?" he whispered in his daughter's ear. "Run along now and let me find out if he's good enough for you!"

Latilla giggled, jumped to her feet, and still blushing, darted past Darios through the door. She left silence behind her. Lalo wondered how to break it. At times it seemed to him that he and Darios had shared one resurrection, but there was no reason the younger man should feel the same.

"Come in," he said finally. "How are you feeling? Have you decided what you want to do now?" Darios sat down on the other bench.

"My own master died, and there's not much left of the Mageguild," Darios said slowly. "What I would like is to finish my apprenticeship with you. . . ."

"But I'm not a mage!" exclaimed Lalo.

"Aren't you?" Darios looked up suddenly, and Lalo saw his dark eyes glowing as they had glowed in the Otherworld. "I know the spells, the recipes, the rules. But what use is that these days, when so much of that kind of magic has lost its power? You have more of the spirit of magic in your paintbrush than the whole Mageguild in their wands. Teach me vision, Master Lalo, and I will take care of the spells."

An apprentice! For the first time in years Lalo remembered that the man who had made him a master had not been a painter, but a mage. There was a pattern here, a power that transcended the gods. Again, inner and outer vision blended, and he glimpsed his life laid out before him like one of the great murals in the temples. He blinked, and it disappeared—like Latilla, he was not yet ready to see.

But one day . . . one day. . . .

Lalo looked back at Darios, took a deep breath, and held out his hand.